MW01148379

#iHunt
By Olivia Hill

Editing By: Filamena Young
Cover Art By: Olivia Hill

Content Warning: This novel contains graphic depictions of assault, drug abuse, blood transfusion, murder, sex, and bodily fluids.

You should join our mailing list. We only send one or two message a month, focused on the books and games set in the #iHunt universe. You can sign up here: http://eepurl.com/dhfD-f.

01
#SWIPELEFT

Have you ever tried cutting fabric with child-safe scissors? This is why good vampire hunters, real vampire hunters, don't do stakes through the heart. It's just not practical. You can sharpen the stake as much as you want, but there's just no realistic way to put it through a rib cage unless you've got a mallet and the vampire's asleep. Only some vampires sleep during the day. So, I prefer the tried and true method—the machete.

I sprint after the fang-fucker. It feels good to chase these guys. They think they're the ultimate predators.

Then what does that make me?

I vault over a concrete and pipe barrier made to keep cars from driving into the park. He's running through the playground, pushing swings aside like the villain in a weaker Jackie Chan movie. As I run up the slide, I wonder if he's trying to distract me. If I were an amateur, it'd be a pretty good tactic. Then again, I don't think he'd be running away from an amateur. He's gotta know I know my shit.

When I hit the top of the slide, I jump as high as I can, raising the machete over my head and bringing it down hard. I won't behead him with a downward slash, but I'll sure as hell stop him from running, and set him up for the kill.

I miss. Damn it. The machete sprays sand and rubber chips all over the place. I break back into a run.

Some people say vampires are vulnerable, weak to beheading. I personally think most everything's weak to beheading. It's just that vampires are strong to most other things. Vampires are weird. There's different families. Each family has different strengths. Different weaknesses. Garlic repels some of them. Some die when exposed to sunlight. Some kill every time they feed. Part of the craft means learning what kind of vampire you're facing, so you can custom-tailor the hunt to the prey.

I hate chasing vampires. They're not completely impossible to catch. They do eventually get tired out. But for the most part, you get tired before they do. I've already got hints of that burning feeling in my muscles. My lungs are telling me to stop it. One of the first things you learn as a monster hunter is that you've got to ignore your body sometimes. I guess marathon runners learn that, too.

He bolts out of the playground, and runs across a big, open field. Big open spaces are terrible for fighting vampires. They're even worse for chasing them. They're tougher, faster, and stronger than you, so you've got to abuse the environment. In a big open field, there's no environment to abuse.

I chase him into the skate park. There's a group of teenagers smoking up. He knows what he's doing. He's trying to shake me. Most monster hunters won't kill in front of innocent eyewitnesses. I haven't decided if I will this time. "COP!" The vampire shouts. The teens snap to attention. They look all over the place, before noticing me. Clearly, I'm the cop. I'm the one chasing the guy.

That's a good plan, gotta give it to him.

Today's prey is a "wolf." In San Jenaro, the vampire families are all named after animals. From our perspective, on the hunt, wolves are the worst. They're strong. They're fast. They're tough. And their weakness, if you could call it that, is that they're territorial. If you fuck with their homes, they go all psycho killer on you. Sure, you can abuse that sometimes and make them fly off the handle. This is good for traps. It's good for ambushes. But when they get like that, they're even stronger, faster, and tougher than normal. It's a trade off.

The kids stare. They move to intercede. They've been trained well by the rising fascism in America. They know they've got to act fast when authority comes down on the people. They all pull out their smartphones and start recording. Under other circumstances, I'd applaud their efforts. I'd cheer them on for holding authority accountable. "Do I look like a fucking cop?" I say, holding my machete up high. They look between each other. When a woman with a machete's chasing a man twice her weight, she probably has a good reason for it. They back off.

Witnesses. My pay's gonna get docked for that. I'm gonna get a shitty review.

No time to think about that. I slow my sprint to conserve my energy. Vampires can always outrun you in a chase. You've got to outsmart them. You've got to wait for them to make a mistake.

He rushes into the park's bathroom.

There's his mistake.

He might have a plan. He's probably preparing for a final showdown, he's probably used to fighting in closed quarters. Vampires are deadly in closed quarters. No guns. No big weapons. So I slow down enough to catch my breath. Gotta be on the top of my game.

I said vampires are terrible in wide open spaces. I also said they're deadly in close quarters. These aren't contradictory ideas. They're deadly. Vampires are really, really deadly. You just have to do different things to survive them in different environments.

I step into the bathroom. There's two sinks, two urinals, one janitor's closet, and one stall. I make a mental map. I commit every single object to memory. When push comes to shove, with a vampire, you have to use those objects. Sinks are great because they're hard, but when you break them, they make really, really sharp things. They're great weapons. Urinals are nice because people will usually avoid them, so if you push them toward one, they'll fall off balance to not touch it. Vampires are just as concerned about touching pee as anyone. The janitor's closet isn't probably that useful on the front end, but on the back end, they tend to have industrial cleaning products. Those make the job a lot easier, and leave you with far less paperwork.

That's figurative. There isn't any real paperwork. But if you leave a mess, you don't usually get paid as much. So a little bleach goes a long way.

He's breathing heavily in the stall. Vampires technically don't have to breathe, but most do. Some do it to look more human. Some just never get out of the habit. I hear there's an owl family that has to breathe during the day.

I knock on the stall door. There's no answer. He's hoping I don't know he's in there. I take a step back, like I'm going to leave. He sighs in relief. At that, I turn on my heel and plant a size 7 Doc Marten into the door and kick, hard. The bolt buckles and the door flies in. These kinds of doors, metal with a little latch bolt, you can almost bust them open by accident. I not only break the latch bolt, but the door swings in and bends the side wall of the stall. I briefly feel bad that I'm wasting the taxpayer money that'll have to go to fixing this. Then I remember how much taxpayer money goes to the military industrial complex, and stop caring about this bathroom stall.

He's perched on top of the toilet so I couldn't see his shoes from under the door. He jumps, panicked. He's young. He looks maybe 25. Maybe my age. That doesn't mean anything for vampires—he could be 5,000 years old. That's not likely in San Jenaro though; we don't have a lot of old vampires in California. He's in skinny jeans, a Metallica t-shirt, and a leather jacket. He's got short black spiky hair. He smells like sweat and smoke. That all tells me he's not 5,000 years old.

"Come on. Let's finish this." I say and step back twice. I don't want to wait. I want to just end it. Unfortunately, you can't swing a machete in a bathroom stall. There's just no space.

He hesitates a moment, and steps out. I move back toward the entrance, just in case he tries running.

"I have money!" He says, pleading. I don't think he's aware that he could probably kill me with even a moderately good strategy right now.

"Oh yeah? How much?" I say, shrugging.

He sighs again, relieved. "Um. I don't know. Let me see." He pats his pants. He fidgets with his pockets—they're too tight to reasonably put a hand inside. He knocks out a few crumpled $20 bills. I see at least a $100. "You can have it all. Just don't kill me."

While he's looking down to his pockets, trying to fish for money, I bring the machete down wide along the side of his neck. His head doesn't come quite off, but it's enough to end him. I bury it about two thirds of the way through. I feel it go through the spine.

I grab his money. I like to call that "the tip." Then I finish the job. I lift the head by the hair with my left hand, and with my right, I put my machete—I like to call it my sword—the rest of the way through his neck. I picture myself as Saint George, killing the mighty dragon. Except my magic spear is a mass produced Ontario Knife Company machete, and my mighty dragon is a 20-something fanged Metallica fan.

"Mission accomplished. 12:42am. November 7th, 2016. Or, November 8th I mean. Forgot, it's after midnight. Gotta change the date." I say loud and clear to the GoPro. I hold the head up next to mine, and with the other hand, snap a quick selfie. I'll filter it later. I like the Juno filter; it brings out the color of the blood and does wonders with my skin tone.

Then, I take the remains out behind the bathroom. I grab some lighter fluid from my backpack and spray it down. I strike a strike-anywhere match and drop it on the pile. Even a young vampire like this one's already decomposing rapidly by the time I get to burning the evidence. I like that most monsters don't leave much for forensics. There's still a bit of a mess inside, so I splash it with some bleach, then turn all the faucets on and plug their drains. Public bathrooms are great for this sort of thing, since they usually have flood drains. And vampires don't bleed much to begin with. I search the janitor's closet for an "Out of Service" sign and put it on the door on my way out.

I sometimes wonder why most monsters fade into nothingness when they die. A lot of church-based hunters say it's because they're being dragged back to hell. I like to think it's a survival trick. They die, but they don't leave evidence. No evidence means no torch-wielding mobs to take down all their families.

#

I get back to my apartment. I pack a bowl. I light it up, and check the iHunt app. Seven new contracts meet my criteria. The bowl is a little weak—it's some stuff I picked up at a dispensary last week. They call it "Swamp Thing." I think back to the Wes Craven classic. I wonder where dispensaries come up with these names. They never really mean anything, but my friend that used to work at a dispensary told me that names are most of what a customer looks for.

"Chupacabra sighting in the Flip. $1,500 with collection. $500 if verified a hoax."

Swipe left. Take a hit. It's almost impossible to verify hoaxes. It's even harder to hunt a goddamned chupacabra. The kinds of hunters who can catch chupacabra, they definitely don't use this app. They're afraid of phones. They think the CIA is watching them through their TVs.

"Client in Palo Verde wants to meet a vampire to consult on her screenplay. $500 after publication."

Swipe left. Hold my breath for a moment. Consultation gigs are never worth it. This one's been sitting unclaimed for weeks.

"Werewolves on the northeast side. Rabies? $750 per head."

Swipe left. Release the breath slowly. Werewolves are way dangerous. Rabid werewolves are even worse. They're worth a few grand. $750 is a fucking insult. That wouldn't even cover expenses.

"This isn't a charity." I say to nobody in particular.

"Fairy circle in Ava Blue. $2000 for the circle. $500 for each confirmed kill."

"Ooooo. Interesting." I stare at the listing for a moment. I swipe left and shrug. "Someone else can fuck with it. Fairies are too complicated."

"Haunting near the shore. $2000 for confirmed exorcism."

"No way. I thought I told them I don't do fucking hauntings."
Swipe left. "And definitely no fucking exorcisms."
"Gang of vampires in the resort district. Corporate contract.
$5,000 per head."

Now we're fucking talking. Corporate contracts are way rare.
They're for the elite. You have to have a consistent average four
star rating over twenty jobs to start getting them. I guess I've
earned my wings.
Swipe right.
I get a pop-up.
"You've received feedback on your most recent gig.
'Witnesses on site, poorly handled. Sloppy cleanup: Police know
to look for ash piles. Wouldn't hire again. 3 stars.'"

*Oh fuck you. The kinds of pricks who leave three star reviews just
don't understand how the gig economy works.*

02
#HUSTLE

The thing about iHunt is, it's got a monopoly. That means it's got its advantages, but it's also got its drawbacks, and they really don't have an incentive to fix the drawbacks. These kinds of apps are all about "disruption," which leaves an industry "disrupted," which is to say "broken," and they come in with their Silicon Valley venture capital to sweep up the pieces. In this case, iHunt "disrupted" the monster hunting business. I've heard arguments it shouldn't be a business, that it should be done out of altruism. But a girl's gotta get paid, and the doctor bills from vampire injuries don't pay themselves.

One of the drawbacks is, if a client decides you didn't do a good enough job, they can dock your pay. They can cut off 25% without anyone batting an eyelash. They can cut 50% if they write a one to three star review, and people won't take gigs from clients who have too many low reviews. It's just not worth it. The worst, the absolute worst possibility is the 90% cut. The kill fee. They're rare. They require a one-star review. If you get a kill fee, it flags your account permanently. You get a suspension, and have to take a test to get your account reinstated after three months. The worst part is, you can't contest any of this. If they decide to fuck you, that's it. No matter how hard the job was.

It's the next morning. SanJayVikes81, the client, flagged me for a 50% pay cut thanks to the witnesses and cleanup. The

$2,000 I expected just turned into $1,000. I think it's total fucking bullshit, but iHunt's a monopoly, and my opinions really don't matter. I take the pay and smile, or I take the pay and walk. Those are my options. So I take the damned pay and I smile. And by smile, I mean I leave a comment on the review.

"Sorry it wasn't to your satisfaction! Thanks for the input! I'll do better next time! XOXO!"

Every time I type an exclamation mark, I imagine myself kicking SanJayVikes81 in the teeth. He didn't have to risk death over this. He just had to input his credit card details. The way we used to do this, at least before iHunt, was we'd visit clients. Someone would put out feelers because their neighborhood, household, company, whatever was being terrorized. A monster hunter would show up, interview everyone, and get to work. There was more of a connection. Now, it's depersonalized. You can do an entire hunt without ever interacting with the employer. They never have to look you in the face, so they don't see you as a person who could die for their safety.

SanJayVikes81 is a cop. Technically, iHunt accounts are anonymized. But once you get used to the signs, you can tell. The initial listing said the footage would be checked for anything that might hold up in court. That's a tell-tale sign. Most clients don't give a shit about courts, because they just want a dead monster. It also had to be done within certain hours of the night. Which means it had to be handled during his shift, so he could take credit for solving the problem. San Jenaro cops are crooked as fuck, and the department hides away a cut of all the cash they take in as "evidence." That money disappears from the books. They use it to hire us, to hire mercenaries, and to hire private detectives to do their jobs off-the-record. The idea is, freelancers don't let shit like "jurisdiction" and "human rights" get in the way of finding the culprit. Don't get me wrong: We hunt monsters. Literal monsters. The cops know we're hunting literal monsters. They know they'd probably die if they tried. But this isn't a noble effort or anything like that; they just don't want to look bad. And keep in mind, we're not the only freelancers they hire. They hire mercenaries for human targets. By mercenaries, I mean assassins. If they want someone to disappear, they grease the palms of a former spec ops guy who specializes in making people disappear. No arrest. No trial.

They're also cheap. Unless you really need the money, it's a bad idea to take a cop contract. They'll nickel and dime you, because they're getting pressure from on-high. I think some of them are resentful, too. Contractors tend to make more than they do, and they know it since they're signing the (digital) checks.

I needed the money.

There's a knock at my door.

Fuck. It's Regina.

She knocks again. "Lana?" She shouts. Definitely her.

I get up and walk toward the door. "Un momento por favor." She knocks again.

I open the door. She rambles at me at a fever pitch. I have no idea what she's saying because of the pace. But I get the point: She wants her money. There's also something in there about marijuana. I can't argue that point. She's easily a foot shorter than me. She's weathered, tough, no-nonsense. She lost her husband a few years ago, and inherited these two buildings, four units each. She's not a terrible landlady, and in her defense, I'm a terrible tenant. I'm a week late. My lease says she can evict me after three days. I've been a week late at least six months out of the past year. I've been reading up on California tenant law, and my lease is totally illegal. But that's one of those things I don't really want to fight, because it'll just be hell and I'll probably still end up fucked and homeless.

"Diez minutos. ATM." I squeeze through the door, grabbing my shoes and locking the door behind me. She's still ranting at me. I point to the bodega on the next block. "ATM."

She stops ranting, and puts her hands on her hips. I toss my pink camouflage Chuck Taylors on, and jog across the street. She stares at me. I don't know this because I look back. I know this because I know. I just do. I can feel it. Maybe it's because I'm a battle-hardened monster hunter. But maybe it's just because she can stare that fucking hard.

I hit the bodega. A loud bell rings as I open the door. It's dark inside, and smells like dust and burned fat. I figure they're trying to save on electricity. I go to the ATM. It's a tiny thing. It looks like an old children's toy with a barely visible green and gold screen. It's covered in magic marker. Names. Phone numbers.

Pictures of crude penises.

I guarantee, the people who draw these penises are the same guys obsessed with making sure everyone around them knows they're totally not gay.

I slide in my card. It pops out. I flip it, and slide it in again. It seems broken. The screen goes dark. It doesn't make any noise. Then there's a weird clicking noise, and it lights back up and asks me for my PIN.

"Lana!" Julio shouts and comes out from the back room. When he opens the door, I can hear a soccer game playing on the TV. He's a good man. He looks like he's about 120 years old. Like a tiny skeleton with slicked back gray hair. He's a sweetheart, always concerned for my well-being. I enter my PIN. I hit another button to tell the machine I understand they're going to take $3, and that my bank will probably take more.

I look to the newsstand by the door. The New York Times: "TRUMP TRIUMPHS."

Fuck. Maybe someone will take a contract out on that monster.

Who am I kidding? Nobody ever takes contracts out on the real monsters.

I grab the cash and count it, carefully shielding view with my back. I walk over to the counter. "Hey Julio. It's that time of the month again. I need a money order."

"$1,200? Anything else?" He says, punching some numbers into an old yellowish computer behind the counter.

"Actually it's $1,275. Late fees. You know. And this." I say, pulling a glass bottle of Mountain Dew from the cooler and putting it on the counter.

"Alright. I'm sorry, Lana, but that'll be…"

I cut him off. "Yeah, I know. Three money orders." I sigh.

"I'm sorry."

"It's not your fault Julio. It's really mine. She doesn't accept checks after the due date." I shrug and count the stack of bills again, and combine it with some others out of my wallet.

"Two money orders for $600. One for $75. $2 each, that's $6. Soda's $2. $1,283 please." I give him $1,300. He gives me $17. "Gracias."

"De nada. See you, Julio!" I smile and wave, taking my money order and citrus sugar water. Julio always cheers me up. He reminds me of the dad I never really had.

Regina's still standing there. She takes a few steps to meet me at the sidewalk. She pulls out her receipt pad. I hand her the money order. She checks it, and scribbles out a receipt. "Next month on time." She says. It's not a question. I force a smile and nod. My phone makes a noise. I check it.

"Reminder: Work at 12"

Shit. Gotta get to work. I've got to shower. No. No time for a shower.

I go back in. No time for a shower. I spray myself with some perfume and wipe my underarms with some deodorant wipes. I grab my purse. I hop in my car and head for the resort district for a shift at the day job.

Yes, I have a day job. People tell me they're jealous of my day job. But it's not enough. Between rent, utilities, food, and student loan payments, that's not even enough to break even. Every year, my rent goes up and it doesn't look like that's going to stop. I tried doing the second job thing, but it didn't work. My job demands that I work weekends, and I have to be flexible with day and night scheduling to get the most hours possible. So, iHunt gives me the chance to work in my spare time, whenever I'm free. While I'm not always on the hunt, sometimes it makes more than the day job. I've considered quitting and doing iHunt full-time, but the contracts just aren't always there. I need a steady paycheck. Especially thanks to poor tax. Rent's already too much. But then there's $75 late fees. Then there's $6 money order fees. Then there's $3 ATM fees on the front end, and another $3 on the back end. There's $35 overdraft fees. It's expensive being poor. With iHunt, I make extra money, sure, but that eats into spare time I could be using to save money by eating in. A $3 dinner at home becomes a $7 dinner at In-N-Out. At least so long as I'm chasing monsters through dark alleys, I know I'll work off that Double Double Animal Style.

03
#THEMAGIC

Work is work. I enter the resort district through the back lots, which the resort uses so all of the poor workers can come in without the tourists thinking we're poor. We get dressed in uniforms and costumes out of sight, out of mind, so by the time the tourists see us, we're chipper and colorful and totally not stressed about getting that fucking stain out of the only nice shirt we still fit in. The resort's all about show business, and pretending poor people don't exist is just part of the magic of showbiz. Of course, they could make poor people not exist by just paying us a little more. But that wouldn't fit the narrative of American exceptionalism now, would it? There's nothing more showbiz than pretending people can work themselves out of poverty.

I'm a tour guide. I drag wealthy families around the MovieLand theme park. I tell them the history of the movies we're celebrating. I smile way too much, all teeth and a pink lip gloss in one of the five approved colors, the closest one to my skin tone—which is still way too light for me. It looks like neon bubblegum smeared on my face and I hate it. I repeat corporate-approved cliches. I lean in close and parrot "hidden secrets" I've accumulated about the park over the years, the same way I lean in and parrot those same secrets to everyone else who comes through. I graciously decline tips when they rarely come up, because corporate doesn't want us competing, and they sometimes send in mystery shoppers to catch us taking money we're not allowed. Anything to keep us from making a fair wage, right?

I even pick up an extra two hours of overtime, since it's holiday season and everyone wants to be in California right now. I know I should be starting the search for this vampire gang. But two hours of overtime? $12 an hour with time and a half, that's $36. I can't afford to say no to that. That's almost half the late fee for my rent. Almost.

Ten and a half hours later, and I'm dead. It's 8:30. I want to go home. I want to relax. I have to be up tomorrow for another shift. I can't. I have to start the hunt. The worst part is, I'm actually hunting in the resort district, but I have to leave completely, walk a half mile to the main entrance of the shopping center—we call it "The Garden Plaza"—and walk in that way in my civilian clothes. I put on some Target jeans and a black t-shirt. I'm fucking invisible. That's real showbiz magic.

It's 9 o'clock by the time I get there, and I have to get food. I get 10% off everything in the resort district, but it's still overpriced garbage. A $12 bologna sandwich becomes a $10.60 bologna sandwich, which is just as ridiculous. These restaurants have a captive audience, because there's no other food for a mile thanks to the immense parking structures surrounding the resort in every direction. If you manage to make it a mile in the California sun, you can reward yourself with day-old heat lamp roller hot dogs at 7-Eleven, or Denny's that still costs about twice as much as any other Denny's in America. The Garden Plaza's whole schtick is trying to look worldly. They end up giving you stuff that looks like it comes from other parts of the world, except without any spice, and starting at about $10 for a glorified grilled cheese sandwich with a pinch of avocado. There's a cajun place where nothing's spicy. There's a Mexican place where nothing's spicy. There's a Thai place where nothing's spicy.

I need protein, and I need it fast. Denny's working the crepe stand. "Holy Crepe" they call it this month.

How edgy. But still not offensive to family sensibilities. I bet a lot of churchgoing teenagers snicker when they see that name.

I get a bacon avocado and egg crepe. It smells divine.

Denny likes me. He likes me likes me. I like Denny because he gives me free crepes. He's sad that I don't like him like him back. He's cool though; he's not a creep about it. He's not *not* cute. He just doesn't really bring up any feeling in me. There's no spark. I even tried a couple of times to picture him like that. Running my hands through his sandy brown hair. Bending my head to the side so he can kiss my neck. Nope. Nothing. I sometimes wish I could like him. He seems like he'd be a nice boyfriend. He asks if I want to go to a party tomorrow. I briefly consider it. Why not give him a chance? But I tell him not this time. Second job. He understands—Denny's also a librarian full-time. Denny's cute, if a little plain. He's skinny but fit. He's got this big brown eyes, and sometimes when he's wearing his glasses, he's definitely worth a second look. I always feel bad when I'm checking him out, like I'm sending mixed signals. I like him aesthetically. I wish that was enough in this culture.

I eat and I walk. The crepe is good enough. Denny added too much avocado though—it overpowers the rest of the crepe, and the crepe itself is over-stuffed so it's sort of falling apart as the avocado cubes poke out the sides. I feel like he did it as a favor, like adding more avocado was a way to show me I'm his favorite customer.

Am I actually a customer if he gave me the meal for free?

I scan the crowd and peer down to my phone. The contract says they're a disparate group that's recruiting heavily. There's at least five members, but probably more. That's at least $25,000. That's life-changing if I make it work. There are three descriptions, with grainy security photos. There's a white guy in khakis and a turtleneck. He's kinda scrawny. Kinda ratty. Like a young Steve Buscemi. There's a black guy, bald, in a leather jacket. Real square-jawed looking guy. Then there's a woman in dreadlocks and a bright puffy jacket. It looks neon, despite the black and white pictures. It's one of those ones that was big in rap videos in the 1990s. It'd go great in a fish eye lens.

I feel like I could point all three of them out if I saw them. Corporate contracts are depersonalized. They're companies defending their bottom lines. With personal contracts, there's more motivation, more attachment. So you tend to get better identified targets. I have nothing to go on with these guys.

RamirezHoldings, the client, probably doesn't know who these vampires are. There's no connection. There's no vendetta here. RamirezHoldings probably just has a contract with the resort to keep the area clean and clear.

I don't know what's going on with the vampires right now, but their numbers are exploding. Word on the streets is, they went from about 80 vampires in San Jenaro last year to about 120 this year. And that's just what we know about. Older vampires are better at hiding. Fortunately, we don't think there are many old vampires in San Jenaro. We work with one of them, we don't know his name. He has agreements in place with the iHunt organizers. He feeds them lucrative contracts. He gets to veto others. I don't know why we're working with the vampires when the job is hunting vampires, but it's not my place to ask questions. Just like it's not my place to argue when the cops decide they're not going to pay me.

I head back to Denny, so I can show him the three vampires. I ask if he's seen them. He shrugs. I tell him to send me a text if he does, and that's what's holding me up from going the party. He says he'll keep an eye out.

As I'm walking away, I see a few guys, big guys, football types, dressed in jerseys and red "Make America Great Again" hats. They're drunk. They're loud. They're loitering outside the giant ESPN store. I briefly wonder if I can pass them off as vampires, take them out, then collect the bounty for them. No. Vampires don't bleed as much as humans. It's obvious. One shouts at me.

"Hey, you!" I assume he means me, since he's looking me straight in the eyes. He does the thing where he sticks up two fingers, and wiggles his tongue between them. If he wasn't white, resort security would be detaining him and getting the police here by now. Bullshit white supremacist double standards.

I flip him off. He and his buddies look between each other. He's definitely the biggest. And in ape families, the biggest tends to be the alpha male. "Damn!" They laugh at him.

Shit.

He puffs up his chest and stomps toward me. I'm pretty tall, but my eyes are still just about to his chin. He's way bigger even than I thought at first. "Why you gotta diss me like that?"

Maybe because it's 2016 and you're a white guy saying diss?

I ignore him. I start walking again.

"Yo. I'm talkin' to you bitch." He isn't getting the clue.

"Just walk away." I say to him, not looking back. Not making eye contact.

Gotta de-escalate, Lana. These guys aren't worth your time.

"I was just payin' you a compliment. You should be thankful." His tone says he knows just as well as I do that he wasn't paying me a compliment. He knows he was being a shithead, and now he's gonna double down on it.

"Thanks. Now go away."

I'm not good at this.

He doesn't slow down. We've got maybe eight feet between us. I grab a hair tie out of my pocket, and pull my hair back in a ponytail.

What's the old Margaret Atwood quote? "Men are afraid women will laugh at them. Women are afraid that men will kill them."

"I said I'm talkin' to you." He thinks I care. He puts a hand on my shoulder. It's hard. Sweaty. Heavy. He could snap me in half if I let him. If he got his arms around me, it'd all be over. All my training, all my experience, that doesn't mean nothing when a guy's got you pinned with a 150 pound weight advantage. I can smell his breath from behind me. Cheap beer. Stale cigarettes. "Didn't you hear? Trump won. That means we get to grab your..."

I don't even think about it. This is practiced body memory for me. Usually, it's vampires. But it works on humans all the same. I drop down to surprise him. I shift on my heel. I turn, and I put every bit of leverage, from my ankle, to my knee, to my hip, to my waist, to my shoulder, to my elbow, to my wrist into my wrist, and I thrust it up and into his nose. Like a machine, throwing a piston into his disgusting Neanderthal face. You know that old myth about hitting a guy so hard you shove his nose bone into his brain and kill him instantly? If it were true, I'd have just killed him twice over. I feel the nose splinter and his lip bust. They say violence doesn't help. But in this case, it sure feels satisfying.

But that's not where my training stops. I rock my hip forward and jam my knee up into his crotch while he's stunned from the punch. He buckles over. I bring my knee back up to his face, plant my foot back down, then swing it up at the side of his head. While he's wavering in pain, I put both hands on his chest and shove him back. There's a bunch of gasps and startled "ooooos" from the crowd as he falls back on his ass.

I see his friends take steps toward us, and I bolt right out of there. They're probably checking on him. But I can't be too sure. I snake through the crowd and sprint toward one of the side exits. As I pass a t-shirt kiosk, I snatch the first thing that looks about my size. Once out of the shopping area, I run out to the parking structure, where I know I can hide and catch my breath. I could probably stay there and claim self-defense when the cops. But those three other guys could kill me before the cops got there.

When you're up against a crew, training only goes so far. A lot of times, training just teaches you how to survive. Winning's all up to chance. Some situations are better than others—if you have them in close quarters, you can bottleneck them and handle them one after another. But in wide open spaces like shopping centers, numbers mean you lose.

I lean against a concrete pillar in the parking structure. My wrist, shin, and knee sting—he was like a god damned brick wall. My lungs hurt from the sprinting. My phone buzzes. I check it while slipping on the t-shirt I stole.

It's Denny. What's he want?

"It's your lucky day. I found your turtleneck guy."

Then another.

"Thankfully he's wearing the same shirt."

Then another.

"Be careful. This guy's a major creep."

04

#WORKLIFEBALANCE

"Lana, maybe you should let the cops handle this guy."

I fire back a message at Denny.

"What makes you say that?"

I walk back toward the shopping center. My wrist still hurts. I'm bleeding a little. Not much. I must have hit his tooth. I hope it doesn't get infected. I have insurance through the resort, but the deductible is $5,000, and I can't spare $250 for the copay even if I didn't have the deductible. A $250 copay on top of a $5,000 deductible is downright insulting. My last ER trip had a $350 bill. Even if I hit the $5,000 deductible that year, I would have only saved $100. I pay $400 a month for the privilege of saving $100 after I've spent $5,000 out of pocket. The only way this could help is if I got cancer. The best part is, I have to pay a penalty if I don't have insurance.

I've picked up a lot since I started iHunt. I've had to give myself stitches twice. I learned the hard way how to reset a dislocated shoulder. My purse has become a makeshift pharmacy, and I keep a more complex micro-pharmacy in my car. I pull out a tiny airplane travel size bottle of hydrogen peroxide and squirt it on the wound. It fizzes and foams up. The wound's not big enough to need stitches. Maybe a half-inch. I wipe it off and put on a band-aid. It's a Sesame Street band-aid.

It still stings like a motherfucker. Even with both Bert AND Ernie's help.

I grab an Oxycontin from a ziplock bag in a hidden compartment in the bottom of my purse. The resort uses drug dogs on the employees every now and again, so I've got to play it safe. Last I heard, the dogs don't detect Oxy.

Denny messages me again.

"He's stalking a girl. Bad. I think he's going to mug her or something."

Shit.

I type back as I walk. Typing makes the band-aid come up. I switch the phone to my left hand, and re-situate the band-aid.

"Keep your distance. He's probably dangerous."

A couple of seconds later, he responds.

"No shit. I took a 15 minute break. Keeping an eye on him. Ready to call cops."

No cops. No cops. No cops.

"No cops. They won't help. I'll be there in a second."

"Just be ready to show me where he's at."

I jog around the resort, and take a different entrance just in case the cops are with the Make America Great Again sleaze bag. I see Denny. He's not very good at subtlety. He's peeking around the rear corner of a Panera Bread. The Panera's open late since it's the holiday season. I look where he's looking, and I don't see the vamp in the turtleneck. So I sneak up behind Denny, and tap his shoulder. He jumps a foot in the air.

"Shhhhhhh." I put a finger over my mouth. "Where is he?"

Denny's eyes go wide, like he wants to lecture me. But he points around the corner. "Between the Panera and the Forever 21. He followed her in the employee entrance." I start walking over that direction. The lighting's terrible. It's a great kind of place to bring a victim. I sometimes wonder if vampires helped to plan the resort for just that reason. I figure it's probably just as likely that the designers were just being lazy. You want to stop vampires? You teach architects about vampires. It's so easy to keep them out. It's so easy to make places too inconvenient for their hunts. Almost nobody does it, though. I guess that's a side effect of the world not knowing about monsters.

"Stay back." I say, then I realize the employee door's locked.

"My ID card can get you in." Denny says, following.

"Do you mind?"

He shakes his head and comes over. He pulls his lanyard and taps the card on the sensor. I hear the bolt open.

"Stay back." I say, opening the door. It opens into a plain beige hallway that goes both directions for what seems like forever. There's a door to about ten different shops on either side, as well as janitors' closets, a few managerial offices, a break room, and a lot of doors without labels. The only things breaking up the beige monotony are a few cork boards here and there with pamphlets advertising federal wage laws, resort employee softball games, and health care premium increases effective January 1st. Those, and a one-off poster of a cat. I can't read the inspirational message in this lighting at this angle—I'm sure it's nauseating.

"Huh?" He looks at me like I'm crazy. Bystanders always do. In their world, vampires and ghosts and goblins don't exist. In their world, muggers and rapists are the purview of police action. If you're white, you call the cops, and they handle it. If you're not white, you hope nobody else calls the cops, because there's a good chance they'll shoot you and let the bad guy off the hook. To bystanders, I look like a fucking ninja turtle chasing down crooks. Vigilantes don't really fit into your average person's world perspective. Imagine if they knew I was doing it to pay the rent.

"Stay back. This guy's dangerous." I whisper back to him.

He stops, but doesn't quite let it go. "That's exactly why you shouldn't go in there alone." He pauses and tilts his head. "Wait. Are you like a spy or something?"

I stop, blinking a couple of times. I look back at him. "Um, yeah. Sure. And that's why you can't follow me. You're not trained to handle this kind of thing. I am. So please. If you're concerned, wait ten minutes, and if I'm not out, call for help." I turn back into the employee hallway.

"Five."

I look back. "Huh?"

"Five minutes."

I grit my teeth, and mumble. "Fine. Five." I put a hand on his chest and nudge him out the door, and close it behind him.

The employee hall is loud. You can hear little hints of everything going on inside the Panera, and you can hear the boring dance pop coming from the Forever 21.

Bump, bump, bump, bump. I could get used to fighting with this kind of rhythm. 4/4, four on the floor. Why don't I get gigs hunting monsters in the club?

I glance both ways. There's movement in a little security office across from the Forever 21 staff entrance. I creep over and glance in the door. The guy in the turtleneck's in there, latched onto a young woman in a purple sweater. She's lazily grabbing his back, like they're making out. But they're not making out. I've seen this before. Most vampire bites are anesthetic, euphoric even. I've heard it's hot. Like, better than ecstasy. But also, it leaves you vulnerable. You can't tell them to stop once they start. Some of them feed from the same people regularly because of it —they build stables of addicts. If you're in the monster hunting game for long, you've known people who have become vampires. Some of my friends became vampires. I keep in casual contact with some of them. I just try not to think of how they eat.

Her head's falling back. He's definitely taking this too far— vampires don't have to kill their meals. I go to open the door, but it's locked. Worse: He noticed. He drops the woman, his victim, and turns to glare at me.

So here's the thing about vampires: They can charm you. They can hypnotize you. They can make themselves super cool, super hot, and make you want to do whatever they say. They go from worst enemy to instant crush with a glance. That's awful if, say, you're trying to murder them. There's a trick though. While they've got you charmed, they can do whatever they want to you. But external threats break the spell. So, bite your tongue real hard, cut yourself, or otherwise hurt yourself, and you're back to reality. It's a little hard to do, actually. You want to please the vampire, so you don't want to break the spell. So you have to get up the nerve and act on pure impulse, and for your average person, just straight up hurting yourself is really, really hard.

I feel it coming on. My body temperature rises. I get tingles all over. I want him. I know it's fake. For one, I walked in here planning on slaughtering him for next month's rent. For another, he's ugly. He's just nauseatingly, painstakingly *wet*. Not unnaturally; there are plenty of guys like him that aren't vampires. He just looks like he sleeps under a porch and doesn't shower.

But I play along. I smile "seductively." I'm not good at seductive. I doubt he knows that. I bat my eyelashes. I heave my chest a few times. While I'm not good at seductive, one of the things you learn in this line of work is how to do a few things that tell a monster "come murder me." He smiles, and opens the security office door. I'm focused on him. Half is because I can't fucking look away from his slimy ass. It's disgusting—I want to give myself to him. I want to kiss him. I want to submit to him. The other half is that I don't want him to suspect anything. I want to check on the victim, but I can't. Not yet.

"Is she okay?" I say, hushed, demure.

"She's alright. We're going to have a good time together tonight."

I giggle. "Okay." *Damn it. I hoped I could check her. Gotta move quick.*

He sidles in to me. It feels nice. I want to stab him. I kind of also want to fuck him. Which makes me kind of want to vomit.

Fuck it.

I grab a pen from the security desk, and jam it into my left arm. I yell out, but bite it down. Turtleneck rapist reels back a little, clearly surprised. I don't think he's surprised as I am. But the spell's definitely over, and I take advantage of his surprise to jam the pen deep in his eye. He screams. I yank it out and go for a second stab, hoping to hit his other eye. He flails out with both hands and knocks the pen away.

Usually I'm smarter than this. I should have thought this through.

I throw a couple of quick punches at his face, then back out into the hallway. They hit him hard. He grabs for his face. He's definitely not a wolf. He's a little too fragile. As he charges me, I grab the cold, metal security office door and slam it on his hand, breaking his wrist. I push into the door and knock him behind it, then swing the door open a couple of times into his face.

With vampires, you have to break bones. You have to try to dismember them. Just hitting them doesn't work. You have to do real, meaningful damage to their bodies. They regenerate, too.

That eye I stabbed out? It'll be better in a minute if I let him regrow it. But for now, he's missing an eye and his wrist isn't going to be a threat.

He lunges forward and hisses. He's got small fangs. Not a rattlesnake. Rattlesnakes can kill you with a single bite if you let them. So that's good. I try to use the door as a shield, but he pushes it and knocks me back. Vampires get real strong when they think they're gonna die. While I'm trying to catch my balance back in the security room, he jumps at me and grabs my arm. I try to twist away, but I don't have the angle for it. He pulls my arm to his face and bites down.

It's everything they say about it and more. Oh. My. Fucking. God.

I freeze. It's too much. Everything feels. Everything's good. Everything's hot. I feel like in that moment, I'd give everything to him. Unfortunately, it feels like I might. I try struggling, but I just can't. My muscles are too weak. It's like trying to run in a swimming pool.

Then there's a loud thud. The vamp pulls back from my arm. I'm bleeding from two pinprick wounds, but still conscious. I shake to attention. I look around. Everything's hazy. It's like that moment when you're just about to cum and the person in front of you is the hottest thing alive no matter who or what they are, and you can't really see anything other than them.

Denny.

He hits the fucker with the wooden office chair. The vampire hisses. Most importantly, he releases me. He reels back in surprise, but glares at Denny. Denny's face goes white, and he starts shaking. One of the other things vampires can do is evoke existential dread. That doesn't work on trained hunters, but it cripples an average Joe. Or an average Denny.

He turns back to me while Denny's crying in fear. Denny slumps against the wall, grabbing his face. He looks like his father just beat him.

I give the room one more quick look. Huge desk. A few computer monitors on top of thin-line client computers. A coffee cup that says "#1 Dad." I doubt that's actually true. The chair Denny hit him with. A rack of charging two-way radios. A cardboard box with "Evidence" written on it in marker—it looks like it's just filled with jackets.

I don't have many options. So I grab the chair. I jam it into his face and chest, pushing him back into the security monitors. He growls, grabs the legs, and tears the chair in half. I toss the pieces aside. He takes another dive for me. I duck out of the way, but grab him by the shirt and toss him into the wall.

Gotta make a plan. Gotta make a plan, quick.

I jump over the security desk, and shove it into him as he's trying to get back up. It knocks him back into the wall. I kick the desk over and jam the top into his stomach, pinning him against the wall. It forces the air out of his lungs in a huff.

"Denny!" I shout, trying to get his attention. It's not working. The monster's trying to break free, I'm holding the desk in place.

Either he's gonna break, I'm gonna break, or the desk's gonna break. My money's on the desk.

I look around. I see the broken chair leg.

That's kind of like a stake, right?

I grab the leg, and slam it into his chest. It bounces off his collar.

Remember what I said about stakes?

He yells, but I've still got him pinned. So I hit him again. Then again. Then again. Maybe the seventh or so time, it goes between two ribs, and he stops moving. I pull out my phone and start recording as he decomposes. The whole process takes about thirty seconds, and then he looks like a prop from The Mummy.

Denny's coming to, but I go to check the girl. "Hey. You okay?" I don't expect an answer. I put hands to her neck and her wrist.

There's still a pulse.

"What's going on?" Denny says, shaky.

"I told you to stay back." I say, picking her up. It's hard. Dead weight's so much worse than a conscious person, and this girl, she's fit. She's got a lot of muscle mass. She's waking up, but not quickly enough. She's grumbling like she's having the hangover of a lifetime. Blood loss is like that.

"I thought you might need help."

"Okay. Well. I do. Help me get her to my car." I hoist her to standing, leaning on my shoulder. I motion to her other arm. He hesitates for a split second, then goes along with it.

"We have to call an ambulance."

I shake my head, and lead him out the back door. "We can't. It won't get here in time. By the time they diagnose her, it'll be too late."

"What can you do for her that they can't?"

"I'm going to get her a blood transfusion."

05
#HEALTHCARE

"You don't even know her blood type!" Denny says. I have no idea why that's his first objection to my proposal for an unlicensed, unsanctioned, person-to-person blood transfusion done in the parking lot of a theme park resort.

"I'm type o negative. Universal donor."

He nods, taking it at face value. I've got my rear passenger door open, and we sit her down on the bench seat. I go to the trunk and pull out my medical kit, fishing through it for some tubing and needles.

"Why do you have a blood transfusion kit?" Denny says, looking around, checking for bystanders.

"Because I kill vampires and other things that poison the blood. You've got to be ready for everything. Sometimes you have to siphon out a venom before it gets to your heart." His eyes go wide. His face is still pale from the vampire's power.

That'll teach him to ask questions.

"You're... not lying, are you?"

I move around to her, and search for a vein. She's lost too much blood. She might not make it. I ignore Denny's question for now, and carefully pierce a vein in her arm. "Make sure the needle stays in. I need to get mine." I don't give him the chance to argue. I tap my arm a few times. The vein pops up quick.

Good. Fang fucker didn't take that much. It's impossible to tell in the moment.

I push the needle in. It stings pretty bad. I've been slashed by werewolf claws. I've been hit by a car. I've broken my arm. I've gotten tattoos and piercings. But needles still hurt, every damned time. I plug the rubber tube into her needle first, which Denny is holding meticulously still, and then into my needle. I pump my fist a few times to get the blood flowing.

"Keep a finger on her wrist. If her pulse slows, tell me." I say, holding my needle in place and flexing to keep things moving. Denny nods.

A few minutes pass. She seems stable. I remove the needles. I stand to put the kit away, and I fall to the side, bumping my head on the car.

"Whoa. We've got to get you to a hospital!" Denny says, moving to help me stand, supporting my weight.

"No way. No hospitals." I feel drunk. But none of the good parts. Just the sick and dizzy parts. I gave her too much. "Can't do hospitals."

"Lana..."

"I said no hospitals." I point to my driver's side door. Like I'm going to drive home.

"Fine. At least let me drive you home."

I think for a moment, then nod. I have no room to argue.

"What'll we do about her?"

I shrug. "Guess we take her with us."

#

Deductibles and copays aren't the only things keeping monster hunters out of hospitals. Probably the biggest part is the uncomfortable questions and mandatory police reporting. If you go into the ER with a bullet wound, cops have to be alerted. Contrary to popular understanding, monsters love to use guns. It helps them blend in and stay hidden. If you're exsanguinated, the doctors just won't let up on it. Exsanguinated, for those who haven't watched popular genre television in the past decade, means you've had your blood drained. Worse, there are monsters connected with some of the hospitals, looking for specific types of injuries so they can silence survivors, witnesses, and monster hunters when they're at their most vulnerable.

Our answer to this is a network of freelance doctors working under-the-table. Most of them are former doctors who have lost their licenses. Just like with iHunt, there's an app for it. MedPDQ lets you plug in your symptoms, just like WebMD. Then it sends your GPS data to the network. All the nearby doctors get an alert. The first one to respond gets your contract, and rushes to wherever you are, or wherever you tell them to go.

There's a lot to be said for GPS and smartphones and the surveillance state. But for those of us on the wrong end of monster attacks, that shit can be a lifesaver. I imagine that at some point in the future, monsters will start using the surveillance state against us. But in the mean time, the girl in my back seat is suffering from critical blood loss and no amount of calling 911 is gonna help. Even if she survived the trip to the hospital, she's black, and the first question they're gonna ask is, "Does she have insurance?" The answer to that question is the difference between a 50/50% chance of survival, and a 5/95% chance.

I fill out the form while Denny drives.

> "Two patients. Massive blood loss. No open wounds. Just need blood."

Within a minute, I've got a ping. I fall asleep for the rest of the ride.

#

Jane's a good doctor. I like her. I've worked with her a few times. She's way better than some of the cretins you get with MedPDQ sometimes. We only use first names in the underground gig economy. Too much liability if someone flips. Jane meets us outside my apartment. With Denny's help, I get the turtleneck rapist's victim to the door. Jane helps us inside.

"Vampires?"

I nod, barely awake.

"You've got to be careful, Lana."

I shrug, help Denny put the victim on my futon, then fall on the floor. Jane checks the other woman, then checks me. "You two are both going to need two units, right away. I'd recommend three."

I groan. "How much is that?" I think I know what she's going to say.

"$450 each. So, eighteen hundred. Or twenty seven if you want to play it safe." She looks apologetic. Of course she does. She's not overcharging me. The Red Cross bills about $150 per unit. And it's not like she can just buy them directly with a Visa or MasterCard. She's got to go through... hell, I don't know how she gets them. But it's not cheap or easy, and she deserves to be paid for her work. And unlike a "real doctor," the price is all-inclusive. She can't go back and tell me the needle was an extra $20 or the alcohol pad was $15.

"Shit..." I sigh.

She pierces the girl's wrist, and draws a small vial. The squirts the blood from that vial into three other vials full of clear liquids. "You know what? Let me call it $400, since you're a repeat customer." One of the three vials turns yellow and starts rapidly clumping up.

"Do you have the blood on you?" I sit up and lean against the futon, looking at her.

She nods, and tapes the needle to the wrist. "Yeah. With all the vampire attacks lately, I've had to. I've also started carrying the antivenom for the deadly ones." She turns and holds up a needle to me.

I shake my head and put a hand up. "I'm O negative."

"Hell. Let me see if I've got enough for you." She gets up and goes outside. A moment later, she comes back in with a large styrofoam camping cooler. "Yeah. I've got enough for both of you.

So, we going for two units, or are we going for three?"

I grit my teeth and think about it.

$1,600 or $2,400. I'm getting paid $5,000 for the kill. That's half my pay, right down the tubes.

I don't get paid until next Friday. Until that, I've got $13 to my name. That's what? It's Wednesday now. So nine days? Er. Tuesday. Ten days?

"Give her three, and give me two." $2,000. Not quite half my pay. That's what? 40%? And that's assuming the contract pays in full. Knowing my luck, it probably won't.

Jane nods. I can tell she wants to argue. She wants to talk me into that third bag. Not for her sake, not for her bottom line, but because she thinks I really need it. This isn't an upsell—this is a woman worried for my health. She taps something into her phone. I get a message from MedPDQ asking to confirm the invoice. I do. I turn my head away and give her my arm.

The blood cools my veins. I hate it. I have Denny give the unconscious girl my blanket, the only blanket in the apartment. I have him get me my one sweater. It's uncomfortable. Nauseating. It goes way too slow. Every few minutes, I look over to the blood bags, hoping they'll be empty, hoping Jane says "we're all done for now." It takes about two hours. I spend most of it passed out.

06
#SELFCARE

I wake to a message on my phone. The bounty went through. All $5,000. It's like Christmas, except I had to murder someone in the back of a Forever 21. Even with Jane's $2,000 bill, that leaves me with three grand. I make less than $2,000 a month at the park, and that's before taxes and insurance. That leaves me with just about $1,500. I want to do all kinds of "self-care". I want to hit up Sephora. I want to get a massage. But right now, I can barely even stand up.

Jane finishes the transfusions. She gives me her personal number before she leaves, and she tells me to ring her if anything changes with the other woman's condition. Denny sits, quiet as a ninja.

"You don't have to stay here."

He shrugs. "It's cool. I want to make sure you're okay."

"Fine. Thanks. Grab me my laptop over there, and we can at least put something on to watch."

We watch some old Mystery Science Theater 3000 episodes. Denny goes down the streets to get some burritos from Alberto's. He offers to treat me, and I'm just not in a condition to argue the point. We eat. We chill. We pass out, Denny on the floor on one side of the futon, me on the other, and our vampire food sleeping beauty on top of it.

#

"Where am I?" I hear a woman's voice. My eyes flutter open. It's dark. I grab my phone and check the time. 4:23am. Vampire food sleeping beauty's sitting up.

I grumble. I groan. My body hurts. It's like a hangover. "It's really complicated. Give me a minute and I'll..."

"No. Where am I? What's going on?" She shakes her head, a little confused.

I get up to my knees and face her, putting my hands out, trying to help her relax. "You got mixed up in some messed-up stuff. We had to pull you out of there. But it's okay now."

"No. That guy. The one in the Garden Plaza... He's a vampire. Are you vampires?" She looks to me, and down to Denny on the floor. Then her eyes go wide. "Is he dead?!?!"

"Yes." I say. She scrambles back on the futon, knocking it over. Denny sits up, startled. The woman crawls back up and looks over the futon, face white as a ghost when she sees Denny. "Oh my god. Did you make him a vampire?!?!"

"Huh?" I look to Denny, then back to her. "Oh shit! No. I'm not a vampire. Denny's alive. I'm alive. I meant the vampire's dead." I realize I just gave up any chance I had for denial. 4:24am is not a good time for cunning, strategic thinking.

She looks to us, confused, panicked.

"Look. I'm sorry. I'm tired. I'm a little fucked up. You and me, we both lost a lot of blood. I can explain everything in the morning."

She tilts her head, then gets up and stands the futon back up. Then she unfolds it to its full bed position. It's way bigger than I remember. It's been months since I've used it like that—I usually just collapse on it when I get home. "Who are you?"

"I'm Lana."

"I'm Denny."

"I'm Vanessa. Look. You guys can get up here. There's plenty of room. No sense sleeping on the floor."

Denny waves his hand and shakes his head. I don't. I get up on my bed and slump to my side, facing away from Vanessa. She puts the blanket over my shoulder; it's nice, warm. I pass right back out.

#

I wake up with Vanessa's arm and knee draped over me. I have to call out sick. There's just no way I can make it in today.

An eight hour shift. That's $96. Fuck.

I grab my phone and dial the employee hotline. It's all clinical. Detached. You go through a menu. You tell them which part of the resort, the park, the hotels, the shopping mall, or the parking facility. Then you tell them which department of the park. Then you hit a number for your section manager. Then you leave a message.

"Tom. It's Lana. I woke up sick to my stomach. There's no way I can make it in. I'm sorry. But Tiffany said she wants the extra hours. I'm scheduled off on Thursday. I'll definitely be in on Friday. I'll see you then."

That also puts me under 40 hours this week. So my $36 in overtime yesterday becomes $24. That makes it a $108 hit. Not $96. Great.

Vanessa yawns and stretches. Then she sits up and rubs her eyes. Denny looks over to us, and rolls his shoulders.

"Oh shit Denny. Don't you have work?"

He shakes his head. "No. I don't work Wednesdays and Thursdays. Besides, I needed to make sure you two were okay."

"Thanks." Vanessa says. She has this thick, long black hair. It's shiny, straight, you'd never guessed she was attacked then slept on it. So jealous. Her makeup ran a little. She's got these soft cheeks you could just get lost in. "I think I'm okay. But, would you two mind telling me what happened?"

I shrug and get up, going to my kitchenette. "Pretty much what you thought happened. A vampire attacked you. We didn't get to you until you were already unconscious." I check through the pantry. Pancake mix. I check the fridge, no eggs, no milk. "We stopped the vampire." I check the pantry again. Cake mix. Brownie mix. Hamburger Helper. "We couldn't take you to the hospital because it's not safe for vampire victims. So we took you here to my place." I go back to the fridge and pull out the leftovers from my burrito last night. I toss them in the microwave.

Denny butts in. "Lana, you're ignoring the parts where you gave her your blood so she wouldn't die right then and there. Then you took her here, and got a doctor to come by and give her an expensive blood transfusion so she'd make it through the night. You also ignored the part where I really didn't have anything to do with it, and you kicked that vampire's ass pretty much all by yourself. I just distracted him for a couple of seconds."

"You saved my life with that chair, Denny." I say, grabbing some hot sauce and a beer from the fridge.

"No way. You were doing just fine. I'm not stealing your valor. She would have died. I wouldn't have gone after him if you didn't first."

I tap my foot as the microwave spins and spins.

Vanessa speaks up. "So, you two kill vampires? For, like, a living? Because haven't I seen you at the Holy Crepes, Denny?"

"I work there part-time. I'm a librarian full-time. I... don't know about Lana. I thought she worked at the resort."

"I do work at the resort. Technically part-time, but about forty hours a week. I freelance as a monster hunter. Pay's not the best. But you know that. You've seen my apartment." The microwave goes "ding." I grab my burrito, and a fork. It's that kind of burrito. Massive. Carne asada, avocado, cheese, sour cream, and french fries. So greasy you can see through the paper bag it came in. Perfect hangover food. Not that I'm hungover, but it kinda feels the same. I look at the beer, and put it back in the fridge. I get a cup of water instead. "Can I get you guys anything? Got fuck-all for food, but I have, um... beer. And water? Sorry."

Vanessa asks for some water, Denny shakes his head. I get a cup for Vanessa, then go back to the futon to sit and eat.

"How do I help?" Vanessa says quickly, eager. I look over to her with a raised eyebrow, chewing. I realize I forgot to add hot sauce. I splash the Tapatio on the plate liberally.

"Yeah, how do we help?" Denny says. I give him the same look, and swallow.

"You don't." I cut another bite.

"What? Why?" Denny says. Vanessa leans in, as if to suggest the same question.

My shoulders slump. "Because it's dangerous. Because I'm stupid for doing it. And I'd be stupid for telling you how to do it. Because I'm trained, and you're not. Because I get that I'm going to die young over this, and that's not just a thing you can decide you're okay with because of one bad experience with a vampire." I take the bite.

Vanessa shakes her head. "But if there's one vampire, that means there's other vampires. And you said you're a monster hunter. If there were only vampires, you'd have said you were a vampire hunter. If this stuff is going on, someone's got to stop it. Besides, I'd be dead if it weren't for you." Denny nods, backing her up.

I grunt. "Yes. You'd be dead if it weren't for me. So, maybe don't go getting yourself killed? That wastes all my hard work, doesn't it?"

"We'll see." Vanessa says. "But he said you had to pay a doctor to help me. How much did that cost? Least I can do is pay you back?"

I shake my head, taking another bite.

Denny butts in again. "It was $400 per unit of blood. You needed three units. Probably would have been more if Lana hadn't given you some of her own blood."

Vanessa chews her lower lip, shocked at that. Maybe the number. Maybe because I gave her blood directly like that. "Um. Okay. Twelve hundred? I can do that. Maybe I can do $600 this month, and $600 next month?"

I wave my hand at that. "No. You don't have to pay for it. You were a victim. Besides, I got paid for killing the vampire who attacked you. It's really okay. I appreciate the gesture." Gotta change the topic, or she'll push the issue. "So I have a question. How'd you get into the Forever 21 office?"

"I work there. I'm an assistant manager. I guess the vampire knew, because he told me to take him there."

"Oh hell. Are you okay? Were you on the clock?" I lean in, trying to get her to open up a bit more. This is a time-honored trick you learn early as a monster hunter. Get them to talk about specific, personal issues, and they'll distract themselves from the supernatural stuff going on around them. When people get mixed up with the supernatural, they either walk away and go on with their lives, or they jump in feet-first. And when they jump in feet-first, they tend to die. A lot of these people, you save them, but then they go and get themselves killed later. It's awful.

She shakes her head. "No. A friend called me and asked me to meet her at the shopping district for dinner. She didn't show up, and wasn't answering her phone. But I was there anyway, so I caught a movie. The vampire was in the theater with me. I didn't think twice about it really; I figured he was just another creep. But seriously, I want to help. If you want me to stay alive, then show me how to do it right. Otherwise I'm just gonna run out and do it anyway."

Guess that plan didn't work.

I glance to Denny. He shrugs and nods.

Son of a bitch.

"Fine." They both perk up a bit. "But I'm gonna make a deal with you: I'll teach you about what I do. But it's one job, and one job only. You kill some vampires. You feel better about yourselves. Then you walk away. You go home. You live your lives. You stay away from the shadows. Deal?"

"Deal." They both say, Denny then Vanessa.

They sooooooooo don't mean that.

07
#BOOTCAMP

Wednesday passes. Vanessa goes to work that evening. So does Denny. I buy a clearance ribeye steak, eat it somewhere between room temperature and rare, smoke a bowl, then sleep for twelve hours.

Thursday, Tom calls and lays the guilt on thick. Tiffany's babysitter canceled, and she'll get a writeup if she misses a day. She covered for me yesterday so I dodged a writeup. So, I volunteer to take her shift. That puts me back into overtime territory at least. I do my eight hours. Tom asks me for another two. I don't feel like he's asking—I feel like he's telling. So I take them. Friday, same thing, but four hours, not two. Saturday, same four hours. Sunday, two hours again. Forty four hours in four days. Every day, a half an hour into the security checkpoints and employee shuttle buses in, a half an hour of security checkpoints and shuttle buses out.

I spend a few hours before and after my shifts, walking the Garden Plaza, looking for the other two vampires. I regret not questioning the first one, or at least searching his pockets. In the heat of the moment, you generally kill first, and ask questions if someone survives. The consequences for not killing your opponent often include but aren't limited to death.

I search, but have no luck. It's frustrating, but this is the big leagues. At five grand a head, I can afford to take a little while searching. Denny gives me a smile and a knowing nod every time I pass by. Vanessa looks for excuses to catch my attention and try to sell me on a shirt or a dress or something. She asks what she should wear to training.

#

Monday comes along. I'm off. I want to relax. But I promised Vanessa and Denny I'd give them a little basic training. I take them to a park in Maplewood that's really ideal for this stuff. Maplewood's full of people who work constantly, so the parks are mostly empty during the day. Sometimes you'll get a drug deal or something, but they're not going to call the cops if they see you doing some combat training. You can say whatever you want, too. If they hear you talking about werewolves, they just assume it's code. I particularly like this park, because it's full of old repurposed tractor tires and stuff. Kids love crawling through it. I love jumping it, crawling through it, and using it to practice hitting things. It's great for parkour, and not full of shit hipsters like the three actual public parkour courses in San Jenaro.

They come together in Vanessa's green Hyundai Elantra. It's a cute car, but easily a decade old. She takes good care of it. I don't blame her. My car gets all roughed up because the job takes me down back roads chasing weird shit at all hours of the night, or I'd take care of mine, too. They get out. She's in scarlet and gold sweatpants and t-shirt, 49ers colors with a big white "7" on the shirt. She looks good. Like, her hips make her maybe the only person in the world who can make sweatpants look good. Denny's in gray sweatpants and a slightly different color of gray long-sleeved t-shirt. I feel like if he's going to go hunting monsters with me, I might have to dress him. But he's cute in a sort of Charlie Brown kind of way. They wave. They're way more positive about this than I was for my initial training. Different circumstances I guess.

"Hi guys. So, alright. I don't want to be a hard-ass about this. But that's kinda the job. You've gotta keep up. I'll tell you some things, but we'll be doing it while working out. All the knowledge in the world doesn't matter if you can't run away from a thing trying to kill you."

They both nod firmly.

They're actually into this.

"So we start off with warmups. Jogging. Let's do a few trips around the park, to get the heart going." I don't give them the chance to think about it. I turn, and start the jog. They follow. Denny's off to a rough start. I don't think he does much running in the library or the crepe shack. Vanessa's right there with me, completely effortless. I feel like maybe she could outpace me. That's both good and bad. A strong start can lead to overconfidence. Overconfidence can kill you in this line of work.

Then again, so can not being capable.

Basically, everything can kill you in this line of work. As a monster hunter, your retirement plan is, "You won't live long enough to retire." On the plus side, you don't have to deal with

Medicare cuts.

So, I pick up the pace. Vanessa has to strain. Denny struggles, and falls behind. "Denny, you've got to push yourself. Vampires won't go easy on you."

"Yes, ma'am." He gasps back at me. He pushes harder. I can tell he's trying. He's gonna hurt himself today. That's for the best, but for now, he's hurrying. He's keeping up. Good for him.

"Lesson one: You learn the most while running. So you have to pay attention while running." They both mumble in understanding. I give them a couple of seconds, then stop and pull a gun, training it on Vanessa. She stops, jumps to the side, eyes wide. Then I point it at Denny. He stops, and puts two hands in the air.

I shout, "Bang!" He blinks twice, his face goes from slight California surfer tanned to stark white instantly. I put the gun away. "Monsters do not take mercy. If you're lucky, they kill you. If you're unlucky, they take prisoners. Prisoners never make it out the same person." He nods, terrified. Vanessa gets up and walks over to Denny, putting a hand on his shoulder. He forces a smile to her.

"That was a cheap trick, I know. But, unfortunately, cheap tricks are like... vampire 101. Vampires are not fair fighters. Vampires will use any edge they can. They like to surprise you." I look to Vanessa. "Do you remember the bite?"

She takes a deep breath and nods. "Yeah. I remember the bite."

"What was it like?"

She takes another deep breath and looks away. She shakes her head and looks back to me, and to Denny. "It was wrong. The moment he bit me, I wanted him. I couldn't fight. It was like even if someone tried to stop him, I'd try to stop them because it was just that good. I haven't stopped thinking about it since that night, being honest."

"Exactly. So, their fangs are a top priority. If they bite you, you're out of the fight. You're as good as dead. And if they kill you like that, you might come back their servant. Then?" I pause for effect.

"Then I have to kill you."

The two look between each other, then back to me.

"You can walk away at any time. If this gets to be too much, there's no shame in calling it quits."

I think back to my teacher. She was tougher. She kept telling me I wasn't good enough. That I'd be murdered. That she was wasting her time by teaching me. She pissed me the fuck off, and I trained that much harder just to prove her wrong. But I don't think I've got that kind of heart. I don't think I can really be that mean to them. I feel like it's going to get them killed. I'm gonna get them killed.

They glance to each other again, then back at me.

"Alright. Let's do these few laps."

#

We run. We do another eight laps around the park. We go

until Denny looks like he's going to pass out, then I call for a water break.

"Denny, you need cardio. No excuses. The resort pays part of a gym membership if you need it, and…"

He puts his hand up. "My apartment's got a 24 hour gym. I've been looking for an excuse to get off my ass and use it."

"Good." I look to Vanessa. "Where'd you learn to run like that?"

She chuckles, blushing a little and looking down. "I was in track."

"Good. It'll help. Your homework's going to be climbing. Lots of climbing."

She nods firmly. I feel like I don't need to get into details with her.

"Next detail about vampires. Their gaze. They can charm you. They can make themselves attractive, distracting. They can go from your worst enemy to your biggest crush with just some eyelash batting."

They both nod. Denny's leaning down, hands on his knees, catching his breath.

"The trick to that is, you've got to hurt yourself. The moment you feel like you want to fuck a vampire, bite your tongue hard enough to bleed, or slam into a wall, or stab yourself. Whatever it takes. There's no harm you can do to yourself that'll compare to what they'll do to you under their spell."

"Gotcha boss." Denny says, standing.

"It's harder than it sounds. You want to please them. And hurting yourself doesn't come natural."

"Fuck if it doesn't." He says, and pulls up his left shirt sleeve. He's covered with scars in a cross-pattern. Self-inflicted—I've seen that before. A lot of hunters were cutters. Most of us had problems with self-harm. Hunting's like therapy if you can't afford a therapist. I don't think I hunt as therapy. That's what the drugs are for. The Adderall, the OxyContin, the cocaine, the Thorazine, the Ritalin—those are therapy. I hunt for the money. I hunt because it's what I know. I'm a fucking weapon, and short of flying off to a country I can't spell to kill the less fortunate as an inhuman, soulless private military contractor ghoul—figurative, not literal—there's not really a lot of room for people like me to make a living.

I think back. I realize I've never seen him in a short-sleeved shirt. Even in the middle of summer, he always wore a long-sleeved t-shirt under his work uniform. I thought he was just hiding tattoos.

I nod. I don't dwell on it. I look to Vanessa. She nods back. I don't question it. Her confidence is infectious. She could be a great team leader. I hope and fucking pray she uses that skill at the Forever 21, and stays away from hunting monsters once we're done. She could be good at this—real good. But being good at monster hunting means you might live to see 40 instead of just 28. She deserves better.

"Next lesson. Self-defense basics."

I walk them through a few simple blocks and stances. Neither of them can fight. But they're both eager to learn. I'm not too rough on them this time. I just want them acquainted with how to knock away a weapon and how to gain the upper hand when surprised.

08
#AGENCY

Tuesday's work. Boring. Mechanical. Same with Wednesday. Same with Thursday. That was, until my last 15 minute break of the evening. I was managing customer flow during the laser light show at 10:45, scheduled to leave at midnight. I got to my locker, and checked my phone. I had a message through the iHunt app.

"I have information on your marks in the resort district. My rates are reasonable."

The message has an attached picture. It features a young woman, a vampire, feeding on security footage. She was feeding on a huge guy, but I couldn't get any details on either of them. Too fuzzy, and a bad angle. It's also blurred so you can't see where it was taken.

One of the most annoying parts of the gig economy is the scammers and the vultures. Any time you take a moderate to good contract, you'll get countless messages offering assistance services. They always want a percentage, about 10 to 25 percent. They promise you a cleaner, easier hunt. Usually they just have some basic information you could get with fifteen minutes of recon. You can report them to the iHunt administrators, but they usually just respond and tell you they're offering legitimate services, even if we don't find them valuable.

In this case, though, I'm pushing 55-60 hours a week at the

day job, and I just can't do that basic recon. So I hit them back.

"What do you have? And what are your rates?"

The response is so quick it feels like they must have been waiting for me.

"Just ten percent. I have information on three marks. Unfortunately two of the other marks you're looking for are already dead, and have been for a couple of weeks."

Hm. That sounds oddly specific. Specific enough that it might help the search. If I catch two of them, that's a $1,000 cut, but I'll still be taking home $9,000. I message back.

"I'll give you five percent, but I'm not agreeing until I see your proof of the dead ones."

Again, they were quick to reply.

"Eight percent. No lower."

They attached a photo. About a 45-degree angle. The other two from my contract, the woman in the pink puffy coat and the man in the black leather jacket. They were disintegrated, but those clothes were pretty obvious. If it was a trick, this person went to a ton of effort to fake it. The two were lying in the streets, surrounded by blood. It was a slaughter. They weren't killed by a vampire hunter—this was vampire-on-vampire violence. Truth be told, that's how most vampires actually die. Unfortunately, they never kill the worst among them.

"Deal. 8%. Send me what you've got."

I get an iHunt alert for a conditional invoice. It acts like a rider on your contract. If you fulfill it, X% goes to a third party. This is a good way to pay for small teams. It's also how these scammers get you. The way they pop up, if they're phrased right, you can accidentally sign away a percent of your earnings without even noticing it.

A few moments later, I get a link to a Tempest folder. Tempest is another app, it's a cloud storage thing like Dropbox or iCloud, but it's ridiculously secure and you get 5 gigabytes free when you sign up for iHunt, with an extra 500 megabytes with every successful contract kill.

The folder's full of PDFs. I flip through. A lot of them are scribbled schedules for the past couple of weeks, showing where three other vampires hang out. They spend a lot of time in Seaside. There's a hostel there called The Adventurer Suites. There's a red X scrawled near it and "DANGER STAY AWAY" in huge letters. They spend most of their time in the resort district though. There's a pretty solid list of where they hunt. They seem to cycle through, hunting about every other night at different bars and shops. They all have favored places to take their victims, along with some photos.

The first photo he sent me, he sent me the untouched version. It was Make America Great Again guy. I wouldn't have recognized him, except for his broken nose and bleeding face. It looks like someone got to him before the cops arrived. Someone in this case was a young redhead, pale, skinny, covered with freckles, and curvy. Pretty hot, if not for the murderous tendencies in the picture. She's holding up MAGA's body while she feeds. It looks awkward since she's a little lighter than me, and he's easily twice my weight, probably more.

The second photo is a… person? It's the kind of person who shouldn't be able to walk around the resort district. It looks utterly inhuman. The skin's pulled tight to the bones. The lips are dried up and stretched back, exposing almost all of its teeth. The eyelids seem nonexistent, revealing huge orb eyes. Its skin was covered in red scratches, probably self-inflicted. It barely had any clothes on, they were all just old, tattered shreds of cloth left over from heaven-knows-what. It wasn't doing anything wrong, per se. But just being in the resort district was a huge red flag though. That meant it was walking around invisible.

I have a brief flashback to one of my first major hunts. An Eastern European lord, a relative of Dracula, came to San Jenaro. I took him down, but he was tough as hell. Near the end of the fight, he looked a lot like this.

This doesn't look like real security footage at a glance. This looks like one of those internet hoaxes like the one about the Russian sleep experiment where they tortured guys into not sleeping for weeks at a time until they scratched off their skin and ate each other or some shit. If it weren't for the very specific context, I'd say it was bullshit. Sometimes you get people trying to pass us hoaxes. Sometimes the client believes it. Sometimes they're just trying to fuck with us. This doesn't look like a hoax, though.

I've never seen a vampire that looked anything like this thing. It looks like a monster. Vampires are usually sexy. Sometimes they're plain average. But this thing? It's something else. I toggle back and forth through the pictures and the documents, but I keep finding myself back at that terrifying image. I can't let go of it.

Weirder still, he goes out in the middle of the day. They both do. Only one family of vampire dies in the sun, but most still do most of their hunting at night. They seem stronger at night.

"Lana?" I hear a man's voice.

I snap to attention. "Huh?"

"Lana? Do you realize what time it is?"

Jake. The shift lead for the light show. He's this effeminate, overly-groomed guy. A tan that says he puts too much effort into tanning, and bleached blonde hair that says he puts too much effort into pretending he's blonde. He's popular with the staff, because he's the kind of manager who it's easy to brown nose. He likes to hang out with "the underlings" as he calls them, and he gives promotion recommendations to anyone that gets drunk with him on his nights off. All the hard work in the world means fuck-all to him, so long as you're the kind of person who goes to play Quizzo with him at Buffalo Wild Wings. I'm not one of those people.

I shake my head. "No. Oh shit. I'm sorry."

"It's ten after eleven, Lana. The show's almost over, and your yellow section is backed up with over two hundred guests." He pauses. "You're ten minutes late coming back from break. Are you high?"

"I assure you, Jake, I am not high. Just, I got a really nerve-wracking personal message, that's all. I'm sorry." I move to dodge around him, to get to the time clock.

He puts a hand in front of me. "This is the third time this month. Do you know the third core company value, Lana?"

"Punctuality." I roll my eyes. "Now, can I be punctual and clock back in?"

He doesn't let me go. "You know, Lana, I think we need to talk to HR about your problem with the core values. You seem to know them. But I don't understand why you don't respect them."

"I think HR leaves at eight, and there are two hundred guests backed up in the yellow section who could use my first core value right about now."

He lowers his arm. "We'll talk about this tomorrow."

"Sure Jake." I go out and smile my ass off for those two hundred people. Which, I might add, were actually only one hundred and twenty. Lying asshole.

09
#COREVALUES

I wanted to hunt Thursday night. I wanted to hit the streets with all that sexy new data, I wanted to find those fuckers, and I wanted to end them. But I couldn't. Not after that full shift. And definitely not after that bullshit with Jake. So I go home, have a beer, spend about ten minutes of quality time with my vibrator, then collapse so I can wake up and waste away another day at the resort tomorrow.

#

When management needs to tell you something, they alert you by way of your time clock. You swipe your ID card, then you get a pop up telling you to report to wherever, instead of the usual, "Thanks for giving our guests a glamorous day!"

"PLEASE REPORT TO HUMAN RESOURCES BACKLOT IMMEDIATELY"

Fucking wonderful.

#

Human Resources is almost insulting by virtue of its very existence. The resort staffing department is this massive, beautiful building full of bright lights and warm colors. The administration offices and payroll are off-site, housed in a building that's nondescript on the outside, but lavish and gorgeous on the inside. Human Resources, however, is a couple of trailers just out of sight. They're way too small to house the staff they manage. The staff is way too small to handle the employees they have to handle. The trailers are a "temporary solution" they've been dealing with for over three years while corporate finds them a better location.

When you go to HR, you take a number, then you sit. Depending on the day of the time, it can go quick, or you can be there for hours. Friday afternoon's rough. This stinks, because those two or three hours cuts into your practical hours. You're on the clock, sure, but that time doesn't count toward bonuses, toward promotions, and toward training targets. I get in at noon. At 3:15, they call my number.

Trudy's at the desk. I like Trudy. Trudy likes me. She's about 68 I think. She's only working here because her 35 year old son has some health problems and can't keep a job, but he can't quite qualify for disability. So she has to pay for his insurance. One time in the break room, she told me Obamacare reduced the premium by half, so now it's only half her take-home income every month. She told me she wished it covered her, too. She has to go without. She sees me, and she winces. She's not happy about this. Shit. It's *that* meeting.

"Hey Trudy." I sit. I look at the picture of her with her son on her desk. Chucky, she calls him. He hates it. He was in medical school for a while, but dropped out. She used to tell me that she'd go to his school events, and he'd get embarrassed when she called him Chucky. But she loves Chucky. And Chucky's why she's got to play by the rules.

"Lana. We got a report that you were late to clocking back in from break last night, which caused guest flow problems. Do you have anything to say about that?"

I shake my head. "It's my fault. I screwed up. I'm sorry. I got a message from an old friend that left me shook, and I lost track of the time. If I went out in front of the guests, I feel like I would have broke down crying."

She sighs, and taps her pen on her desk. "Lana, Lana, Lana." She glances away from me, then shuffles the paperwork back into a stack. "Your department manager gave a recommendation that you undergo a three-day suspension, and submit a drug test by three this afternoon."

I can't pass a drug test. There's no way in hell I can pass a drug test.

"It's already 3:15. I got here ten minutes before my shift at noon. I can't do that. I came right here."

She nods. "I know. And I can write in my recommendation, explaining that you were here in good time, and made every possible effort. But, new company policy says we administer the tests here." She gets up and walks a couple of feet to a filing cabinet, and pulls out a ziplock bag with some papers and a cup. She comes back to sit down. "You can take this to the restroom over by guest services."

The HR department doesn't even have their own toilets. If they don't consider toilets a resource for humans, what qualifies? Or do they mean the humans are a resource, like the company has all these different kinds of resources, and humans are just one of them?

"California law says I can't be subject to a drug test unless I'm injured on the job, or I agree to take one voluntarily." Check and mate.

"I don't know if you're right or wrong, Lana. If you're right, you can take that up with an attorney. All I know is that company policy says if my screen says you're supposed to take a drug test, you're supposed to take a drug test. And according to my notes, you're not allowed returning to work until the results are in."

I clench the armrests of my chair and look away. I grit my teeth until it hurts. If I fail a drug test, that could burn me. Marijuana's not criminalized, but it might as well be for service workers. They can't put you in jail, but they can sure as fuck fire you for it, and make sure you can't find another job. It's not like I have a legal leg to stand on, either. I signed a disclosure form when they hired me, which said I could be subject to a drug test at any time, for any reason. They wouldn't have hired me if I didn't.

"Lana, I'm sorry. You know this isn't personal. If I had any say, we'd stop these tests. But corporate…"

"Yeah. Corporate." I stand. "No offense Trudy, but fuck this. If the company doesn't trust me, I can't work here."

"Lana, rethink this. If you don't give your two weeks' notice…"

I cut her off, shaking my head. "Then I'm not eligible for rehire. I know. It's not like I have a choice here." I snatch my ID card off my lanyard, and drop it on her desk. "Bye."

#

My march out isn't quite as sexy as I pictured it when I left. I get about thirty feet from the HR office, and four security guards come at me, grabbing my arms.

"Whoa. What in the fuck? I'm leaving."

An older, black-haired, short woman responds. She seems to be the senior officer. "We're escorting you off the premises. Company policy."

"Yeah. Company policy. Always company policy. At least let me get changed. Don't want to take my uniform home. Company property, right?" I don't even know why I'm getting in their shit. It's not going to score me any points. Nobody's watching. But I'm furious. I want to fucking scream.

"We'll send the contents of your locker to the address you have on file with HR. We'll also send you a postage paid box. Put your uniforms and any other company assets in the box and send it back. If we don't receive them within the next fourteen days, they'll be taken out of your final check." She's got this speech down. She must say it a couple of times per day. With 30,000 employees, that's pretty likely.

#

It's like insult to injury, having to leave work in my uniform after being fired. It also keeps me from walking the shopping district, since security will stop me for being in-uniform off the clock.

Fuck it.

I don't even get in my car. Too much anger. Too much energy. I want to hit something. I jog down the street to a little tourist shop, the kind of place full of "California" clothes. Hawaiian shirts. Screen-printed t-shirts. Gaudy shorts. Beach towels with Marilyn Monroe fucking the California Republic bear or whatever. But, most importantly, cheap, quick clothes.

I grab a black Route 66 tank top, and a pair of dark green cargo pants. They beat the denim shorts with the fake fraying bottoms, and the palm tree pattern swimming trunks. I get a pair of fake Sketchers since I might have to run, and I have to wear uncomfortable-assed loafers to the park. I tie back my hair, and hit the shopping district.

#

With the schedules, with the lists of hangouts, it just takes a couple of trips across the Garden Plaza before I catch sight of the redhead from the picture. She's in black fatigue pants and a red halter top, with combat boots. Kind of like a perverted mirror of me right now. She's all fucking business, prowling. She's scanning, scoping, her eyes hit a hundred people a minute. Just like I'm doing. I don't think she's hunting, at least in the proper sense. She's not showing any signs of hunger—she's not particularly pale, I don't see any visible veins, she's not especially tense, her fangs aren't extended—and she's not taking some pretty easy marks. The kind I'd go for if I was a vampire.

Maybe she's just picky?

Part of hunting vampires is putting yourself in their shoes. Trying to think what they're thinking. It's harder than it seems. As you learn more about them, you can start to predict feeding patterns, but every vampire has their own specific preferences. It makes sense though. Late-night resort staff tends to eat after their shifts. But some want Taco Bell, some want McDonald's. The shift leads have a little more money, so they might go to the Buffalo Wild Wings. It's all about context. This means I spend a lot of time asking myself, "What would I do right now if I was a vampire?"

Long story short, she's not hunting. There's no way.

Then what in the hell is she doing?

I feel something heavy on my shoulder. It squeezes, damned near crushing my collarbone. Then I hear a voice, low, mean. "You should have said thanks for the compliment, bitch."

10
#MAGA

The grip around my shoulder tightens. I feel stress on my chest and arm. There's a stabbing pain down my spine. "FUCK!" He's not human. Not even a little bit.

I do what I'm trained to. I fall. I prepare to shift in place. But when I drop my weight, he doesn't go down with me. His hand's holding tight to me, like I'm no heavier than a bottle of soda he dropped and caught.

Then he throws me.

Being thrown by a superhuman monster is a little like it is on TV, only faster. You fly. You slam into something. It knocks the wind out of you. You roll a bit. If nothing's broken, you catch your breath and you get back up. It actually looks worse than it is. You've got to think, even vampires can't throw you faster than gravity, and people survive ridiculous falls all the time.

Doesn't mean it doesn't hurt—It hurts like a motherfucker.

I slam into a wall. I feel and hear plaster crack against my back. I don't know what wall I hit. I don't know what direction I was going, or even what part of the Garden Plaza I was at. The worst part is that spiky stucco shit they put on the walls to make it look rustic. That puts all these little dents and tears in your skin where it hit. It also probably ruined my new shirt.

I try to get up. My vision goes blurry and spins. I fall face-down against the sidewalk. Gonna need to wear some extra concealer for the next few days. Out of the corner of my eye, I see his shoes. Massive, size 930 Nikes stomping my way. I briefly consider telling him that his shoes are made in a country Trump plans to cut trade to. Instead, I force myself to my feet. It's not badass. It's not graceful. It's not dramatic. I barely even manage, with all the nicks and scrapes and blood.

I take that back. It's actually pretty badass.

As I'm standing, I realize my left arm's out of socket. It hurts, but survival instincts are telling me pain doesn't hurt. I rock my chest back, and grab the shoulder to brace it. I roll the shoulder, and it proves to me that—yes—pain does in fact hurt. But it pops back into place.

"I'm gonna give you one warning." I say to him. Vampires react one of two ways to ultimatums and threats. Sometimes, their survival instinct takes over, and they back off. Smart vampires know when to back off. Other vampires, they go ballistic. They think they're King Shit, and they've gotta prove it. So they charge, they hiss, and they go for the throat. Against pretty much any human, that means they win. Even against a trained soldier with an assault rifle, it means death.

Against a vampire hunter, it means an opportunity.

And, spoiler alert, Mr. Make America Great Again goes ballistic.

He lunges forward with hands the size of medium pizzas, and fangs the size of, I don't know, lipstick tubes. Or at least it looks that way in the moment.

I try to dodge to the side—to use his momentum against him. That's 101 shit. Vampires are strong. Vampires are fast. You're not. So you've got to use what they've got as a weapon.

I fail, miserably. I trip over a green rubber hose. I don't fall, but I also don't dodge out of the way. MAGA slams his palms into me, going for the grab, but he knocks me over instead thanks to my lack of balance. I fall back on my tailbone.

Fucking fuck fuck fuck sonofabitch fuck.

I don't even tell my body to, and it jumps back up to my feet. I put my hands up for an instinctive, rough defensive stance. MAGA goes low and barrels into my stomach like a football tackle. He lifts me off the ground, and I start kicking him in the stomach and pounding on his back. It's all I've got from this position.

He runs, charges into the wall right where he threw me a moment ago. His shoulder pins me, crushing my stomach, knocking the wind back out of me. After the initial surge of pain, everything goes numb. My body goes limp.

He stands, hefting me and tossing me forward to flop against the wall. As I slump down, he grabs my shoulder again. I see his face. His blue eyes. His fangs. I feel the tell-tale exhilaration—he's trying to charm me. I've got nothing. I don't think I could respond even if it worked.

He hisses, and slowly goes in for the bite. Fucker's savoring it. This is him claiming victory.

Not today. Not now.

I don't have much strength, but I've got one impulse left in me. I reach up with one hand, and grab his face, burying my middle and index fingers into his pretty blue eyes, and I hook my thumb into his upper lip. And I clench. I dig. I grab him like he's a winning lottery ticket about to fall in the ocean. I squeeze his face like a lump of clay in a community college art class the day after a breakup when you were begging her to stay, even though she broke up with you and not the other way around, but she wouldn't and you know she's going to move right in with that dude-slut.

He screams. I don't stop. I grab harder. I put everything I've got into it. He releases my shoulder, and I push his huge fucking face away from me. He stumbles back. He grabs at his bleeding eyes, and pulls his hands away like he wants to look at them. You know, except without eyes.

I think about Jake. I think about HR. I think about $5,000. I think about drug tests. I think about dying to this newbie garbage piss monster vampire. I think about what'll happen to Denny and Vanessa if I disappear or turn up dead. I kneel down with my right leg back, then swing it up hard, putting all my weight into it. I connect with a loud crack of broken bone and cartilage, and my shin makes the fucker's face great again.

Fun tidbit: When you punch a person in the mouth, you can get an infection from their teeth. It's called "fight bite." While vampire fangs are harder and sharper, you can't get infections from them. Their saliva's antibacterial. I guess that's to protect their victims and keep the local blood supply safe. That means there's just about zero arguments for not knocking out a vampire's teeth.

I expected to knock him back, but mostly I just stun him. His face is covered with blood. I not only kicked his teeth in, I shredded his lips. He looks like he made out with a weed-wacker.

I don't take time to admire my art. I drop my right foot to the ground, spin, and plant my left foot in his solar plexus, knocking him back. A lesser monster would fall to the ground. But this caveman's a goddamned tank. He buckles over at the stomach. I drop to my left foot, then raise my right leg back up vertical to my chest, and bring it down on his collar. Classic axe kick. Brutal. Inelegant. But it does the trick. He falls to his knees.

I draw a fist back, ready to smash his face again and again. Then I realize everyone's looking. There's a circle forming around us. People scream. People are filming with their phones.

Shit. Gotta think fast.

This looks like murder. You have self-defense rights in California, but any time you use self-defense against a vampire, it looks like excessive force. "Reasonable force" isn't enough to stop them, ever. Anything short of "excessive force" means you're dead.

I punch him a couple more times in the face. This is partly to keep him stunned while I think. This is partly because I really, really want to hit this motherfucker.

I look around. There's an Old Navy next to us. It's got this cute little scene outside, with a picket fence and a family of those frightening mannequins with the disturbing huge smiles, barbecuing. I guess they're trying to sell tourists on the California weather. The barbecue grill's on the ground in pieces. I think maybe that was because of me. If MAGA threw me like three feet over, I would have hit the glass floor-to-ceiling windows instead. That would have been much cooler.

This is the moment where—if I were in a cartoon—there'd be a lightbulb over my head. I've got a plan.

I put my fingers into some of the holes in my new Route 66 shirt, and tear it right off and rip it in half. That, of course, gets even more attention. But it's a noble sacrifice. I wrap the bottom half around my face kind of like a ninja or some anti-fascist black bloc type, covering my mouth. I tie it in the back. I figure with all the quick movement, hopefully nobody's gotten a good, focused shot of my face.

Then, I put my foot through the prop picket fence. It's a gamble, but it pays off—it's actual wood, not particle board. The slats fall apart. I grab one of the long boards and put my foot on it, right dead center. It's thin that it bursts in half with just slight pressure. Half a board is kind of, *kind of* like a spear. Kind of.

MAGA's getting up again, so I swing out my leg and smash him across the face. He reels. It's just enough. I wrap the top half of my Route 66 shirt around the board/spear thing to make a makeshift handle. I lift it up over my head, I jump, and I bring the point down on his collar, right next to his neck.

Stakes through the heart are hard, right? The chest is almost impenetrable. It's just a massive pain in the ass. I've said this before. But it's also possible. But if you really, really want to put a stake through a vampire's heart, you go through the collar. So long as you get the tip in between the clavicle, it's all tissue. It's not easy, but it's way squishier than the ribs. I love this trick—I've done it to way stronger vampires before.

I bring the spear down through his chest. He screams, and spews blood from his mouth. Vampires are like this. Messy. Disgusting. Just like in Lost Boys, vampire never go out clean. Everyone starts freaking out, screaming, shrieking. MAGA's trying to stand, trying to grab at me. Fortunately, I can keep him at spear length here. I take a step back, holding the makeshift handle, and I run forward and drop my weight, pushing it in further. He growls and grabs the shaft, trying to pull it out. His eyes are now red—glowing red.

One more time, heave-ho.

I howl out, and run forward, thrusting the spear in further. I push him back. His screams stop, that's how I can tell I hit the heart. But I don't stop. I push a little more, I keep pushing until he's pinned into the fake lawn of the Old Navy. His body begins rapidly decaying, crumbling into nothingness, just ash and chunks. I feel like there's probably some social commentary here.

I stop and look at the crowd. They're all wide-eyed and frozen in place. I shrug. They blink. I start clapping. Hesitantly, one or two start clapping. Then the whole rest of the group claps.

"Thank you! This was our practical effects exhibition. We're trying to use this to sell our new television show to the studios, kind of like a 2017 Buffy the Vampire Slayer. What did you think?"

And the crowd went wild.

"If you want to hear more, you can like Santa Zavala Studios on Facebook." I wave.

Sell the cover story.

That was the name of my would-be film production company when I made a couple of shorts in community college. It has enough pictures of me to be believable.

"What's it called?" One of the audience shouts out.

I shrug. "We don't have the working title yet. This is all just proof of concept filming."

11
#15MINUTES

I snap a couple of selfies with the audience, conveniently positioned to prove the kill. Gotta make that payday, right?

Instagram. #MovieMagic #LanaTheImpaler #SantaZavala #Vampire #FemaleLead #IndieFilm

Fortunately, the contract said nothing about being noticed or filmed. Logistics support is one of the big benefits of a corporate gig. The movie studios will back me on this one. They'll toss some lawyers at the witnesses. Money. Empty promises. I don't know, it's not my problem.

I head out. I quickly realize I lost track of the redhead. But hey, $5,000 isn't bad for a day's work. It takes an edge off the sting of being fired. Once I catch my breath, the pain sets in. Everything hurts. My side's covered in flecks of blood, mixed with little bits of dust and mud. My knuckles burn and ache. My ankle's torn up pretty bad from all that Making America Great Again.

In this line of work, you kind of have to be your own mobile clinic. Sure, you can hit up the MedPDQ if you're really torn up, but that's expensive and it takes time. When you're bleeding, when you're in pain, you've got to act fast. So, monster hunters have to be expert collectors. Except instead of stamps or coins or Beanie Babies, you collect illicit prescription drugs and whatever makeshift medical supplies you can scrounge. My kit's in my car, in the hidden compartment for the donut tire. I rifle through it. I grab some hydrogen peroxide. I look through the kit. It's full of so many felonies if I get caught. OxyContin for pain. Amoxicillin for infections. Benadryl for allergens. That one's not illegal. Epinephrine for really bad allergens. That one is illegal. Some generic loperamide for diarrhea, also not illegal. You'd be shocked to find how much of a problem that is. Rehydration powder. Dramamine. Ciprofloxacin. Albuterol. Iodine.

I pop a couple of the OxyContins, and start scrubbing clean with the peroxide. I get a couple of weird looks from others in the employee parking lot. I just shrug. They move on.

As I start my car, my phone buzzes. It's Denny.

"Hey Lana. Don't want to be the bearer of bad news, but you're famous. Hope that was part of your plan."

I pull out, and punch in a text with my off-hand. I briefly consider the dangers of texting while driving. Then I remember the vampire that almost murdered me earlier.

"Yeah. I got filmed by a couple of people. I passed it off as a movie shoot. I think they bought it."

He responds almost instantly.

"That's an understatement. You're viral. Resort employee posted it to Reddit. There's already fan art. They're shipping you with the woman from that Van Helsing show on Netflix."

That ship would never work.

I type back.

"Sad to say, their dream movie isn't happening. Anyway, I killed another vampire. And I've got leads on a couple of others."

I drive. He responds, but I give it a few minutes before I read it.

"The redhead in the red tank top? She's really obvious."

The problem with the supernatural is, once your eyes are open to it, they can never close. Any time you're in a big, crowded place, there's a good chance you've seen a vampire, a witch, or something worse. You just didn't know, because you didn't know what to look for. Once you know what to look for, you see this shit everywhere. When you see a pair of shoes and pants tossed behind a bush, you know that's a werewolf who had to dump her clothes before she changed. When you see a wall full of graffiti, and one otherwise normal tag is written backwards, you know that's witchcraft. When you see mushrooms growing along the side of a busy street, that's a budding fairy circle. You can't un-see the supernatural. Denny has spent less than five minutes around monsters, and he can already identify a vampire on the prowl. This never ends well.

"Yeah. Don't follow her tho. Don't let her know you know. I'm serious."

He'd better fucking not. I can't fight another vampire. Not

tonight.

"I won't. I promise."

Is that the "I'm totally going to do it as soon as I put down this phone" version of "I promise," or is it the actual, you know, "I promise" version of "I promise?" I reply.

"Scout's honor?"

Ten seconds. Fifteen. He's totally lying. God damn it, Denny.

"Skirt's honor."

That's better.

"Typo fail, Denny."

The first rule of monster hunting club is, you can't take yourself too seriously.

"Is it really though? :)"

I roll my eyes. I send him the eye roll emoji.

"So. There's a party Saturday. It's going late. Maybe we could go after your shift?"

I type a response. "Not this weekend. Too busy." I delete it. "I don't know, let me get back to you." I delete it.

"Actually I just got fired. Where's it at?"

I hit send.

#

Friday's uneventful on the hunting front. I avoid the

immediate resort area and patrol around it, hoping I run into something. I don't. I'm not gonna lie, I spent a good amount of time trolling through the news and trending topics about killing MAGA. The consensus was about half and half.

Half thought I should be immediately scooped up for a big budget superhero flick. People were Photoshopping me into Wonder Woman, Black Canary, Supergirl, and all sorts of other costumes. Of course there were Buffy comparisons. I accidentally seeded that one myself. I even saw one that said I should star in a Terminator reboot. Guess I could have a career after monster hunting if I wanted. Who am I kidding? I'd be lucky to land a stunt woman role. I'm too muscular for Hollywood—I scare fragile men. Also? Not white enough. I'm about half Brazilian, and half Japanese; if there was a movie about my life, Emma Stone would play me. Maybe Scarlett Johansson. I'm not old enough to get whitewashed by Tilda Swinton.

The other half thought I should be tried for treason because the guy I killed had a Trump hat. "Social justice warriors are taking over!" Um, no buddy. Monsters have taken over. We're just trying to level out the playing field a bit. These guys swear they're boycotting a movie that isn't even happening. Their outrage is delightful.

If this goes viral enough, I wonder if Donald Trump will whine about me on Twitter?

I realize I'm bored at around 6pm. Lonely. I message Denny and Vanessa. They're both working past midnight tonight. The joy of the holiday season. They won't even have a customer between 10pm and 11:30. They've just got to be there to handle the last minute rush after the laser show ends.

I decide to hit the gym. On the way, I get a message from my mom.

"I saw you on Facebook. You're trying to make movies again? You know there's no future in that."

I only ever hear from her when she realizes I've done something she disapproves of, or she wants money. I reply, then regret it the second I hit send.

"It's a fun project, it's good pay, and it's not my only work."

I tell myself I'm not going to read it when she replies. But I do.
"A million pretty girls like you go to California hoping to get into movies. They all end up pregnant or on drugs."

I am on drugs, mom. And I'm happier than I've ever been.
I ignore her and keep jogging.
She'll apologize in a few seconds. That's her pathology.
My phone buzzes.
"I'm so sorry. I didn't mean it like that. I miss you. We all miss you."

Of course you do. And next, you're going to ask me for money.
"It's just that your daddy's on hard times. You know the shoe factory closed, and Janine's beating down our door for the rent."

Of course she is. She is every time you think I've got any money.

"I'll Western Union you $500. That's the best I can do."

She replies immediately.

"Bless you. I'll pay it back as soon as I get my tax return."

No you won't. Stop pretending you will.

Five minutes later, I check my Facebook. She's shared a meme about lazy millennials who mooch off their parents, and how they killed a chain restaurant she's never been to. Hashtagged #MAGA. I wish she'd take that $500 and buy some self-awareness.

#

"You're the girl from that video!"

I'm punching a bag. I kind of wish I was punching this guy. He's kind of cute, except for the part where he's in my face, and I've given him every possible subtle cue to get out of my face.

"Yeah. I'm just trying to work out, y'know? Gotta keep in shape for the camera, right?"

He nods, putting his hand to his chin. "So, how'd you do that part where the guy crumbled to dust on the ground? That was so tight!"

I punch once, twice, three times. I picture his face. I grunt out, "Plaster and spirit gum."

He nods, and furrows his brow. "That makes sense. So, what about..."

I stop. I cut him off. I put a hand up. "Look. I'm gonna get out of here. I'm off the clock. I'm really not interested in talking shop. This is me unwinding."

His eyes go wide. "That's not a way to treat a fan. We're why you're successful. You should be *thankful*."

I blink twice, and bite down to stop myself from screaming. Successful. From my nonexistent movie. Where I almost died. I shake my head and start to the door, grabbing my bag.

"You don't get to just walk away. No fucking way."

Can't punch a human. Can't punch a human. Can't punch a human.

The thing about hunting monsters is, you train your ass off to be a lethal weapon. It isn't about self-defense. It's about eliminating the threat as quickly and as brutally as possible. This means if you turn your skills on a normal person, you will fucking murder them. So, you have to be careful. You have to be smart. Use your words.

I stop. I turn around to face him. "Look." I say, as loud as I can without screaming. About half the gym turns to look at me. "I told you I'm not going to fuck you. You need to keep your hands off me, and you need to leave me alone, or I'm calling the cops."

His face goes red. He looks around, shaking his head to the people, glaring at him accusatorially. I use the opportunity to make my way out.

12
#DOLLADOLLABILLS

I wake up Saturday to tons of messages. Facebook, Twitter, Instagram, email, whatever, it's all flooded. Some women in sci-fi and fantasy website wants to interview me. Deleted. I have about seventy marriage proposals. Deleted. A couple of companies "offer" to host my video on their Youtube channel, promising a bajillion views, and they'll just take a modest seventy percent of the ad revenue. Deleted. An agent wants to represent me for a future career in film, so long as I'm willing to do some "tasteful adult scenes." Deleted. A "content creator" convention asks if I'll be a guest of honor. They'll even get me a free badge, I just have to pay for the plane ticket and the hotel room. Deleted. I even have an email from a mid-level studio interested in publishing my movie. They said they're willing to discuss a budget of 2.5 million. For the hell of it, I tell them I'd like to hear more.

I go out to grab some clothes for the party. It's a house party in Ava Blue. That means it's a rich kid whose parents are away. Those houses are all basically mansions. They've always got great medicine cabinets if you get there before anyone else. No generics. Full to the brim, because their platinum-level health insurance plans mean they get over-diagnosed all the time. I build a little shopping list, things I hope to find. Klonopin would be nice. Some Demerol maybe. I can even sell any surplus—always gotta consider the hustle.

I hit the Park Town Mall over near the resort district. It's the kind of mall that was a Real Big Deal twenty years back when they built it, but now maybe a third of the stores are closed, and another third have "Final Clearance Everything Must Go" signs.

I bounce from shop to shop, looking for bargains. Then I see something I like. It's white. White's not really my color. It's also like $140. But it stands out, and it's cute. Besides, I deserve it. I've made like ten grand this week. I'm a fucking baller. If I don't spend money on myself, something else will take it. A bill will come up. My car will need some repair or another. It's this cocktail dress that hugs just right, with thin straps and a slit up the side. Most importantly, it's the right side, which is not the side where I'm all torn up from the fight on Thursday. It perfectly shows off my tan. If I'm going to this party, I'm going like a goddamned princess. On the way out, I see the redhead. She's watching me. Once I spot her, she ducks into an employee hallway. I check, but she's nowhere to be found. I dodge out before security figures out I don't belong there.

With a little Dermablend, some Ben Nye powder, and moderately thick pantyhose, you'd never know that I probably should have gone to the emergency room less than 48 hours ago. It's a trick I learned from a Reddit page from some domestic violence victims. I stop by Sephora, and grab some frozen yogurt on the way out.

#

I'm early. Not early enough. The medicine cabinet's already empty. The parents could have just emptied it before they left. Who am I kidding? They didn't. Someone else got the stash.

The early bird catches the Wellbutrin, Lana.

I'm way early in the actual party process though. 7pm. Denny's not here yet. There's a few dozen people, but maybe a tenth of what'll be here when the night winds down, or when the cops arrive to break it all up.

"Oh hey. You're the girl from the video!" Time and time again. I counted seventeen. That's not counting the ones who said it, then brought over a couple of friends to tell them, and they all said it. None were as pushy as the guy at the gym. Most of them offered to "buy me a drink." Which at a rich guy's house party means "go to the bar and tell them you want a drink." Not exactly buying. But I appreciate the sentiment. I take three beers over the first couple of hours. Pace myself.

By 10:15, the place is crowded. It's too loud to hear much of anything. I'm sitting on a sofa, nursing a beer in a Solo cup while a bunch of people around me tell stories about college life. I feel old. I've got a few years on most of the people here. I forgot that's one of the reasons I kept shooting Denny down when he asked me to do these things. Speaking of Denny, I get a text.

"I'm here. Where you at?"

Hoping to alleviate the boredom, I type back like my life depends on it.

"Livingroom. From the main door, make a right. Sofa in the far corner."

A moment or two later, he pushes through the crowd. He's in tight jeans and a blue button down shirt. It looks okay, but a little too tight for my tastes. No room to move. He'd be dead in a vampire attack. I briefly resent that my idea of sexy requires tactical utility in the face of supernatural menaces. I nudge people on either side of me. They look and see him, and defy physics to make room. He sits, all smooshed up against me.

"Nice party?" He says, damned near shouting just so I can hear.

I lean in to his ear. "It's okay. Boring. Everyone wants to talk about the stupid fight video."

He shrugs. "It was pretty awesome."

"Yeah whatever. All in a day's work." I flip my hair back, all action hero-like. I look to his empty hand, then back up to his face. "You don't have a drink."

He shakes his head. "I don't really drink. Addictive personality. It's a bad idea, y'know?"

"Yeah, I get you. I'll just drink enough for the both of us." I finish my current red cup of beer. He nods. We sit there. It seems like five minutes of dead silence (you know, aside from the music and yelling and everything else in the background) but it's probably just about thirty seconds. "So, um, how was work?"

"Work's work. Not closing, which is cool." He shrugs and looks to the crowd. And by the crowd, I mean the ass that's about a foot away from his face, smashed up against another ass to its left, and another ass to its right. We could drown in all this ass. Everything smells like sweat and pot smoke. It makes me wish I was at home, smoking pot away without all the sweaty meat in my face. "What about you? Why were you even working at the resort? You seem to make more than enough from hunting monsters."

I shake my head, and shout back. "Nah. This is the best-paying contract I've ever worked. It's unreliable. Sometimes I go a month without a contract. I guess maybe I can do it full-time now. But I really prefer to have a reliable paycheck. Rent's too much to fuck around and risk it."

"You ever considered getting a roommate?"

I shrug. "Nah. I mean, I've considered it. But it's not feasible. Most roommates have a problem with you rolling in at 3am with your mob doctor friends, doing makeshift surgery in their kitchenette."

He laughs, a little weak. "But what if they're like... in on it?"

I freeze. I really, really don't want him and Vanessa to get in too deep.

They're already in too deep. I hope they don't die.

I shrug and stand up. "I really don't wanna talk about work right now. I'm gonna grab another drink."

He stands right after me. "Lemme get it?" He knocks the ass in front of him, who knocks the ass beside her. They all sort of lose balance, and one turns and splashes a little beer on us.

I put my hands up while the beer's owner apologizes over and over, and Denny's trying to wipe the drink off my dress. "I'll get it. I'll be right back." I push through the crowd, practically swimming through a sea of flesh toward the bathroom. Once I get there, I do my best to scrub out the beer, then dig through the cabinets. I grab a hair dryer, turn it on, and pray it doesn't shrink my new $140 dress. My phone buzzes. It's Denny.

"You okay?"

I sigh, shake my head, and punch out a response.

"Bathroom. Cleaning up. Chill."

The dress perseveres, except for this one fucking part, right down the center. It's a little warped, and a little yellow. It might come out in the laundry. Maybe.

Can I even wash this dress? Or is it dry clean only?

My phone buzzes again.

Fuck I can't do this right now.

Someone pounds on the bathroom door.

"Just a second!" I say in my chipper resort employee voice. Might as well take advantage of the skill since I won't be using it at the resort anymore.

I'm all over the place. I'm staring at the toilet paper roll. Then the mirror. I see every single one of a million little blackheads on my nose. I look at my phone.

"Sorry :("

I roll my eyes. I fish through my purse for a tiny ziplock bag with two Adderall and a Coumadin. I need the Adderall to deal with tonight. The Coumadin's just a hunch. I toss them on the marble counter, and pull a little piece of metal out of the purse pocket. It's a strip of maybe aluminum, maybe steel? I don't know. It was part of a hose clamp I broke off, just a thin piece of metal covered with holes. I push it down on the pills, and run it back and forth a few times, turning it into powder in seconds. I pull a five dollar bill out of my wallet, and roll it up. I hate, hate, hate using money for this stuff. It's filthy. But it's all I've got right now. I used to carry a straw. I stopped when I told myself I wasn't going to do this anymore. It makes me feel like a more casual user if I don't have all the necessary supplies on me at all times.

I pull the reddish orange powder into a line, lower my head to it, and inhale hard. It burns a little, but I'm used to it. My eyes water. My passages start filling up with mucus. I sneeze. But the rush is instant. All my muscles tingle and give in.

OhEverything's right again. My stupid job doesn't matter. Vampires are stupid. Denny's texts are actually kind of endearing, not pushy.

Oh yeah, Denny.

I type out a response.

> "It's okay. Be right back."

I stop by the bar on the way back, and grab a gin and cranberry. No more beer tonight. The crowd sort of fades away. They're background noise. I feel like a ballet dancer, gliding through them. I'm perfectly aware of all their bodies, all their shoulders, and all their fucking drinks.

I like Adderall, because it feels the way they describe being a new vampire in a trashy vampire romance novel. Everything buzzes a little. You feel sexier, more graceful, stronger. It's like being a Disney princess and an action hero all in a little pill, and it's perfect.

I poke though the last little crowd, and wiggle my fingers to Denny. He smiles wide, and slides over enough to give me about a fourth of a sofa cushion. I glide down, squeeze in, and drape a leg over his.

"Oh hi." He squeaks out and blushes. "Everything okay? You look great. Or, I mean, your dress looks great. I don't see any beer on it."

I turn to face him, and suck on my tiny straw. "Which is it?"

"Hm?" He raises an eyebrow.

"You said I look great, or my dress looks great. Which is it?"

He's all the way red now. "Your dress. I mean, both. You look great. But, your dress looks clean. And great. It's a great dress, I mean. On you."

I laugh out loud. He smiles nervously. Again. Exactly how they describe vampires. I totally get why most of them have power trips.

He blurts out, "You get what I mean..."

I put my free index finger to his lips. "SHHhhhh. I get it. It's cute. Thank you." We laugh together. "So I'm just gonna get this out of the way and say this is stupid, and goes against pretty much all my personal rules. But whatever. I'm not gonna make a big deal out of it."

His eyes strain. They almost go wide, but he's trying very, very hard to play it cool. "Rules? What do you mean?"

"I mean, doing this sort of thing with someone I'm working with. Like, working-working. It's a stupid idea."

"What do you mean... this sort of thing?" He gulps, his face still red in a way that'd have a vampire licking her lips right now. Seductively. Hungrily. In complete control.

Or me. What I'm saying is I lick my lips.

I bite my lower lip and I grin. I probably ruined my lipstick, but that's okay. I'll figure it out later. "Drinking. Partying. You know. *This*." I play with him. I tap his upper lip and run my fingertip down his mouth, dragging his bottom lip a little. I say my "this" is in my faux 1950s movie starlet throaty teasing voice. I think it's so stupid and goofy that it's hard to do it with a straight face. But it always works. I take my hand back and sip some more of my gin and cranberry.

He does one of those things where he pretends to yawn and stretch, but awkwardly puts an arm around my shoulder. Because of how we're crushed on the couch, he has to squeeze his hand between my shoulder and some other woman's back. That removes any even remote sense that it's coincidence.

It feels nice. I kind of want to snuggle into him. Everything's a little tingly and warm. But I also want to fuck with him. "You tired? Because we can call it a night. I know you've got a shift tomorrow."

"Oh, no, no." He shakes his head. "I'm okay. Just a long day. It's good to unwind."

I nod. "Yeah. Good." I take another sip. "So why do you do these things? You don't seem like the big groups of people type."

"What gave it away?" He runs his thumb in wide circles along my shoulder.

I slide my ankle up his, and tug up the cuff of his jeans with my toes. My flats fall off. Whatever. I wore the flats because, deep down, I had to be practical. There's always the chance of monsters. And that means running. And heels mean not running very well. "You're a librarian. Also, you don't seem to like the music, nobody here knows you, and you've not said a word to anyone but me. So. Why do you do these things?"

He shrugs. "I dunno. I guess I go to pick up women."

I chuckle. "Does it work?" I don't even really find it funny. I'm just trying to distract myself. My heart's racing. I could really, really use a cock right now. There's one like six inches from me right now, and he's being a schoolboy.

He shakes his head. "No. But, it's not like there's a class you can take or whatever. I mean, there are classes. But those are all creepy pickup artist guys. I don't think a gorilla mindset really suits me. Pounding my chest in the library. Spraying urine all over the resort district. You know." As he speaks, his face goes back down to an almost peach shade instead of blood red.

"Hot." I sip my drink.

"Sorry, I mean, I just…"

"Stop it. Seriously." I laugh. "You don't have to apologize. This is me flirting. It's okay."

And then he's red again. "Sorry." He puts his hand over his mouth. "Shit. I mean, I'm sorry. I'm not sorry."

I grab his wrist and tug it away, then lean in, close my eyes, and I kiss him.

He freezes in place, and closes his eyes. I don't know how I hear him over 85 or so decibels of Tupac's California Love drowning out everything around us, but I swear I hear his heartbeat speed up to just about machine gun level. Adderall-fueled vampire powers, that's how. Rawr.

A couple of seconds pass, and he takes his hand back and puts it on the side of my head. Too little, too late. I lean into him, and wrap the leg I had draped over him around his lap and pull up into his lap.

"You not into this?" I mumble through the kiss, breaking long enough to take a breath.

"I am." He nods. "Just…"

"Just what?" My breath is hot. His is too. It's like a pressure cooker between our faces right now. His glasses are coated with steam.

"Nothing." He kisses me back, but I feel like I'm maybe eight times stronger than him. I feel good, but everything good right now is happening because of me.

I take his hand from my face, and bring it down to my ass, and squeeze. He takes the hint and grabs a little tighter. "Better." I grumble, and slip my tongue out. His lips are pressed, but open slowly. I feel him smile—he pushes up against me, and runs his other hand up my hips and waist, cupping my ribs.

I wiggle in a little closer. I kind of hope my dress falls off. I don't even care that there's a million people in this room right now. I kiss along his cheek and down his neck. He quivers. I give his collar a little nibble. He coos and tilts his head to give me a better angle.

If I was a vampire, I'd be so fucking good at it.

The ones that are the best at it are the worst. That's why you've gotta watch your shit, Lana.

I'm wet. Like, if I weren't on Adderall I'd probably be a little embarrassed. I whisper with my lower lip against his earlobe. "Let's go upstairs. Find space in the bedrooms."

He laughs, weakly, and kisses my cheek. "This place is crowded. There's no free rooms. Maybe we should go back to your place. Or mine."

I grind my hips down against him. He's hard. His crotch is hot and pulsing. I feel like I might accidentally get him off in his pants if I'm not careful. "No way. I can't drive for at least a few hours."

"I'll get an Uber. We'll get your car in the morning." He brings his hand up my back, and combs his fingers through my hair. Good. He's learning.

"Uber's shit. They exploit labor. I can't leave my car here.

Murder kit and all that." I take his other hand, and bring it around to my thighs. I spread my legs a little, and coax one of his fingers to my panties. I don't figure he'll do much, but maybe he'll notice that I'm ready now, not when an Uber gets here.

"Shit..." He whispers. Not sure what exactly he's responding to. "Just so many people, you know? It's weird."

I sigh. I sit up and look around, then back to him. "Fine. We'll take your car."

He shakes his head and winces hard. "I don't have a car. A coworker dropped me off."

"Ugh." I say, and drop my forehead down against his. "Drive my car?"

"I don't have a license." A fucking Boy Scout, but he didn't even bother to get the god damned driving merit badge?

I grind my teeth, and sigh again. "I kill people for a living. I don't really care about licenses." I stand up, and realize I dropped my gin and juice on the floor, on my shoe. It's soaking wet and stinks.

I look back down to Denny, who is now starting to stand up. "I'll..." He's looking over my shoulder. His eyes go wide.

He sees a monster.

I try to turn, but a sharp, orgasmic feeling jolts up and down my spine, and my muscles give in.

Shit.

I muster up enough strength to reach back behind my head. I grab hair. It feels nice. Silky. I roll my eyes over to look at the hair, the curls I've got twisted and entangled between my fingers.

It's the redhead. I only need to see the hair. It's the redhead.

13
#ONCEBITTEN

It's good. It's so fucking good. Being bitten's one thing. But being bitten on Adderall is like a whole new world. She's drinking, and I can't manage much of anything besides groaning and pushing back against her.

I want it. I want her. I want to give myself to her. I want to cum for her. I want to die for her.

My eyes flutter. Denny's panicking, yelling something at me. I can't hear him. I don't want to hear him. I wish I could turn around and touch her and make her feel the way I'm feeling right now. I'm about to explode. There's a numbness and a fire in all my nerves.

Then I remember the Coumadin. I remember the Coumadin and I smirk. I grind up against her one last time.

Why not enjoy the moment while it lasts?

The redhead pulls back, releasing me and hacking. My senses come back, and I picture myself turning around like a motherfucking superhero, and kicking her ass right here in front of everyone. I don't. My body just isn't there for it. I fall forward. Denny catches me, and then falls back into the sofa. I turn to look at her. People are giving her the stink eye, and parting with profanities since she's ruining their good time. She's grabbing her throat and spitting up blood.

You see, Coumadin is a blood thinner. They give it to people at risk for strokes. And when a vampire drinks from someone on Coumadin, it fucking wrecks their shit. It quickly spreads through all their blood, rendering it useless and volatile. If you can trick a vampire into feeding from someone on Coumadin, killing them is almost too easy, since if they even survive the tainted blood, they're usually catatonic on the floor.

It was a weird hunch. I saw the redhead. I figured she'd attack later. So I took the Coumadin. Part of monster hunting is trusting your gut. This time, it paid off.

Redhead's not quite catatonic. Not yet. But she's in pain. Her body's betraying itself, attacking her own blood like it's an invader. It looks excruciating.

Kind of feel bad for her.

Whoa. Not okay. She was just trying to murder me.

I realize the sensation's mostly her trying to charm me to help her. That's another benefit of the Adderall—it helps you focus when a vampire's superpowers are trying to give you the business.

I lean forward from Denny just enough to grab redhead's wallet, poking out of her back pocket. I shove it in my purse, then collapse back into Denny, into the sofa.

"Lana." I hear Denny, but I'm focused on the redhead. She's trying to make her way for the door. I want to get up and follow her, but I just can't. I can't get up. "Lana! You're bleeding really bad."

Oh shit. The Coumadin.

Coumadin's a blood thinner. It doesn't just thin vampire blood. It thins human blood. So if you've got Coumadin in your system, and someone takes blood out of you and leaves you with a couple of open wounds, you bleed—it's bad, and it's potentially deadly.

"My purse." I shake my head, and start patting my body, like I'm somehow going to find my purse on my dress.

Shit. I left it upstairs in the bathroom.

"Denny, I need you to find my purse. Upstairs bathroom." I roll off of him. He gets up.

There's no fucking way that purse is gonna be there. I'd be shocked if it went five minutes before someone took it.

Denny runs upstairs, pushing through the crowd. I must look terrible. I put my hand to my neck. It's hot. Wet. Covered in blood. Yeah, it's bad.

A couple of people notice, and start fussing me. I put up my hand. It's covered in blood. There's no way I'm ever going to be able to wear this dress again. They panic a bit, I shake my head. "I'm okay. My friend's getting a bandage." They don't seem convinced.

"SOMEONE CALL 911!" The music stops.

I stand and shout back, "No! NOBODY CALL 911! I don't need fucking 911. I'm okay!" I don't blame them. I probably look like I need 911. I mean, really, I do need 911.

I consider telling them to turn the music back on. But

honestly, it was too much. I make my way to the stairs, slowly. It's hard. I'm dizzy. But, I've got to pretend I'm okay. I stop at the banister and pull out my phone. I open MedPDQ, and click through my symptoms. I say I'll be at my apartment in 20 minutes. That's a tight deadline, but honestly I'm not thinking too much about the logistics. I see Denny at the top of the stairs. He's got my purse. "What took you so long?" That was probably unfair. I can't believe he even has it.

"It was in the trash. I think someone went through it."

"Shit." I take it and rifle through it. I pull out the tiny emergency medical bag, and grab a zeolite bag. "Get this on the wound. Quick." I tilt my head. I get dizzy, I almost fall over, but I prop myself up on the banister.

"There's too much blood. I can't see." He says, grabbing the little gray square and holding it near my neck.

"Wipe it off!" I snap. Again, probably not fair. But, also, I'm dying.

He takes the cuff of his nice blue shirt and wipes off my neck, then situates the sticky gray square. It feels tight. The skin pulls a little. Zeolite's this powder—a mineral or chemical or something—that helps blood coagulate quickly. It's good for really bad wounds, at least until you can get more intensive care.

"Alright. Get me outta here. Jane's on the way to my apartment." Denny gives me a shoulder to lean on, and we start to the door. "Wait." He stops. "Where did she go?" I look around. He looks around. The redhead is gone. But there's a massive pool of blood where she fell, and there's a woman passed out on the sofa where we were sitting. She was the one pressed against me when Denny put his arm around me. She's got a bitten collar, but there's no signs of blood around her. I consider telling them to call an ambulance, but she's dead. Very dead. Redhead took so much blood, there was none left to bleed.

I shake my head. "Let's go. She's gone." I motion to the door, and Denny leads us out. A few people watch us leave. A couple move in to try to help, and I wave them away.

This is bad. This is really bad.

As soon as the door's closed behind us, I motion down the street to where I left my car. Denny speaks up. "What happened? Was that girl dead?"

"Yeah. Dead. So…" I sigh, and we wander off toward my car. "Quick vampire biology lesson. Vampires happen in two different ways. Both ways result in a different type of vampire. First way is, if you die with vampire blood in your system, you come back a vampire. Like, full vampire. All the ones you've seen so far are those types."

We get to the car, I hit the button to unlock it. Denny opens the passenger door for me. I slump in. "So." He looks over to me. "The second type?"

I hand him the keys. He starts up the car and pulls out. "The second type are sorta not really vampires? We call them ghouls. Other vampires call them the Hungry. Vampires like to use terminology that makes themselves sound like they're less monstrous than they really are. Ghouls happen when someone dies from a vampire bite. Not every time, but sometimes. Ghouls are more like zombies. They're mindless animals. They'll just kill anything in front of them."

"Hell." He says, driving. "So, she's going wake up one of them? Shouldn't we stop her?"

"This is one of those cases where we can't intervene. Stopping her would mean beheading her. Even if we didn't do it there, we'd have to get her body somewhere private. And when she turns up dead, fifty witnesses tell the cops she was last seen with the woman on the viral vampire killing video. And..."

He sighs, nodding and driving. "Yeah."

"Besides, it's a slim chance. The stronger the vampire is, the more chance it has of making ghouls. Redhead was pretty weak. If I had to guess, she's not even a year old." As I think about her, the rush comes back. The feeling of the bite. I want it. I curl up in my seat, and bite my lower lip. The feeling of the Adderall's gone now, and I feel empty. I feel cold. I wish she was here. I shake it off.

This is how vampires work. They're like drugs. They make us feel. They make us want more. We know they hurt us, but it's just so good, and we're just so fucking empty that we'll do anything for a pleasurable death, since it's so much better than a boring life.

Denny looks over, merging onto the highway. "You okay?"

"Hm?" I look up to him. I'm really cold. I must look terrible. I'm surprised I'm even conscious, honestly.

"You were daydreaming for a minute there."

"Yeah, I'm fine."

#

Jane suggests three units of blood. I agree. $1,350. That's a huge dent out of the $10,000. Or $9,000 after the agency fee. $7,650.

Jane then lectures me about blood loss, about taking care of myself, and how blood isn't just something I can afford to lose and replace every week or so. I feel like a jerk for just nodding over and over and saying, "I know, I know." She's right. This isn't okay. Human bodies just aren't designed for hunting monsters. I guess that's why we call the monsters monsters, and not prey.

14
#SATISFACTION

"I think I should crash here." Denny looks to the door, then to me once Jane's gone. He's standing over by the kitchenette bar. He's been since we got here. I've changed into shorts and a t-shirt. I set a reminder on my phone to take the dress for a futile attempt at dry cleaning tomorrow morning.

I fall back into my futon, and nurse an orange juice. Doctor's orders. "Yeah. Sorry stuff was so messed up at the party. We can pick up where we left off?" Even with the blood transfusion, I'm cold. Needy. Empty. I want to be touched and licked and fucked so hard I can't remember my name tomorrow.

"You're in no condition. You heard Jane. You should rest."

"No offense to Jane, but I know my body. I'm fine. I'll have a snack. I'll be okay. I slept in this morning, there's no way I'm sleeping for a few hours." I pat the futon next to me. He hesitates a moment then comes over. I rest my head against his shoulder and put an arm around his waist. He's warm. It's not like before, with the Adderall—but it's nice.

He pets my head and puts his other arm around me. My eyes close and everything fades a little. Part of me wants to sleep. But I'm raw. Frustrated. I slide in a little closer, and kiss his neck, and nibble on his earlobe. He tugs away slightly. "Lana..." He sighs.

I want to scream. He's been chasing after me for almost two

years. Now I'm up for it, and he's hesitating. "What? I thought you wanted this."

"I do. It's just..." He pulls away and looks to my face, hands on my shoulders, keeping me at distance.

It's just what?

"You're high, aren't you?"

I bite down and take a sharp breath in. I swear to God, I am so not here for this right now.

"You are." He says with a sigh.

"Well." I say, trying to find my composure. My first instinct is to deck him. "Since you asked, no, I'm not high. I was earlier tonight. But that all subsided with the near-death experience. Turns out, nearly bleeding out's pretty fucking sobering. Second off, why's it your business if I am?"

He winces. I don't think he was expecting me to get in his shit about it. "Because it's wrong. If we have sex, I'd be taking advantage of you. You can't consent when you're high."

"Okay." I grunt. "Well. I'm not. And I'm really, really uncomfortable with you telling me when I can and cannot consent."

"I'm sorry." He leans in and kisses me. I don't really kiss him back, but I also don't fight it. "Besides, I'd prefer our first time to be sober, so we can really enjoy each other to the fullest." He kisses me again. Again, I don't do much of anything in response.

"Oh my God." He pulls back a little to look at me. I realize he's trying to be cute and romantic. But I'm not having it. "Our first time? No offense, Denny. You're cool and everything. But this isn't about first times. I was in the mood. I was having a good time. Like, I just wanted to hook up. Why does it have to be a big thing? Why can't we just enjoy now?"

He swallows. His face goes a little red. Something I said hurt him. I feel a little bad. But I also don't regret it. "Oh." He looks away, over to the door.

"Denny..." I say and pull back. I look him over. I've got to do something quick. No sense in fucking this up any worse than it already is. "It's just that in this line of work, you meet a lot of people who end up dead. Okay? It's not that I don't like you like that. It's just that I've got to be careful. I've lost too many people. If I just want to fuck or whatever, it's not because I'm not into you. It's that we've got to take what we can get, when we get it, you know?"

He's thinking. Hard. Processing. He's like a computer with the little spinning beachball. This is the hardest part for someone new to the supernatural. It's one thing to consider that vampires and zombies and ghosts are real. It's another to consider that they'll probably end up killing you. That's a lot to take in. If I let him, he'll dwell on it all night. Maybe for weeks. Some hunters dwell on it until the day they die. Which is usually way early for those types.

"Here." I say, and pull up to sit on his lap, facing him. He looks me in the eyes, and I put a hand to his cheek, and run it back through his hair. He smiles, and I pull back off his lap. I sink down to my knees in front of him, and rub his thighs and his cock through his jeans.

His eyes don't leave mine. "Are you sure?"

I nod. "Yeah. And I'm sober." Within seconds, he's hard as a rock under my hand. I slide up and go for the buttons of his jeans. They're tight as hell, so I take his hip in my other hand to nudge him up. He gets the hint, and I unfasten his pants and tug them open. "Like, do me a favor and let me determine if I'm okay to make choices for myself?"

He nods pensively, and strokes my hair. I fold open the flap in his boxers, and tug his cock out. It's not huge, but it's bulging, tight, like a balloon filled up enough to pop with a little tap. I kiss him just below the head. He gasps. I put my tongue near the base, and run it up the shaft. He groans. I take his head in my mouth and suck.

"Lana..."

I look up to his eyes, lightly bobbing and suckling. "Mmmmm?"

He runs his fingers through my hair. It feels great. The tingling, the warmth is all coming back, a little at a time. I go down on him, flicking my tongue against the underside of his shaft, and he squirms every time. A lot of times you have to work to find just where a guy likes it. But he's easy.

I don't think I could fuck this up if I had to.

He says my name over and over. I switch to my hand every few moments when my jaw gets tired. He's into it, but I don't think it's going much further like this. Some guys are like that.

I pull off and sit up. "Hm?" He mumbles. I move to rummage through my end table, and pull out a condom. "Oh." I sit down next to him on the futon and kiss him as I tear open the condom pack. He turns to face me and kisses me back, much more eager now. All the shyness is gone.

I grab his shaft and squeeze and tug a couple of times. He groans. I stretch the condom open, slide it over his head, and roll it down. There's a satisfying snap as I release it. I sit up on my knees, looking down to him, and he's kissing my mouth, my cheeks, my neck. He's running his hands up and down my sides and back. I slide off my shorts and kick them out of the way. I take his right hand and put it on my breast, squeezing lightly. He takes the hint, and squeezes and massages it.

I close my eyes. I see the redhead. I see her hand, touching me. I see her face, she's kissing me. I fall back into the futon and moan, wrapping my legs around her and pulling her close. I feel her curly hair fall against my face and I smell it and god damn.

I gasp and my eyes open. Denny's there again. It's confusing and weird and disorienting so I just lean up to kiss him, and use my legs to pull his crotch up against mine. His shaft slides against me, my clit, my thighs, and I feel empty. I feel hungry.

He grabs his shaft and rubs his head against my clit and smirks down to me. It's cute. It feels nice. But right now, I can't wait. No fucking way.

"Just fuck me."

He freezes, blinks, then nods. He adjusts so his head's teasing at my opening, and pushes in. It's good, if a little underwhelming. I feel like I'm too eager, too open, and he's just sort of... there. I squeeze my legs to pull him in deeper.

There it is.

I throw my head back and close my eyes. He pulls out and pushes in again. It's awkward at first, but he gets a rhythm with my assistance. He speeds up. I feel and hear his balls slapping against my inner thighs. That's maybe the best part. The rest, I just don't feel that much. Like he's not hitting anything inside of me.

It's not working.

I put his hand back on my tit, and squeeze around my nipple. He squeezes and holds it for a few seconds, then puts his hand beside my head to prop himself up again.

I take his other hand and adjust to make a little room between us, and put his hand on my pubic mound. He rubs me, my hair for a moment, then removes it. He takes my hand and pins it to the futon beside my shoulder.

He speeds up. His face is red. His eyes are trained down on me. He's gasping and moaning. I feel like he'd be exactly the same even if I weren't here right now.

I take my hand back and put it between us. I slide it down and find my clit with two fingers. I massage it with little circles, but his pubic bone keeps knocking my hand out of the way.

He groans loudly.

Can the neighbors hear him?

I feel his muscles all clench and harden. It's kind of nice. He feels strong in that second. Then, he relaxed before falling to jelly. He kisses me hard but lazily, and falls over to the side, rolling beside me. "Thank you." He whispers. With the two of us side-by-side, the futon's crowded.

Should have unfolded it beforehand.

"Yeah." I lean into him, not done yet. Open, eager. My heart's all over the place.

He makes a little snorting sound.

He's fucking sleeping.

Not ten seconds, and he's passed out. Snoring. Didn't even take the condom off. I want to scream, but priorities are priorities. I put my hand back down to my clit. I close my eyes, and picture the kissing, the fucking, the breath against me. I move my hips, and think about the rhythm and the heat.

It's not happening.

I freeze. I chew on my bottom lip, and I grunt. I look over at him. His snoring's nothing short of obnoxious and distracting. I nudge him in the ribs. He smiles, and turns over to face the back of the futon.

"Can we unfold the futon?" I say to him. He nods and groans, but doesn't wake up.

I get off the futon, and grab my blanket and pillow. I spread it out on the floor and lie on my stomach, cheek against the pillow. I put my hand back down and start again. It's better with more space, but it's still hard to not focus on the frustration, on his snoring.

I picture the redhead. I think back to the feeling, to the bite.

This is disgusting, Lana.

I push the thought out of my head. Thirty seconds later, my back's arching, I'm whimpering, and I'm awash with ecstasy. Another two minutes, and I'm asleep.

15

#PRINCESSPROBLEMS

I'm up at 7. Denny's still asleep. I toss some cookies and cream Pop-Tarts in the toaster. Breakfast of champions. I grab the half gallon of orange juice from the fridge. I consider getting a glass.

Fuck it.

I pop off the lid and drink from the jug. I tried the princess thing last night. Fuck of a lot of good that did me.

I hear the futon springs. Denny's getting up.

Don't come in here.

He walks in to the kitchenette. I keep facing the toaster. He puts his arms around me from behind, and squeezes to me. "Morning, sunshine." He smells like sex. I try to focus on the Pop-Tarts.

"Hey." I pull a foil pack from the box and hold it up. "Want a Pop-Tart?"

"No thanks. But I do want you..." He says and kisses my neck. I force a light laugh, put down the Pop-Tarts, and take his hands off my stomach. "We could go again. Then maybe go get lunch in a little bit?"

"Not right now. Anyway, you've got work today." I open the pantry and start looking around. I'm not looking for anything in specific, I just don't want to look at him right now.

"It's an evening shift." He says and takes a step over to me and puts a hand on my hip.

"Denny." I say, taking his hand off me. The Pop-Tarts spring up from the toaster. I put them on a paper towel and go to sit down on the futon.

"What's wrong?" He says, following me in.

What's wrong is you are a completely selfish prick and I'm not gonna get you off again and leave myself hanging.

"Nothing. Just, let's relax a bit. I've got some stuff to do. If you want to take a shower or whatever, that's fine. Thanks for driving me home." I take a bite of my Pop-Tart. My stomach growls. I guess I'm hungrier than I thought.

He sits down beside me. "Last night was really good."

I nod, and turn a little away, taking another bite of the Pop-Tart.

He sighs and puts a hand on my shoulder. "Seriously, Lana, what's wrong?" I roll my shoulder back to push his hand off.

"I really don't want to talk about it." I take another bite, then get up and throw it in the trash. I don't even know why.

"Did I do something?" He doesn't get back up this time.

More like you didn't do something.

"I'm just not good with this stuff, okay? It's me." I'm struggling to keep calm.

"That's not true. You're upset about something. What is it?"

I stop. I turn to face him. I feel my temper rising. My body warms. "Look. This? I don't think it's going to work out. So, can we just be cool? You're a good friend, and we probably shouldn't have done this. So, can we try and not let this fuck things up?"

"Yeah. Whatever." He says and stands. He mumbles something, and walks to the door.

"Denny..." I say, watching him as he opens it. He shakes his head and slams the door behind himself.

I flip the door off. I don't think it cares.

#

I shower, I get dressed, and I run the dress to the dry cleaners. They think they can fix it, and it'll just be $40. I tell them to do it. The $140 dress just became a $180 dress. But it's a $180 dress with a story. That's somehow better, right?

While I'm at the dry cleaners, I realize I don't have my wallet. Someone must have taken it from my purse at the party. I do have the redhead's wallet though. The redhead's name is Natalie Walsh. She's my age. Both born in early April. Both Aries. She's got about three hundred in cash. Not quite enough to replace the blood she took, but it's a start.

I spend the next two hours on hold with my bank and two credit card companies, telling them to cancel cards and send me new ones. Of course that means I'll be without access to my accounts for 5-7 business days. Great. And it seems like someone's already gone on a shopping spree. "Did you spent $1,200 at Foot Locker?," they ask me. "Did you order $300 worth of pizza last night?" At least they should be able to figure out who did it.

Who steals someone's credit cards and orders pizza delivery?

I drop Denny and Vanessa a text. I figure if I just focus on work, maybe Denny will get that I'm not blowing him off, I just don't want to make this a thing.

"You guys up for Wednesday? I'm gonna do some recon. I want to corner one of the vamps. Strength in numbers."

Vanessa gets back to me quickly.

"I'm in for some action. I'm free all day. Can we maybe meet in the mean time? I'm also off on Monday."

Twenty minutes pass before Denny replies.

"Yeah. I think I can do that. See you then."

I send a thumbs-up to Vanessa. Then I respond to Denny.

"I'm sorry that was awkward."

He doesn't reply. Maybe that's for the best.

#

I wander around the resort. I don't go in—I'm not interested in the attention. It's okay though; Natalie—the redhead—and the monstrous-looking one spend some time out there hunting according to my intel.

I do some digging online while I wander. I swipe through forums on my iPhone. I poke through the mons2 boards. They're anonymous, which means there's a lot of misinformation. But they're also a treasure trove of real information if you're willing to sort through it.

It doesn't take long. I find out that the really monstrous vampires like I saw in the docket are basically invisible. They walk unnoticed. Wherever they go, people just overlook them. They notice a vague person, but they don't notice any of the details. The vampire just comes off as the most random, nondescript person you can think of. But there's a trick. The effect is very immediate. So even a camera or mirror will still have the same effect. But, if you catch them on camera with a slight delay, at least a second, then you see them plain as day. Once you see them, you can't un-see them. The power just stops working once you've broken it once. It's the same way with their charm bullshit.

I download an app they recommend. It just plays your iPhone camera with a one-second delay. Simple, elegant. Then I prowl, old-school. I go from bar to bar, diner to diner, hotel to hotel, combing the entire neighborhood around the resort. I used to do this all the time, except without staring into my phone screen.

Five hours, an order of supreme nachos, a frozen margarita, and a Red Bull later, and I spot the monster. It's walking off-site, to a shitty motel called the Tropicana. I follow it from a distance. Some assholes drive by and do that thing where they wiggle their tongue between two fingers, whistle, and call me mamacita. They call me puta when I ignore them.

Because ignoring these guys who can only get consensual sex by paying for it definitely makes me the "whore" here.

I follow it into the Tropicana. It's a disaster. A few years ago, a Congresswoman's daughter filmed a documentary about this place. It made a little buzz. The city talked about tearing it down and making a new parking lot for the resort. But it just never happened for whatever reason. As I pass through, there are kids playing all over the place. This isn't really a place where you stay for a vacation or a business trip. It's a place you live if your credit's so bad you can't get an apartment, or you've got a criminal record so you can't pass a background check. It's cash-only, and the crime rate's through the roof. But you get HBO for free. That way you can hole up and watch Game of Thrones to pretend even worse shit isn't happening just outside your door.

This place is a stealth nightmare. It's a giant C shape, with maybe eighty rooms all facing in to the courtyard. The courtyard has a big, greenish and blackish swimming pool, and a volleyball court full of cat shit. There's almost nowhere in this motel's grounds where you're not in plain view of forty or more windows. Maybe that's beneficial to a monster who can walk unseen.

The monster prowls. I don't think it's hunting—it goes to a stairwell up the second floor. I watch it casually, and I walk over to another area to evade suspicion. It goes to room 214. It's got the keys. That means it comes back here.

I could follow it. Right here, right now. Corner it, and end it.

No. Bad idea. Gotta give Vanessa and Denny their chance. And if I can bottleneck it, that means they get the best possible chance for surviving this. This is valuable. Gotta be patient.

I make my way toward the street, out of the Tropicana grounds.

"Hey." A woman's voice rings in my ear. It's pleasant, but I try to ignore it. Either she's not talking to me, or she's trying to sell me something I'm not interested in buying.

"Hey." This time it's closer. I stop. Maybe I dropped something.

I turn around. It's Natalie. I clench my fists. I don't go into an obvious defensive stance, but I focus and I think about it. She's standing there, hand on her hip. She doesn't look like she's going to attack. She in tight jeans and a pink camisole with black lace trim.

"It's okay. I'm not here to kill you."

"Oh? Then what do you want?" My eyes jump from place to place, looking for exits. I realize I should have looked for those beforehand.

That's just fucking sloppy, Lana.

"That's just fucking sloppy, Lana." She almost smirks. It's cute. But then she stops herself. I realize what just happened—she can read minds. I feel like maybe I should be pissed about it, but I'm not. "Sorry. That wasn't fair." I blink at the apology. It's somehow more sincere than Denny's litany of apologies for literally everything.

"Oh?" I think about her bite. I think about the feeling. The rush. I realize she can probably tell what I'm thinking, so I start singing the old Sherry Lewis Song That Never Ends in my head.

This is the song that never ends. It goes on and on my friend...

"You asked what I want. I want you to back off. Leave us

alone. We'll leave you alone." She takes a couple of steps forward. "I don't want to hurt you, Lana."

I don't move. I watch her. "You kill people. Even if you don't want to hurt me, and I don't believe that, you hurt other people. You murdered someone yesterday."

I mean, also, your head in a bag means five grand in cash.

"I lost control. You poisoned me. And yes, you poisoned me because I bit you. I deserved it." She says and stands maybe two feet in front of me. Her voice lowers to a whisper. "But it doesn't have to be that way."

She slowly moves a hand up, like she's going to touch my cheek. I gently push it away. "Don't do that." Fuck if I don't want her to.

This is the song that never ends. It goes on and on my friend...

She withdraws her hand and nods. "Five thousand dollars? Is that what I'm worth to you?"

"It's a little more than money."

It's really not.

"It's really not, though." She shakes her head. "Look. What if I pay you? Seven grand. Just leave us alone, and I'll pay you. No questions. No fighting. Just cash in hand."

I think about it for a moment. Maybe a moment too long. "I don't know. It's more than that. It's five grand per head. And I know there's a lot of you guys."

"You... You're in over your head if you think there's more of us you can just kill. I... You're a smart woman, Lana."

"Thanks?" I raise an eyebrow. She's really lovely. I wonder briefly if it's the charm, but it's not. She's got a warmth, a sincerity to her. Her cheeks, her freckles, everything just comes together. I want to be her friend.

"It might take me a few days. I'll get ten grand. You leave me and my brother alone. And in addition to the ten grand, I'll sit down with you and explain just why you can't go after the others. As much as I'd want you to."

She means this. She's not threatening me. I mean, what's the harm in taking the money? There's nothing to say I can't go back on the deal...

This is the song that never ends. It goes on and on my friend...

"Alright. It's a deal. You know my name. What do I call you?"

"Natalie."

No fake name?

She shakes her head.

Natalie and I exchange numbers. She says she'll text me when she gets the cash together.

16
#SIDEQUEST

I wake up Monday to an alert from iHunt. $7,500 for a rush gig. Tight deadline—it has to be completed tonight. I bring up the details. The job's in San Maria Cay. There's a werewolf. They've provided a couple of pictures. Yeah, definitely a werewolf. Hairy. Huge. Terrible. All that. There aren't any pictures of it in its human form though.

Apparently, tonight's the last night of the full moon, so tonight's the last chance to catch this thing for a month. The client, Medi-Cor, needs the werewolf captured with a special sedative. If it's dead, there's no pay. That's unfortunate. Killing werewolves isn't particularly hard. Catching them? That's tough.

Werewolves are huge. Transporting one's not a one-woman job. I message Vanessa.

"Hey. You said you wanted to train today. Want to do a job with me tonight?"

She gets back in a few seconds.

"Love to."

I tell her to meet me at the gym.

#

My gym's not that close to my apartment. It's in Palo Verde, near a lot of the old movie studios and the tourist bars catering

126

to the studio fanatics. I go there because it has small, private rooms with weighted bags. You can beat on a bag without a ton of attention.

The funny thing about it is, it's run by a vampire. He's a hot Middle Eastern guy named Ari. He teaches Krav Maga and self-defense classes, mostly to women in the area. He feeds on some of them, but it seems to be mutually beneficial, and I've not gotten a contract on him, so I leave well enough alone. I don't think he knows what I do, and he's the type of vampire that sleeps during the day, so we only rarely see each other anyway.

Vanessa shows up ten minutes after I get there, fifteen minutes before I asked her to be there. I take her to a room.

"So tell me about the job." She says, putting down a duffel bag and pulling out some training clothes. It's a cute, designer set of sweatpants, black with a royal purple stripe down the side. Totally jealous.

I slip out of my clothes, and put on my $3 clearance sweatpants and a blank gray t-shirt that came in a bag. "It's a werewolf in San Maria Cay. We've got to sedate it and bring it in to the client. It has to be tonight, since tonight's the last night of the full moon."

"Werewolves are real, too?" Not gonna lie, I watch while she changes. She's fit. Tight. Strong. She ties back her braids then stretches her arms up.

I nod. I get up and throw a couple of weak punches and kicks at the bag to warm up. "Yeah. Usually if you're trying to stop a werewolf, you find out who they are, and you hunt them while they're in their human form. If you get the jump on them, you can take them out before they change. If you get them square in the head or the heart, one silver bullet will do it. But this one, we've got to bring in alive. The client's got a sedative they want us to use."

"Sounds fun. Is it injected? Or do they have to eat it or something?" She gets up, and mimics my movements. Except her hits are much firmer. She's much more serious about this. She rocks the bag a little when she hits it. It's kind of impressive.

I see her hit the bag, and I step up my game a little. I go from little warmup taps to direct hits. I feel like I've got to do whatever she's doing, and a little better, just out of principle. I'm the teacher, after all. "I don't know. Listing didn't say that. I have to go by their offices this afternoon to pick it up."

We quickly pick up rhythm together. We're hitting in turns, I kick, she kicks, I punch, she punches. She's a natural. "Mind if I get something off my mind, boss?"

Boss? Sounds nice.

I can't help but to smile. I stop, then start with very specific strikes—palm strikes, the kind you might use to stop a rampaging monster. She watches, nods, and imitates me. "Sure? Go ahead." I like working with her. She's keeping me accountable. No slacking off allowed.

She doesn't break pattern. She keeps hitting. "I'm not thrilled with what went on with Denny. I don't want to make a big deal about it. But I think it was really unprofessional."

I stop. She stops. I look away, then back to the bag and sigh. "Yeah. It was a stupid mistake. I was feeling needy. He was there, and he's been trying to hook up with me for a couple of years." I shrug, and start hitting the bag again.

She follows me again, hitting the bag in time. "He's really upset. And I'm worried that'll put him in danger, or you'll make a dangerous mistake because of it."

"Yeah. Me too. Trust me. I don't feel like I can just tell him to not hunt with us, though. That'll make it worse. He'll just go hunting alone, and he'll definitely get himself killed. So I've got to take him on this job, and make sure he knows that's it."

I don't know what job I'm talking about. I just agreed not to kill the vampires he thinks we're killing.

"Good choice boss." She says, hitting hard enough to put a full-grown man on his ass. She glances to me. "You okay?"

"Me?" I move into kicks, slamming my shin into the side of the bag. "Yeah. I'm fine. Truth be told, he was just a really, really bad lay. That's all."

She smirks, holding back a laugh. "I kind of expected that. Say no more. So, about this werewolf?"

"Werewolves." I put my weight into every kick. I think back to my Muay Thai training. I move to demonstrate, to show her how to land the hits, shin first. "The biggest threat with werewolves is getting scratched by them. So it's best to keep them at a distance."

"What happens if they scratch you?" She says, adapting to my examples.

"You run the risk of becoming a werewolf yourself. So, distance where possible. We'll also make sure we're wearing thick clothes just to be double safe."

#

We train for about two hours. It's relaxing. It's cathartic. No pressure, just exercise, and an eager, capable student. We hit up the army surplus store and pick up some black fatigues for sneaking around, and matching stab vests just in case we take a werewolf claw to the chest.

Afterwards, we head to the Medi-Cor offices. The office is well outside of town, in an industrial park between like four of the suburbs. It's this huge, nondescript office complex, gated off from the world. You have to buzz your way in and give them a code word. Once we're in, we see armed guards—guys in black uniforms with assault rifles which I swore were outlawed in California.

What kind of medical facility needs mercenaries?

We go exactly where we're told. We park in a spot 126 like it says on the tag the mercenaries gave us. We go to the door they told us to. We swipe the card they gave us. We go down the hall they told us. Inside, it's all very clinical. It looks like a hospital, with medical supplies all over the place. I briefly consider stealing some drugs from one of the trays in the hallway, but then I remember how armed these guys are.

Vanessa's sweating bullets. These guys scare her more than the werewolves and vampires. Truth be told, I feel the same.

We go to office 32B. Nothing here has a name. Everything's just a number and a letter. I wonder if the staff even calls each other by numbers and letters.

Office 32B is the most plain little office possible. An older woman, maybe in her fifties, sits at a nondescript desk. Behind her, there are a few nondescript file cabinets. She asks for our contract number. I give it to her. She messes with her laptop for a moment. It's an ancient, huge black thing. I can hear the fans inside it. And it has one of those special screen covers so you can't see what's on it unless you're leaning in real close from just the right angle.

She nods, gets up, and rifles through the filing cabinets. She pulls out container with six little vials full of green fluid. It's almost neon. It looks like the kind of stuff that turns pet turtles into the teenage, pizza-eating variety of turtle. She puts it down on the desk. Then she goes through another cabinet, and pulls out a ziplock bag with a small thing that looks kind of like a hot glue gun and a plain white book. She puts it down next to the vial container.

"This compound is a sedative, as mentioned in your contract. It'll need to be administered to the subject directly. You can use this applicator to administer the compound. You'll find full instructions for use within the manual." She motions to the bag.

"Um, I..."

She cuts me off. "Do excuse me. I'm neither authorized nor informed to answer your questions. If you find the contract sufficient, you'll find all relevant information within the manual." She gets up and gets two clear file folders out of a third filing cabinet, and sets them down before us. Each has a form within labeled AGREEMENT OF NON-DISCLOSURE. She opens the folders, and motions to a signature line, then flips through the forms, showing another which says AGREEMENT OF NON-LIABILITY, another which says AGREEMENT TO MEDI-COR PRIVACY POLICIES, and a last which says AGREEMENT OF WORK-FOR-HIRE.

"Do we..."

She cuts me off again. "Sign these four forms if you agree to the terms of the contract."

I glance through them. I look to Vanessa. She looks to the papers as well. The language is so dense it's hard to even make out what they're saying. I'm not terrible with fine print, but this is plain eldritch. I have no idea what it's saying. But, I do suss out that apparently *each* of us will get $7,500. That's not usually how these contracts work. So, I'm much less resistant to signing. I sign, then Vanessa signs.

Then, we make our way out of the Medi-Cor compound.

17

#BADWOLF

Werewolves change shape during the full moon. Some of them can change at other times, but as far as monster hunters know, they all change for the full moon. The full moon, at least for these purposes, lasts for three days. I don't know why that is. Astronomers say the full moon is a one-day affair. Lycanthropy disagrees.

Our mark has been seen for the past two nights in a specific neighborhood of San Maria Cay. The Cay's one of the trashier suburbs. It's filled with trailer parks. Whereas San Jenaro is full of hippie liberal voters, The Cay would all die off if you told them they could vote for Ronald Reagan again if they just walked through lava. The Cay is full of people who a lot of time complaining about Mexican immigrants stealing all the farm jobs, even though they wouldn't be caught dead on a farm.

Needless to say, I avoid the Cay like the plague. I don't even go there to ironically watch monster truck rallies. But $7,500 is worth it. Probably.

Our mark's been spotted twice in the same apartment complex. Fortunately for us, this is the kind of place where the cops assume everyone's on drugs or mentally ill, and thus ignore their complaints about werewolves or giant dogs or aliens or gay rights or whatever they're going on about this week. That means the locals will be on alert, and receptive to anyone offering to help. At least I hope.

We drive. We hit The Cay by 3:30. I wanted to get there early so we could get a lay of the land, but the sun sets around 4:30 this time of the year.

Rancho Amiga is technically a gated community. Except both the gates are broken and don't close. The signs that say you'll be towed if you don't have a parking pass have been sprayed over with graffiti penises and swastikas and phone numbers and stylized gang names. There's at least ten layers of tagging. It reminds me of high school geology class, where we had to look at the layers of rock at the Grand Canyon. I feel like you can track entire eras of racism and sexism in this place if you chip away some of the paint.

"Classy joint." Vanessa says as we drive through the parking lot. A good fourth of the cars in the lot are up on bricks, or sitting on flat tires. A stray dog darts across in front of us and I have to stop to not hit it.

"Yeah. With this kind of thing, you've just got to remember the paycheck. Smile and nod, right?" I find one open space. I feel like it's a stupid idea to park here. Like the guy who normally parks here will come back from his trip to the corner store to get smokes and Four Loko, realize we've taken his unmarked spot, and slash my tires.

We get out. We get a couple of looks. A couple of stares. There's a group of five white guys that won't stop watching us.

One of the guys is bald, with arms as wide as my waist, and a Nazi eagle tattoo. Two non-white women who don't live here? We don't belong here. I wonder if maybe it *isn't* worth $7,500. I picture him changing into a werewolf and I smile to myself.

"What?" Vanessa whispers to me as I grin.

"Huh?"

"You're smiling. You don't see that Hitler motherfucker over there?"

"Oh yeah. I see him. So we'll go that way instead." I motion to another part of the complex.

As we make it around to another entrance, there's a woman in her forties, Hispanic, walking around with a hand on her waist. She's definitely packing, but she's not with the gangs. She's patrolling. She's looking out for something.

"Hey." I say to her.

She looks to us and stops, watching us for a couple of seconds. "Ain't seen you around here."

"Yeah. We're here to do some work. Heard there's been some problems here the past couple of nights." I approach. Vanessa follows, just a step behind me.

She's watching us with a raised eyebrow. "Oh yeah? What kind of problems."

"Weird problems." I say, and we stop about six feet from her.

"Don't gimme weird. What are you looking for?"

I take one more step in for effect, and speak softly. "Werewolf?"

Her face contorts. She looks distressed. "Magic fucking word. You with Agent Roth?"

"Agent Roth?" I tilt my head a little.

"Yeah. FBI guy. I take it you're not with him. I was gonna tell you to get his ugly motherfuckin' van off our street."

"I can still tell him to get his ugly motherfuckin' van off your street." I tease. She doesn't seem amused.

"Seven people I know of saw it. Turns up a few times a night. The cops don't care. They tell us to call animal control. Ain't no animal control that's gonna stop a werewolf." She pulls her gun out. It's a huge revolver. Shiny. Scary. .356 Magnum. Random lady in a place like this, she has no business with a gun that big. If I had to guess, that's about a $4,000 piece. There's a lot of people living here that don't make $4,000 in a year. "I found these this morning. Normal bullets don't cut it." She pops open the cylinder, and removes a bullet. Silver. It's got that sort of dull gray you can't miss when you hunt monsters for a living. And an "Ag" is engraved into the bullet.

"Silver bullets. Nice." I say with an appraising nod. "Where did you spot it? We're trained. We're here to stop it."

She motions over the other way, deeper into the complex. There's an empty, fake creek running through the complex. It leads over to a clearing with a small playground with rusty old equipment.

"The playground? Not good." I sigh. She nods along.

She hands the gun forward, handle first. "Those FBI guys,

they're not here to stop it. They're just trying to keep it under wraps. They don't want it to make the news, that's all."

I push it away. "You keep it. When I walk away, you're gonna be here to pick up the pieces. You've gotta keep your community safe."

She nods, and puts the Colt back under her shirt.

"You wanna do me a favor?" She nods once. "Go to the nearest carnicería. Get me a slab of pork. Biggest, cheapest cut you can find. Bloody." I pull $40 of Natalie's money out of my purse.

The woman pushes it back the way I did with her gun.

#

It's just about 5. The woman, Maria, brought us a pork head. Smart. Big and cheap, just what I asked for. I tell her to make sure everyone's inside. Kids can't be out playing. Not tonight.

Vanessa and I sit on top of the slide, with the pig head at the bottom. It stinks. We smoke a bowl together to get over the smell and to chill our nerves. I hate my bowl. It's one of those awful glass tie-dyed things. An ex-girlfriend left it at my apartment a while ago, and I sort of laid claim to it when I lost my old one.

While Vanessa smokes, I check the green serum gun. Apparently it's less like a gun-gun, more like a staple gun. You have to use it from up-close. You slam the barrel into the target, and it injects them. Great. I was hoping not to get anywhere near it while it's conscious.

"Bad idea." She says, holding in a breath and handing over the bowl. "If I get hurt at work, it's a same-day drug test." She exhales slowly.

"You're telling me." I take a long hit and hand it back over. "I just lost my job because I refused to take a drug test. Half the fucking resort's high. It's the only way you can put up with the tourists."

She laughs and moves to perch on her tiptoes. She's watching the area like a fucking hawk. "Yeah. But hey. $7,500, right? That's like two months' pay. If I lose my job, I'll be okay for a while. And this is all under the table, right?" She takes another hit and passes it back.

"Yeah. All under the table. It's not bad work, if you don't mind dying." I shrug and inhale a little more. Off in the distance, the bushes rustle. I put up a hand. I mouth, "Dog? Maybe?"

We both watch, staying stationary.

A huge brownish/black blur bolts out from the bushes to the pig head.

Werewolf. Definitely werewolf.

The plan was, Vanessa would make noises, throw things, and otherwise catch its attention while I went for the attack. The second it grabs the head, Vanessa shouts out the weirdest sound I've heard in a while. I jump down to it with the gun in hand.

Or at least, I try. The old rusty slide isn't made for two grown-assed women and a werewolf. When I jump, the ladder and slide buckle under me. Vanessa falls to the side, I fall to the other side. I land in the playground sand. It could definitely hurt worse. I feel like the biggest danger here is ringworm. The beast growls and looks between us. At first, all I see is its eyes, glowing red and green under the street lamps. Then I see its body. It's massive. If it stood on its hind legs, it'd probably be eight feet tall. It's definitely heavier than one of those little two-person electric cars. Its breath sounds like an angry horse.

It looks to Vanessa. It bends down to pounce. I rush to my feet, and she crawls back away.

"Don't try to run!" I shout at her. The monster doesn't pay attention. She doesn't, either. I look around for the gun. It fell about ten feet over, near the merry-go-round.

The monster jumps at her, and knocks her over. She rolls to her back, so she's looking up at it when it pins her down into the sand. I can't risk it. Can't go for the gun. I sprint forward and slam into the werewolf with my shoulder. It's like running into a brick wall with fur. It doesn't move, but it stops for a second.

"HEY!"

It looks to me, so I do a full swing and smash my shin into its snout. It yelps and stares at me in disbelief. Vanessa swings a leg up right between its hind legs. It howls out sharp, and she squeezes out from under it.

Has she seen Monster Squad? Or does she just instinctively go for the ball kick?

I sprint for the gun.

While I'm situating the vial and running back over, it snaps its jaws forward, nicking Vanessa's back.

So glad we grabbed those stab vests.

As I get to the monster, I thrust the gun forward into its back. The black plastic shatters in my hands. It hurts like a son of a bitch. The vial bursts, and the green shit goes all over the place. Where it doesn't go, though, is inside the fucking werewolf.

He swipes wide at me with claws the size of Filipino folding knives. I jump back out of the way. It tears a palm tree's trunk about half way through instead.

I shout to Vanessa. "Go for the car!" I throw her my keys.

She catches them, looks to them, then to me. "I can't leave you!"

"GO TO THE FUCKING CAR. I'll be there in a second!" I somersault out of the way of the thing as he pounces.

Vanessa runs to the parking area. I jump behind the merry-go-round. The monster grabs the edge of the metal disc, and yanks upward, ripping the merry-go-round out of the ground. While he's trying to scare me, I pull my survival knife out of my boot, and another one of the six vials. I snap open the vial. They're not made to be opened by hand, so I cut my thumb open on it.

As the merry-go-round flips and flies up into the air, I duck underneath it and charge the werewolf. I slash into his leg with my knife, and with the other hand, I shove the vial into the wound.

"Let's see if this works..."

I duck under another swipe, then run after Vanessa, jumping

over picnic tables and barbecue grills. The monster dodges around them, but I manage to keep ahead of him.

Vanessa gets into the driver seat, and starts the engine.

There's no way we can get in that car if he's right behind us. He'll grab it and flip it and we're as good as dead.

I turn 90 degrees away from the car, and run deeper into the parking lot. I look everywhere, for anything, for an idea. What I see is a semi truck with trailer. I lower my center of gravity and sprint as I get to the cab. Then, I jump sideways, feet first between the cab and the trailer. The rampaging werewolf goes straight through.

The trick to fighting werewolves is to remember that they're never subtle. They never take the long way around if they think they can just go through. You can use this to your advantage if you're creative.

Now, he's jammed between the cab and the trailer. He's bent the metal on both sides. He won't be there long, but it's long enough for me. I jump up and grab the edge of one of the garages, and vault to the top. Then, I run. I dash across the top of it back toward the car. "OPEN MY DOOR!"

"Gotcha boss!" I hear the door open, and I hear the tires squeal. She's ready to go, lined up facing the open gates. The passenger side's across the alley from me, so I jump down from the garage, onto the car roof. I feel it dent under my feet.

That won't be cheap to fix.

Then I jump down into the passenger seat, slamming the door

behind me. "GUN IT!"

"I KNOW!" She squeals out. I can see the monster in the rear view mirror.

18

#CHASECARES

The monster's running after us. Vanessa's pulling out into the San Maria Cay streets. He's gaining on us, but we're about onto a straight stretch.

"Okay. So. We can't let him catch us." I say, climbing over the passenger seat into the back.

Vanessa's speeding up, but not fast enough. "I'm down with that plan. But how do we do it? Your car can only go so fast."

I trip the latches on the back seats, folding them down so I can access the trunk. "I think I'm gonna shoot him enough to slow him down."

"Slow him down? How about you shoot him enough to kill him?" She's pressed back into her seat, intense and tense, concentrating on the road.

"For one, we don't get paid if we kill him." I pull out the first gun I find. A MAC-10. I hate using these things, but they're useful sometimes. One of those times is when you need to put about thirty bullets into a rampaging werewolf. "Second off, normal bullets don't kill werewolves." I check the magazine. It's full.

"Okay. You're gonna slow him. But what do we do once he comes back after us?"

The car's getting faster. He's gaining slowly, but not as much as before. I lean out the rear passenger window and spray a few bullets back at him. A couple clip him, but it's not doing much. He's still charging. He doesn't look like half-man, half-wolf. He looks like half-wolf, half-gorilla. Every time Vanessa turns, he jumps on top of cars to close the gap. "Stop turning! We've got the advantage when we go straight. Hopefully by the time he gets to us, I'll have an idea."

Shit. I've got an idea.

She snaps back. "Sorry boss, but it'd better be a good one. I'm not dying on my first night out on the job."

"You're not gonna die. I've got a plan." I put the MAC-10 into my other hand, and grab another vial of the serum. I hold it in the same hand as my knife, and lean out the window.

"Don't tell me I'm the bait, Lana. You better not tell me I'm the bait."

"No way Vanessa. I'm the bait. But, I need you to slow down. Not a lot. You gotta keep moving. But we need him to catch up with us. The West Cay Park is nearby. I need you to drive straight into it."

"We passed that on the way in. Aren't there concrete barriers?"

At least she didn't object to my plan outright.

"Yeah. That's why I need you to go through the fence. My car can handle a fence. It can't handle a concrete barrier."

She keeps driving, but a little slower. The monster's gaining on us. She takes two deep breaths and nods. "I hope your plan works."

"Me too." I lean all the way out the window, then shoot back at the wolfman a few more times. Then I make a big dramatic show, pretending the gun's jammed. I toss it, and hold my knife at ready. "Come on, fucker!" I swing the knife a few times in the air, getting his attention straight on me, not the car.

Vanessa blows through the fence. I almost fall out, but grab the passenger seat headrest to brace myself. "Stop now!" I shout. She hits the brakes. The werewolf jumps on top of the car. The back window shatters and a fat hairline crack goes down the windshield. Vanessa screams. I stare the monster down. He snarls, and I hold the knife and snap the vial with my thumb.

Timing's gotta be perfect.

His jaws go wide. I lean back, but throw the knife and the vial into his mouth. His jaws clamp shut an inch in front of my nose. I fall back out of the car and cartwheel, bringing my foot up to kick him in the jaw. I don't know if it helps, but it sure feels like the right thing to do. The monster gags and spits. I jump back a few more feet, watching him.

"Vanessa, get my med kit! Grab a syringe!" She freezes for a solid second, but then nods and reaches back to the trunk space.

The werewolf jumps off the car, and lowers like a bull ready to charge. Then it vomits.

"Little bit quicker!" I shout. I look around and grab a cinder block from the edge of the baseball diamond. I heave it at the fucker, and it bounces off his shoulder. He snorts and glares. His head is spinning a little. He's dizzy. The serum's working—just not enough.

"Got it!" She says, holding up a needle kit.

"Great. I'm gonna need you to catch."

She thinks about it and nods. I grab another cinder block. He starts his charge. I throw the vial container wide in an arc over his head, and I spin with the cinder block, smashing it into his face as he gets to me. He yelps and reels back. I see Vanessa get out of the car and run across the field.

Bad throw.

I grab the cinder block in both hands, one in each of the two holes, and I swing it into his face again, this time smashing a corner into his eye. The eye splatters. He shoves forward with his shoulder and throws me from third plate half way to home base.

So glad I'm not trying to do this in a white dress.

He starts another charge. Vanessa's got the syringe in hand. She pours the green fluid into it, then starts running toward us.

"I'm gonna let him pin me. You get him in the back of the neck!"

"Got it boss."

I swing the cinder block wide this time, hitting him in the shoulder to buffer his charge. I dodge to the side of his jaws as they clamp down next to me. But he still barrels into me, knocking me over. I hold on to the cinder block for dear life. He jumps on top of me, and brings his mouth down to my head. I thrust the cinder block up in the way, and shove it in his open mouth.

I see Vanessa's braids fly up over his shoulder. She grunts. He stands up tall, throwing her back. But as he turns to face her, I see the syringe in the back of his neck. He stands there, huffing, gasping. Then, he falls. I roll out of the way, so as to not get smashed.

He shrinks down. His fur absorbs into his body. It takes about thirty seconds, but once the transformation's done, he's the skinhead.

Why didn't I just trust my gut?

Vanessa spits on his face. "Fuckin' wereHitler."

"Yeah. WereHitler. Ha ha. Did Nazi that coming." I say dryly. "Help me get him in the car?"

She nods, and we throw him into the back, and bind his wrists and ankles with cable ties.

#

Vanessa drives. I check my phone. Natalie texted me.

"Is tomorrow okay? I've got the money together. We can meet at your place."

I text her back.

"No offense. I'm not telling you where I live."

My bank emailed me. They're telling me they're launching an investigation into the fraudulent activity. They said they saw mysterious deposits that are significantly more than I usually deal in, so they've blocked the transactions. They said if the transactions are valid, I can request they be reviewed, and they'll be fixed within four to six weeks.

They didn't, however, block withdrawals in the amount of a few thousand dollars from MedPDQ and J&R Consulting, as they appear valid. They regret to inform me that these charges have put me significantly into arrears, and that I'm encouraged to deposit about $5,000 to bring my account back into the positive within the next 24 hours, in order to avoid penalties, account closure, and legal action due to the amount of the debt.

My bounties. Fuck. That's rent. That's groceries. That's bills. That's everything.

I get a response from Natalie.

"No offense. I know where you live."

Of fucking course she does.

I respond.

"Fine. Tomorrow. Noon?"

She agrees.

I call the bank. It's after business hours. Because of course it is. I respond to their email, telling them to clear the goddamned payments. I set a reminder to call them at 8am sharp.

#

Medi-Cor pays. Even though Vanessa agrees, they can't send my pay to her account because of some company policy or another. So of course the payment's going to be blocked by my bank. I go through the iHunt support line, and tell them to not deposit the pay, and to just issue me a check. They say I'll get a check issued in seven to ten business days. I tell them I need it tomorrow. They ask me if tomorrow for me is seven to ten business days from now. I hang up on them.

19
#TWOGIRLSONECOP

From 8am until 11am, I'm on the phone. Mostly on hold. The rest of the time screaming. I demand to speak to their manager. When the manager can't help, I demand to speak to their manager. Every single fucking person I talk to assures me they understand how frustrating this must be, and promise to do everything they can to help me. In the end, they do fuck-all. They tell me they can remove the deposit block on my account, and I can just request the payments be processed again.

iHunt client services tells me they can't re-process the deposits until the blocks have been fully resolved, which my financial institution can help with.

My financial institution tells me my employer can absolutely re-initiate the deposits, and that the blocks are resolved.

iHunt sends me a printout of my account information, where it says my bank is still sitting on the deposits, and has yet to cancel them.

The last time I talk to my bank, they tell me I should wait 48-72 hours for the cancellations to fully process, and then they let me know that I've had multiple charges that have just gone through with Escobar Holdings LLC, 7-Eleven Corporation, Taco Bell, Netflix, Client Services Incorporated, Sephora, Orange Julius, Shell Petroleum, MedPDQ, McDonald's, and Carver's

International. It's a total of 20 charges at $34 in overdraft fees each, so that'll be $680. They warn me that every five days, the charges will repeat so long as my account's in the negative. I tell them I need those charges waived since clearly I have the money, it's just held up thanks to this fraud situation. They tell me they can't waive the charges, and that these policies are in place to protect me.

Then they ask me if they can do anything else to help me.

I put a fist through my wall. I wasn't going to get my security deposit back, anyway.

#

I catch my breath. I chop up some kratom and make a tea to calm my nerves. I realize Natalie's gonna be over in forty five minutes. I grab a shower while my tea cools down to drinkable temperature. I do a quick and easy makeup look. Nothing too extravagant; I just liven things up and get rid of the bags under my eyes. I take a Coumadin just in case.

I toss on a little black dress and toss a denim jacket over it for some simple accent. I sip my tea and grab some Pop-Tarts, since I realize I forgot to eat breakfast while I was yelling at the banks. As I clean up, I realize I got Pop-Tart smeared into my dress somehow. It manages to show up even though it's on black fabric.

Fuck.

I try to scrub it out. It just makes it worse, smearing cookies and cream goo all over the place. It's 11:52. I run to the closet, toss everything off, and start digging. Nothing's clean. Everything's in the hamper. I grab the few things still on the rack. Nothing matches. I'd be set if I wanted to wear swimming shorts and a sweater I've never worn because I live in goddamned California.

The doorbell rings.

"Just a minute!"

I have no idea why this is such a big fucking deal.

I slip on a pair of jean shorts and a t-shirt I got from some local metal act called La Mortal. I think they broke up a long time ago. They were opening for... I don't even remember who.

I shut the closet and turn to the door. "Hey." I open it. Natalie's standing there in black capris and that same pink camisole with the black trim. Her lips match, with this sort of bubblegum-colored gloss.

Vampires are so good at not looking like murderers.

I step aside to let her in. "So, hey. Could you do me a favor?"

"Not read your mind?" She says and steps inside, looking around.

"Yeah. That. You know I can't do much about it. But..."

"Courtesy. And yeah. It's fine. Besides, I'm not really into Lamb Chop's Play-Along songs."

I blush and close the door behind her. "Have a seat?" I motion to the futon. It's the only place to sit. I don't really have company here too often.

She does. She seems nervous, she clenches and opens her

hand three times on the way to the futon.

"You alright?" I say, going over to sit with her.

"Not really. No offense. I'm in a vampire hunter's home. I'm a little nervous." She says, and digs through her little pink faux leather purse. She pulls out a stack of $100 bills that's maybe a little over a half inch thick. It's wrapped in an orange paper ring that says $10,000 on it.

My eyes go wide. It's not every day you see ten grand in cash, outside of heist movies. Vampires must see this kind of thing all the time. "You don't have anything to worry about. I'm not going to do anything. Also, fair warning just in case, my blood's dangerous."

She shrugs and hands over the stack. "Excuse me if I don't trust you with my life. You're a mercenary. Nothing's really stopping you from taking my money, killing me, then claiming the bounty."

"Yeah. Well, technically. And I imagine optimism doesn't get you too far in the world of the undead. So what's all this about the other vampires? Why shouldn't I go after them?"

"Because you'll get slaughtered. And this isn't one of those things where I say it's impossible, and you just suit up and tell me it's just never been done before. I'm saying that they're a cult. They're huge. And they're sociopaths. The worst things you think about me and the ones like me you've killed, that's nothing. They're in the middle of taking over the city."

I turn a little to face her, to watch her while she talks. She's not just sincere, but she's afraid of these things. "Taking over the city? What do you mean? Just like being the vampire leaders?"

She shakes her head. "Not just like that. It's worse. They're building captive blood supplies. Basically slaves. It's really awful. And they're moving in on the werewolves, too. They're basically treating them like a food source."

This is all new to me. From everything I'd heard, vampires and werewolves more or less leave each other alone. "Werewolves? Why? Just better blood?"

"It's special. Werewolves can build these really strong family units that are obsessed. Packs. They'd all die for each other without hesitation. And if a vampire drinks from a werewolf, they can build packs like that, too. So the leader of that compound, her name's Elisa, she's got all these slobbering soldiers at her beck and call. They're gonna march on everyone that's against them. It's gonna be bad. You don't want to get in the middle of a vampire war." She turns to look at me as well, pulling a knee up onto the futon so she can face me better.

Vampire supremacists and all that aside, I just kind of stare at her. I watch her lower lip for a moment. Then I look back to her eyes. Green, bursting out like those metal sparkler things you get for the Fourth of July. I feel for her. I want to console her. "What about you? Which side are you on?"

"I don't have a side." She says, resting her elbow on the back of the futon, and her head against her hand.

I remember the party. The way her hair felt in my hand. It's gold and shiny and silky and smooth and... "Oh?"

She shrugs her other shoulder. "They made me as part of this fucked-up political move. They made a ton of new vampires in hopes they could sway a lot of us to vote for them. At least for now, the city's a democracy. The other side, the old guard, they won the vote. Elisa still said she's taking over even though she lost the election. I don't really much like either of them. I want to do my own thing. I guess that's more the opposition stance, the old guard. But everyone's all 'you're with us or against us' right now, so that's hard."

"Must be a pain in the ass." I say, but I'm distracted by her eyes.

I wonder if she's reading my thoughts right now.

I'm totally going to kill you. Gonna take your money, then take your head and cash you in like a carnival prize.

A couple of moments pass. She shrugs again.

We should fuck. Just, right here. Right now.

If she's reading my thoughts, nothing in her face says it.

What time is it?

I think about the clock. I could look over at it. Check the time. But I just can't. I can't look away from her. I don't wanna look away from her.

Oh shit. She's doing the thing.

I stand and clench a fist.

"Whoa. Totally not cool. I can't believe you'd fucking do that here."

She looks up at me like I'm stupid or speaking Esperanto. "What? What are you talking about?" She backs up a little, like I might kill her.

If she was charming me, I couldn't stand up.

"Shit. Sorry. Thought you were doing the vampire charm thing."

She chuckles and raises an eyebrow. "What makes you think that?"

There's a knock on the door. Loud. "San Jenaro PD. Open up."

Natalie's eyes go wide. "Did you...?"

I shake my head. My hands shake. "No idea what the fuck they're doing here. But I should get it. You know."

She nods, and goes to my bathroom.

I open the door. Kinda dopey, kinda vaguely handsome cop. Big guy. "Detective Garcia. SJPD. Are you Lana Moreno?"

"Um, sure. Can I ask what's the problem, officer?"

"Last night, there were reports of a blue Honda Civic in a driveby shooting in San Maria Cay. A woman fitting your description was seen firing a machine pistol near Third Avenue. Where were you last night around seven pm?" He's doing that thing where he's edging his head in so he can peak around my apartment without getting a warrant or permission. I step to the side to give him a better look; I figure I've got nothing to hide in here. I definitely didn't leave a submachine gun on my coffee table.

"I was with friends. I don't know anything about any

shootings. And I mean, one person to another: Do I look like the kinda girl who would hang out in San Maria Cay? Or the kind of girl who could afford a gun like that?"

He steps back and looks me over, like that matters. Then he looks out to the street. "What happened to your car? It looks like it was in an accident. The reports suggest the car drove through the West Cay Park, suffering significant damage."

"It was gangs. You know this isn't the best neighborhood. They sometimes vandalize cars."

He tilts his head. He's not buying it. "Ms. Moreno, I think I'm going to have to ask you to come into the station for some further questions."

He looks over my shoulder, curious. Natalie steps up beside me. "Thank you for your time officer, but I don't think you're going to find anything useful here. Some kids took Lana's car for a joyride, and wrecked it. She was with me all last night. You checked my alibi. We were bowling. She beat me. She teased me about my terrible score. You're going to take whatever evidence you've got, and file it away as illegally obtained in violation of the suspect's civil rights. Lana's off your suspects list."

He nods, and tips his hat. "Well, ladies. I think I've got everything I need. Sorry about what happened to your car." He smiles to us then steps back and walks to his car.

Why'd she do that? She could have been rid of me. She could have walked with her cash and never had to worry about me again.

I close the door behind him, sigh, and fall against the wall.

"Oh my god, thank you."

My heart's fluttering. My goddamned knight in shining armor. With fangs. Who tried to kill me a few days ago.

"No problem. So, are you going to leave those cultists alone?"

"Yeah. I don't think they're part of the contract anyway." I slink back into the corner, between the front door and the wall. She's close. I don't know what to do. I want to hug her. I want to just thank her over and over until she tells me to shut the hell up.

"So the other thing I wanted to tell you. The contracts you're taking. You know they're from other vampires, right?"

"Huh?" I tilt my head. I reach forward a little. I kind of want to touch her hand. But I don't.

"Yeah. When we kill each other, it's basically an act of war. So we go through intermediaries. The three vampires you were contracted for originally? One of them created me as part of the democracy thing I told you about. Those three vampires were messing with some people on the old guard side. So, the leader of the old guard, technically the leader of the city, he hired you to kill them off. He knew a couple of them were already dead, so he made the contract broad enough that you could just kill anyone hunting in the resort district and thin their numbers."

"Well hell." I sigh.

"I know money's money. But it's maybe good to know these things."

I reach forward and grab her hand. She doesn't stop me. I hold it between us for now. "Why'd you make that creep a vampire? The one who jumped me?"

"You know how we can make people do stuff?" She looks to our hands, then back up to my eyes.

I nod.

"That's not just humans. Someone made me do it. They saw you fighting with him, and forced me to turn him. I'm sorry. I didn't want to. Once the command wore off, I realized I'd be held responsible for him, so I was trying to teach him the basics when you ran into him that second time."

"And the girl at the party?" I say.

What's come over you, Lana? Are you begging her to justify herself? To make herself not seem like a monster?

"Like I told you, I lost control. When a vampire's about to die, instinct takes over. Everything goes black, and if you survive the night, you come to the next night covered in blood, not knowing what happened. I don't know anything about that woman. I don't even know which one you're talking about." Little drops of pinkish, watery tears come up at the corner of her eyes. "Do you know what happened to her? Did she awaken hungry?"

I shrug, and squeeze her hand.

"I should go." She looks to the door, and pulls her hand back.

"You don't have to."

She shrugs. "I should." She opens the door, which kind of corners me against the wall.

"Hey."

She stops. "Yeah?" She's looking away. But I see the trails of pinkish tears down her cheeks.

"Text me if you wanna talk about it."

She takes a long breath in and swallows. She glances to my eyes and nods, then steps out and closes the door.

20
#AUDIT

Wednesday rolls along. I tell Vanessa and Denny I have to cancel because I don't have any leads to pursue. Denny responds with "K." Vanessa asks if we can train. I tell her we can after I go to the bank.

So, I go to the bank.

I wait in line for twenty minutes in order to give them about $8,000 to cover the negative balance. I'm not broke, but from my perspective and for all intents and purposes, the single largest chunk of cash I've ever seen, ten grand, just turned into two grand. It's like magic. Bank magic.

Vanessa and I train. It's great, but a bit exacting. She's wound up all to hell. I feel like she might break the bag a couple of times. If she keeps this up, she's gonna put me to shame. I teach her some blocks, some holds, and some throws. We talk about specific techniques for killing different types of vampires. She's giving it 110%. She accidentally hurts me a couple of times.

I should note, this is weird. I mean, I'm not fighting her for real. I'm not giving it my all. But she's strong, fast, and mean. I've got to rethink the curriculum at this rate.

A week passes. We train some more. Vanessa's really interested in getting back out on the field. I tell her I'll keep an eye open.

During the week, the blocked deposits roll off my account. I tell iHunt to re-process them. They say they're taking a 3% penalty. I want to protest, since that's more money I really can't part with, but I know it's just not worth it. The house always wins with this shit. I get a few bounced payment notices from a few of the stores. Taxed on the front end, taxed on the back end.

Then, I meet Agent Gardner.

#

"Hello. I'm Agent Gardner, IRS. Can I come in, Miss Moreno?"

I'm just gonna long story short.

The IRS has a process they call "civil forfeiture." This happens when you make a number of deposits that are all under $10,000 but combine to exceed $10,000. When you make a $10,000 deposit, you trigger some flags, some paperwork has to be done. So a lot of criminal groups use smaller deposits to evade IRS attention. So, they've been looking for people trying to evade that attention, and they use this process called civil forfeiture and take the deposits from you until they can confirm they're legit.

This is big, big business for the IRS. They've made nearly $300 million in the past decade through this process.

iHunt processes a lot of payments under $10,000. In fact, they've never processed a single payment of $10,000 or more, Agent Gardner explains to me. This is very suspicious.

But, in the interests of good, hard-working people like me, the IRS is on the case. As a way of hitting iHunt for avoiding IRS scrutiny, they're going to seize my money. This includes the $8,000 in cash I deposited last week.

I explain that it's contract work, consulting work. It's like Uber. He doesn't care. He says if it's legitimate, it'll be back in my account as soon as the investigation concludes. He reminds me that freelance income is taxable income, so I should be extra careful come tax season.

My first year on the job, I traveled to the mountains and fought a Wallachian vampire lord who impaled his enemies and bathed in their blood. My second year, my teacher brought me to a village in Cambodia that was subject to top secret US military experiments which created a zombie outbreak. I've seen slave rings run by warlocks, where the slaves were branded with eldritch runes and would die if they spoke ill of their masters.

I'm hard. I can deal with shit.

As Agent Gardner line-item detailed everything they were taking from me, I cried. It took everything I had to not put a boot through his jaw. I wanted to put a stake through the heart. But stakes through the heart only stop vampires. If I kill Agent Gardner, they'll just send bigger, better armed agents. These people are worse than monsters.

Vampires are just parasites, doing what they must to stay alive. Werewolves are cursed to become something they hate every month. The IRS? They live to bleed innocent people. They don't need to do it. They could stop. They could walk away. They're not cursed. They're not just surviving.

#

That afternoon, I cry. I cry and I throw up and I scream and I kind of hope someone calls the cops and they come and bust down the door and find drugs and I resist arrest and they fucking kill me or lock me up so I never have to worry about where my next meal or rent payment comes from.

I take two beers and an Adderall, and hit up some of the cutesy tourist bars on the resort district. I find a guy, Tommy, who's here on business. He sells frozen cappuccino machines or something, I don't even care. He's from Florida, god damn shut up. He's married and hiding it, but I also don't care. He's not very funny, but he looks okay, at least drunk and on Adderall. He gets the hint when I'm smiling and nodding and looking at the clock, and he invites me back to his hotel.

I ride him for about twenty minutes. It's okay. I manage to not think about anything else for a couple of hours. That's all I really need. Eventually I pass out. He wakes me at 5am, tells me he has a meeting, and that I need to leave. I roll my eyes and start getting dressed. He rushes me out, and says it's really important.

Whatever.

#

iHunt sends out this long-winded apology explaining that they were blindsided by this whole thing with the IRS. While they can't do anything about existing payments, they will conduct future payments through money orders or wires, which of course we'll eat the fees on. If we're in a city with a branch office, which

I'm not, we can visit their liaison for a cash payment instead. Right now, branch offices exist in... Northern California. And New York. And Shanghai.

Of course.

I flip through the current offerings since I'm gonna need money, and soon. Who knows what the next bullshit manufactured crisis is going to be?

It's all just poor tax. I should be winning. I'm making more money than I've ever made in my entire life. More than I thought I'd ever be able to. And now I'm broke. These barriers are made to keep me broke. They're made to prevent even meager class mobility. And they fucking work.

"Palo Verde. Small gang of vampires near the historical movie district. Five fully-detailed marks. Any one qualifies."

Oh wow. This is promising.

I tap to read more, since the pay information's not on the main ad.

"Audition gig. Corporate client."

Fuck.

Audition gig means no pay. It's an "exposure" gig, where if you do a good job, theoretically, they hire you for another job that actually pays. Unfortunately, as more people join iHunt, who are willing to work for less and less, we can't really do anything about these gigs, since there's somebody who will take them. Some desperate schlub will ruin it for everyone who demands to be paid for their hard work.

I swipe left.

I get up to grab a snack. The Pop-Tart box is empty. There's some salad in the fridge. I go to pick it up, and it's sludge. The granola bar box is empty. Back in the fridge, I poke through some takeout containers. The first, the one in the front, has some fuzz growing inside—that means they're all ruined.

My stomach growls.

I forgot to eat again. What was the last thing I ate? It was before I hooked up with that guy. What's his name? Tommy, right?

I find my wallet and flip through numbers on my phone. I'll order something. Delivery means a $10 minimum. I have $2,000 to my name, and rent's up in a week. What's that? $800? After phone, electric, gas, water, sewage, trash... Is that enough?

I can't spend $10 on food. Not right now.

My stomach growls.

"Jobs, Lana. We're looking for jobs. Gotta find work to eat." I say to nobody in particular.

I flip through another gig. It's one I rejected a while ago. Repost. I might be able to negotiate a higher rate.

"Client in Palo Verde wants to meet a vampire to consult on her screenplay. $500 after publication."

After fucking publication? When will that even be? The listing doesn't say. But I can't turn down work. It's not like I won't need $500 in six months, a year, or two years. I swipe right, and tell her we can set up a time to meet.

I flip through some more. I head out and across the street to Julio's bodega. I can eat cheap there.

"Demon in Schuster Park. $2,500. Can be killed, exorcised, or bound. Discretion if currently possessing victim."

I hate demons. Hate them, hate them, hate them. But, I need the money. Swipe right.

"Lana!" Julio's all full of cheer.

"Hey Julio." I go to the counter, and grab a couple of beef jerky packs and a Mountain Dew. "Can I get some cicciarones?"

"How much? Half pound?"

I motion to the largest in the cabinet. "Nah. Just get me that really big one right there. That should be fine."

He puts the big one on the scale, prints a barcode, then puts it and a few more in the bag.

"You don't have to take care of me, Julio." I smile. "But thanks."

"Someone's got to. That'll be $3.79."

I reach for my wallet. I pat my clothes.

Fucking forgot it.

"Shit. Just a minute, I forgot..."

"Don't worry about it. You're good for it, Lana." He shoos me off.

I check for other gigs.

"Succubus in Ava Blue. $3,000. $9,999 if captured alive."

Well shit. That's some fucking cash.

I swipe right. Then I realize why they want to capture it alive. *Perverts. Fucking rich motherfuckers want a pet succubus.*

Then I remember why I can't let my morals or dignity get in the way of a paycheck.

I look down to check on other gigs. I get a text message from Natalie.

"Hey. Was that offer to talk just a platitude, or did you mean it?"

I chew on a cicciarone as I cross the street, staring at the message. A car honks. I give the driver a dirty look and keep walking. Then I type back.

"Yeah. You free tonight? I need to get out."

She responds a few seconds later.

"Yeah. Got something fun in mind? I'm a bit down."

I think for a moment. I consider what we can do for free.

Fuck it. Fuck free. If I don't spend this, the IRS or the Illuminati or the bank or the cops or some other motherfucker will take it.

"Yeah. Amusement park. I don't know if you eat, but I wanna treat you to coneys, beer, and churros."

She sends back a sticker of a Rainbow Bright laughing.

"I do eat. It's a date."

21

#TERMSANDCONDITIONS

I go back by Julio's. He says he won't take my $5. I get a $1,200 money order for Regina though. This is the first time in months I haven't had to pay the late fee. I feel like I'm jinxing myself, like if I pay early, I'll need that money for an emergency in the mean time. But I also feel like if I don't pay it now, I'll spend that money on stupid shit and I'll be up a creek next week.

Regina's shocked to see me. When she answers the door, she tells me she's not providing any extensions anymore. I show her the money order through the peep hole. She opens the door with wide eyes. She thanks me about seven times, and wishes me a Feliz Navidad, even though she's like three weeks early for that. Although I guess I really only see her every month come rent time, anyway. I put a reminder in my phone to get her a present a few days before Christmas. I know it must be hard losing your husband and being all alone with shitty tenants like me.

The screenwriter gets back to me. She wants to meet me tomorrow for coffee. I tell her that works.

I consider hitting up Schuster Park for a while to look for the demon. I decide against it. I don't want to get into a fight. Not right now. Not a real fight. Instead, I head over to Ava Blue to scope out their succubus problem.

As I go for my car, I get an email from Keller Pictures, the studio that wanted my totally fake story. They said they're willing to option my story for $5,000 direct, with an additional $10,000 a year for three years. They say if they buy it, it'll be for $75,000 with some fine print about residuals. I have no idea about any of that, so I do a little Googling while I drive. It sounds good, so I tell them I'm in. I ask how quickly they can send a check.

#

A lot of people think succubi are demons. They're not. They're actually thought forms, which are basically creatures created by the human mind. Someone with psychic powers or just really strong feelings under the right occult circumstances can create thought forms, either on purpose or more commonly by accident. Usually thought forms are strange and unique to the creator. Succubi really aren't. There are some differences, mostly cosmetic, but by and large succubi work almost the same all over the world. The only places they don't exist are places which don't attach cultural shame to sex. Which is to say, they exist more or less everywhere. We even call them by a gendered term. Sometimes we use the male-coded version, "incubus," but that's far rarer. Because, surprise surprise, our culture has issues with women fucking, and has for fucking forever.

A succubus is a thought form who bleeds psychic energy rapidly. Since they're made up of psychic energy, this is a problem for them. They can only replenish that psychic energy by absorbing two emotions: lust and guilt. This is why the classic stories have them appearing as beautiful women who seduce married men in their sleep or whatever. Sometimes, the stories have incubi impregnating women. Spoiler alert: That never actually happens—thought forms are not fertile. The woman gets pregnant by someone she's ashamed to have fucked, and the thought form feeds on the lust and the guilt. But as psychic entities, succubi are terrifyingly good at finding out exactly what you want, and more importantly what you're ashamed to want. For example, a succubus might know that I kind of want another season of *Dharma and Greg*.

Most people either ignore or don't know about the guilt part. They just like to tell stories about the sexy dream ladies who wreck homes. The people in the know, they know that succubi have unique powers to inspire lust. They can take whatever sexual feeling you've already got, and crank it up to eleven. So sometimes you get rich people who have it all, who want a little bit more. They summon, create, or try to trap succubi. Considering the average house in Ava Blue goes for about $2.5 million, I think it's safe to say that's what I'm dealing with here.

The house I'm supposed to meet at, it's not in the $2.5 million range—if I had to venture a guess, I'd say it's probably in the $25 million range. It's huge and fucking gorgeous. I think they call it "Italianate Revival." It's three stories, and a couple of the ballroom windows go from floor to ceiling. It's god damned absurd, is what it is. As I get out of my car, a cobalt blue Aston Martin drives by, and I'm pretty sure I've seen a shitty movie starring its driver.

I get an email from Keller Pictures. They've attached a PDF

contract. It says they'll pay within two weeks of signature. Not to seem too needy, I sit in the driveway and sign it on my phone. As I'm signing it, an old man comes out in an expensive-looking red silk bathrobe. The kind they make fun of in Old Spice commercials.

"Excuse me, miss?" I look over. He's probably 75. Maybe he's the one looking for the succubus. Maybe Viagra just isn't cutting it anymore.

"Oh, hello. I'm here about the… procurement job?" I put away my phone. I can't help but to scan the house. I don't belong here. This neighborhood is full of people who have never wondered whether their electricity will go out, and they'll have to replace a fridge full of food. "Nice house."

"It's a classic. Designed for some of the golden age directors. It's passed hands a few times, from movie stars to gold tycoons to powerful attorneys." He holds the door open. "Come in. Let's talk."

He doesn't have to tell me twice. I lock my car, wondering why I even bothered. There's not a car in this neighborhood that's not worth ten or more times this one. Nobody here wants to steal my piece of shit. "So which are you? Movie star, gold tycoon, or attorney?"

The inside of the place is more majestic than the outside. The floors are all green marble with silver inlay in all the cracks. There's a fountain dead center the foyer, with a statue in the middle of maybe Athena or Hera or… something Greek or Roman.

I was never good with that stuff. Every few feet along the wall, there's a table with some statue or pottery or whatever. I'm sure it's all very amazing if you have an art history degree. I just think about what it'd be like to bust a $20,000 vase over someone's head.

"Sorcerer." He says, walking through another wide open door to a library. It's the kind of place you see in TV. Massive, with three stories of books, and wheeled ladders all over the place to get to the top. A lot of the books look older than America.

"Sorcerer? Then why do you need a hunter to get a lowly succubus? Can't you just do a binding ritual?" I don't know much about sorcerers, but I do know that they can make quick work of thought forms, spirits, and demons.

"To make a long story short, I've lost my *to ti esti*." He says that with an accent, maybe Mediterranean. I can't place it. "The spiritual essence which fuels my sorcery. This would normally be a career-ending problem. However, if I can procure this succubus, I have uncovered a ritual which can return my grace."

"Deep." I say, poking around through the books. He goes over to a series of leather sofas in the middle of the library. "So if you need it alive, why are you still willing to pay if it gets killed? Wouldn't that be a deal breaker?"

He hesitates a moment. "I need it resolved, one way or another, because I summoned it. A local, a rather terrible man, was looking for love. Thanks to my sorceries, I knew he'd killed his last wife. So, I thought to curse him. He knew of my sorcery, at least in the loosest sense, so he asked my help through magical means. I gave him a potion that I told him would solve his problem."

"And it solved his problem by plaguing him with a succubus?"

"Yes." He clears his throat. I look back. He seems a bit distressed, a bit embarrassed. "Frankly, I wanted the succubus to drain him dry. To leave him a husk. He deserved it. However, when I lost my *to ti esti*, I became incapable of restraining the thing. It's now terrorizing the neighborhood, gaining strength. And you know how these things are."

I nod, and go to sit down on the sofa across from him. How they are is insufferable. They'll keep growing and growing until something stops them. "To capture a thought form, I need a soul stone. I don't imagine you have one of those sitting around, do you?"

"Indeed I do." He says, and pulls a green silk bag from his pocket, then hands it over.

I grab it and peek inside. The crystal inside is warped, deformed, about the size of a golf ball. It's green, black, and blue, glowing and strange. Soul stones don't look like any normal rocks, or any real thing, actually. When you look at them, they feel... *wrong*. Not like evil or anything like that, but like they don't mathematically fit in the space they fill. Like they're infinitely empty, but also infinitely dense. It's not the biggest soul stone out there, but it should do the trick. "Where can I find it? Does it have any patterns?"

He nods. "It's been avoiding my home. I think it knows that if it intensifies my sensation, I'll regain my power, and its life will be forfeit. She's still plaguing the Chadwicks. I have no reason to believe she'll be changing that pattern. The man of the house, Frederick, our resident wife murderer, is still in the early stages of her spell. His new wife doesn't suspect anything." He scribbles down an address and a rudimentary map. Maps are easy in Ava Blue, since every property's its own distinct block.

He's lying. He's just plain fucking lying. I have no idea what's really going on here, but this is total fucking bullshit.

"Good. I'll look into it. Talk to you as soon as I hear anything." I force a smile and stand up.

As I'm on my way out, I get a message through iHunt. Ramirez Holdings, the shell company that hired me for the resort district vampire gang, wants me to "CEASE AND DESIST" if the subject line's any clue.

I open it as I get in my car. They're telling me that I cannot sign an option for that story, and I can't make any money or sign any agreements over the vampire killing video. According to the fine print on the iHunt ad—as they've highlighted for my convenience—I agreed that all work created during the execution of that job, including research and cover identities, would be property of Ramirez Holdings without exception. That my work for them would be considered "work for hire," and that I am disallowed from any sort of secondary income from the work. They tell me they've reached out to Keller Pictures and told them they'll be taking over the contract from here onward. They'd also like me to know that further breach of contract would be handled to the extent allowable by law.

22
#NOSFERATU

I drop Vanessa a message telling her that tomorrow I'm hunting something interesting, and could use her help. Why not, right?

I get changed into a faux snakeskin skirt and jacket over a red tank top. I clean up a little, then dart over to the resort district, and grab a parking spot. I mingle with some former coworkers, and get one to agree to let me and my friend into the park without paying. Derek likes calling himself my "gay best friend" when we hang out every three to six months or so. I don't want to break to him, but he doesn't hang out with me because he's my gay friend—he hangs out with me because I'm the only non-white person who'll put up with him. He hugs me whenever he sees me. Today's no exception. I feel crowded. Like somebody's watching the hug. I appreciate it, but I can't wait for it to end. I feel vulnerable there in his huge bear arms, four inches off the ground.

Just around that time, I get a text from Natalie.

"At the park. Where are you?"

Then another.

"N/M CU"

She's waving from the other end of the front gate line. She's in black jeans and a green turtleneck that matches her eyes. She looks upset, but trying to hide it. Her makeup's covering her freckles enough that it looks like she was trying to cover up the fact that she's been crying. I motion her over to the ticket booth.

"Hey. Everything okay?" I say, and Derek motions us through the turnstile.

"Yeah. I mean, no. But yeah?" She shrugs and follows along. She carries her weight low, and shies her gaze away from me as we enter the park.

The park, in this case, is MovieLand. Celebrating the golden age of cinema. The main entrance looks like Palo Verde in the late 1940s. It's gorgeous, with boldly lit cinema marquees and vaulted champagne-colored arches all over the place. I could see the "Make America Great Again" argument if you were just talking about making everything look like this again. Except the part where I couldn't own property, drink from the same water fountains, or swim at the same beaches as everyone else. Or the part where my entire family would be kept in an internment camp. You never see that stuff in this golden age revival shit. In a way, I kind of wish they'd address it. I wish people would stop whitewashing the past and all the terrible shit that happens here. On the other hand, it's kind of nice to have this, to be able to enjoy something that was denied to my family during even worse times.

Natalie's got her arms crossed, which is totally awkward while walking. She's looking at the pavement. Which is kinda nice for pavement. It's clean. They added little sparkly bits, so it's always glimmering in the California sun, they way the old crooners used to sing about it. But she's definitely distant. I don't blame her; I feel eyes on us from everywhere. I guess it makes sense, there's thousands of people in here. But I feel singled out. I imagine if I was undead, I'd feel that even more right now.

"Seriously Natalie, what's wrong? You said you wanted to talk. You've got stuff on your mind. Out with it."

"Not yet." She says, shaking her head. "Can you... just talk to me for a little bit? I'll talk about it later. I just have to get the words together, y'know?"

She's miserable. It hurts to see her like this. Sometimes you stumble on vampires who are doing the dark, brooding, loner schtick. The "woe is me I'm the undeath" bit. That's not her. She's hurt. There's no general malaise here. She's specifically, fundamentally hurt.

"Yeah. I don't really know what to talk about. Life's been a wreck lately. Work is crap. I lost my real job a few weeks ago over stupid reasons. Money's terrible, and the banks and the IRS and everyone keeps taking and taking. But I don't want to get all negative. You're dealing with enough."

I lead her into a tiny theater. There's a dozen of them, each playing short clips of classic silent films. This one's playing the 1922 classic Nosferatu. I wonder if I subconsciously chose it. They're playing the scene where Max Schreck's shadow is climbing the stairs. Natalie puts a hand over her mouth to cover a laugh. I put a hand on her back and rub it.

"You can tell me whatever. It's okay. It's more about listening to someone else talk right now. Doesn't monster hunting make pretty good money?"

I shrug. She leans her shoulder against mine. "It's okay money. But it's weird the way it's set up. And the IRS is doing a crackdown, so a lot of my accounts got frozen and stuff. So while right now I'm making the most money I've ever made by a longshot, I'm also broke. I also just found out I can't sell the movie rights to my video."

"The one where you killed Chet?" As she speaks, I nod. Her hair smells nice. Jasmine maybe.

"His name was Chet? You put your fangs on a guy named Chet?"

She nudges into me playfully. "Trust me, if I had any choice in the matter, I wouldn't have touched him. He was slime."

"What kind of person do you prefer?"

She pulls away and looks to the door of the tiny theater. "I don't really want to talk about that. No offense or anything."

"It's okay. Sorry." I walk to the exit to guide her out. As I'm distracted with her, I bump a big wall of a guy in a hoodie. "Sorry!" I turn to face him to see if I knocked anything out of his hands, and he's gone. "Did you see the guy there?" I glance back to Natalie.

"No. Sorry. Wasn't watching."

#

"Can you keep talking?" Natalie says as we walk, breaking a moment of silence.

"Yeah, sorry." I look over to her face. She looks like she's pleading with me, this desperate, pathetic look.

We wander over to the Napa Valley area of the park. It's probably my favorite. It's all made to look like vineyards. Truth be told, I've never really been to Napa, but I imagine this is just as much what Italy looks like as Northern California.

"So. I'm doing a job right now in Ava Blue. It's a little weird."

"Oh?" She perks up a little, but pensively, like she's waiting for another shoe to drop.

"Yeah. This old guy, he's a sorcerer, he's trying to get me to catch a succubus for him."

She raises an eyebrow, curious. "Wait. A succubus? Is that slang for a vampire family?"

I shake my head. "Nah. It's an actual thing. A psychic entity that preys on guilt and lust. They're relatively harmless in the scheme of things."

"Wait." She cuts me off. "You're hungry. You want to get dinner?"

She's right. I forgot to eat since the cicciarones from Julio. How many hours ago was that?

"Um yeah? But how did you know?"

"Your stomach's growling. I heard it."

"Well, then, yeah. Can't ignore biology." I lead her to a little counter service Italian restaurant called Avalon.

Wasn't Avalon in England? Glastonbury maybe?

As we walk up to the counter, she puts both hands on my arm. She's now paying full attention. "So tell me more about this succubus."

I grab a tray and a couple of plates and some pasta and salads. "Well. They basically feed on psychic energy. So they drain people by… you know, overexerting them. Then they move on to others. This one doesn't seem particularly bad as far as they go, but he wants it captured because apparently it's the key to getting his magic powers back."

A young couple are clearly listening in to my story, giggling to each other. They're both model skinny, but not model hot. White with surfer tans. They belong together. It'd be kind of cute, but they've got that sort of soulless look in their eyes, like there's no depth whatsoever. I imagine they have strong opinions about The Big Bang Theory.

When I was training, one of my mentors told me to always speak of the supernatural in secrecy, in code. To always use symbols and metaphor, for fear of the populace discovering the truth. I've found that to be a worthless exercise. You can talk about anything in front of anyone, and they'll write it off. This couple probably thinks I'm talking about my novel, or some movie I watched.

"That's really weird." Natalie says, grabbing a couple of prepackaged red wine glasses. Plastic, sealed containers. Single-serving indulgence. "So how do you catch a succubus?"

"There's like a ritual and stuff. It's strange. You have to draw them out, which is pretty easy since you generally know what they want. Then you use the ritual real quick and trap them in a magical soul stone. That's really the hardest part. It takes a pretty experienced sorcerer or witch to make one of those. Or you can get them in a deal with a demon. And I imagine you know how that goes." I lead her over to one of the little standing space trattoria tables since all the sit-down space is taken. Then I set out the plates and she arranges the glasses.

"Yeah. Be careful what you wish for shit, right? So do you have the soul stone? Is this a thing you do alone?" She starts taking the plastic covers off our pastas and salads.

"I've got a partner I'm working with for this gig. Usually I'd do it alone. But you take whatever help you can get." I pop the lids off our wine glasses and lift mine. "Cheers?"

"What are we drinking to?" She lifts hers as well.

"Fuck if I know. Not having real jobs and overpriced crappy wine and good company?"

"I like that. To good company." She smiles, and taps my "glass." The plastic kind of thuds.

We eat quietly. Glancing back and forth throughout. We don't talk, but we communicate. We connect. Every time we steal a glance, she warms up a little—she gets more comfortable. We both laugh a couple of times. No jokes shared, but it's like we did. It's nice. Pleasant. Relieving.

#

After dinner, we wander. It's fully dark now. The park's best at night, with creative lighting everywhere. This place ran the company about a bajillion dollars; it has to ooze atmosphere to turn a profit.

"Have you ever been on the gondola ride? Or the ferris wheel?" I say, looking over to her as we walk.

"I've never been here before." She shrugs.

I look over at her like she said she's from Mars. Or is a fairy. Or a vampire. "Really? Did you not grow up around here?"

"I did. Just, my family couldn't afford it. Never cared to."

"Wow. Just... different strokes. My family couldn't afford it either. But in high school, my friends and I would jump the fence. They have security measures in place specifically because of the stupid shit I've done to get in here without paying."

She laughs. "So, which first? They both sound fun."

23
#ROMANS1-26

We opt for the gondola ride first. It's lovely, if a little crowded. They put twelve people on a gondola, and inevitably you can't see over half their heads. So you end up looking behind yourself to get any sort of view.

"Maybe it wasn't ideal for private talk." I say to Natalie quietly as we ride. Make no mistake, the ride's beautiful. It takes us through fake buildings from all over the Mediterranean, through vineyards and fake mountains and all sorts of art. Even surrounded by hot, sweaty tourists, it's still gorgeous.

"We can talk this way." I hear Natalie's voice in my mind. I look over to her, meet her eyes. They shimmer in the firelight from one of the torches we're passing. She nods.

I experiment. I think back. "This isn't a thing all vampires can do, is it?"

She shakes her head, and I hear, "No. Just some of us. We're all really different. But you know that, don't you? Because you kill us." Her face goes red. "I'm sorry. This is… a little more direct and honest. You don't have the same floodgates with thought that you do with speech."

"It's okay." I think, and reach over to touch her cheek. I don't hear anything from her, but I feel warmth and relief. "You're not wrong. I do kill vampires. I don't even know why you're here with

185

me right now, but I don't plan on hurting you."

"I guess the other part of this is that I trust what you're saying because there's no floodgates. We can lie to each other like this, but it's really hard. I appreciate it." She smiles and reaches up to touch the back of my hand with her fingertips. Then she looks around to the ten other park guests in the boat, and the rower, and puts her hand in her lap.

I jump to react, thinking sharply. "It's okay Natalie. Nobody's gonna judge you here. We're alright."

"I don't know if you mean that or you just don't know."

I tilt my head and think, "What do you mean?"

"There's a guy behind us." I hear her, and glance back subtly. "He's judging us right now. He's thinking we're abominations. That the bible says we should be put to death." It's a big guy in a flannel shirt. His wife next to him's giving him an elbow, like she's embarrassed because he keeps staring at us. And he does.

"Oh." I think, and look to the water. It's clean. Too clean. I can smell the chlorine. They go overboard, so the only moss is what they paint on.

"And the ride operator guy thinks he recognizes you. He wonders if he can get us in a three-way. Because, and these are the exact words he's thinking, bi girls are sluts."

I grit my teeth and swallow hard. I don't know the rower's name. I've seen him around the park.

I hear Natalie again. "You can't beat them up, Lana."

"I don't want to beat them up." I think, and look back to her.

She puts a hand on mine, rests my hand in my lap, and squeezes it. "Yeah. You do. And you can't. It won't fix anything."

"Mind reading sucks, doesn't it?" I think, and audibly sigh. She nods.

We stay quiet through the rest of the ride. I try very, very hard not to think about violence.

\#

"I didn't mean to fuck up your night." Natalie says as the gondola stops. I shake my head, and get up quickly to make sure we're the first ones off the ride. I tug her gently to the side as the guests shuffle off the boat.

"Can I kiss you?" I think to her, squeezing her hand.

She tilts her head, looking at my eyes. "I guess?" She thinks back.

As the guy in the flannel hoists himself up the stairs to leave, I take a step back in his way. I tug Natalie in, then I close my eyes and I kiss her, full-on.

"What are you doing?" She thinks loudly, surprised, her face red and warm.

"I asked. You said it was okay." I think through the kiss. I don't push in though, just in case there's a problem. The guy in the flannel's eyes go wide and he shakes his head. I think I hear him say "Sodomites." I might just be imagining it.

"It is okay. I just didn't think you were planning to weaponize it." She pushes back in, tilting her head and putting her arms around my shoulder so as to tell me it's still okay.

"I guess I could see how it looks that way." I break the kiss and grin to her.

"So this is a thing?" She whispers, taking a deep breath in.

"Whadda you mean?" I say, release, and start the way out to the park walkway.

"I mean like, is it a thing? Or were we just making a point to the bigot?" She puts her hands in her pockets and looks up to the moon as we walk. It's a big, bright half moon.

"It was a real kiss." I look to her, and put an arm around her waist, resting my hand on her hip. She smiles, but keeps attention on the sky.

We stop by the trattoria again and get some more wine, then walk toward the World's Fair section of the park. I never understood why there was a World's Fair section of a park dedicated to classic cinema. It's cute though, a little bit Atomic Age, and a little bit cheesy carnival.

I point over to the ferris wheel line.

"Now that we're on the same page." She says, then slams into me in a blinding flash. I go rolling across the pavement. It hurts like hell. I think I feel my shoulder pop out of place, but I'm not sure. I know I'm gonna have some bruised ribs, definitely. I slam into an old man's legs, and I hear seven variations of "watch yourself!" I grab the stake out of my purse.

I knew this was a possibility. Fucking knew it. God damn it, Lana. Why the fuck did you trust a vampire?

I look up to where Natalie hit me. I'm ready to charge. But

she's on the ground, being beaten all to hell. It's the couple from Avalon, the surfer tanned ones who were laughing. And from out of the corner of my eye, there's the big guy in the dark gray hoodie from the theater, running at me like an NFL offensive tackle. He's fast. Strong. Gotta assume he's a vampire.

The best thing about a stake to the heart when someone's charging you is, it doesn't really matter if they're a vampire. That stake's gonna do the trick. It's also nice when they run straight for you, because that gets rid of a lot of the difficulty that comes with trying to ram a stick through a fucker's ribcage.

People are panicking, running. Tourists and rich people, they don't like to stand around when there's danger. Nobody here wants to be the first one to call for help. He dives, trying to crush me under his weight. I do some quick mental math, roll a couple of feet to the side, and put the stake on the ground, pointed end up at about a forty five degree angle facing him. He smashes into it with his chest, and since he's squishier than the pavement, it goes straight through. I feel like if it was longer, it would have gone out the back side, too.

People scream. He starts decomposing. I look around and shout. "Y'all act like you ain't never seen a vampire before." It doesn't really help.

The man of the couple is still kicking Natalie—she's covering her head, balled up in a fetal position. The woman dives down to bite her leg.

"Oh uh uh." I dash forward and slam the tip of my right Chuck

Taylor into her jaw, and send her rolling back.

"Oh you picked the wrong fight, Buffy." The man kicks Natalie harder, tossing her against a trash can, which practically explodes with the impact.

"Okay. I am *so* not Buffy." I say, getting into a defensive position. "Two reasons. Wanna guess?"

He flashes his fangs and flexes. He nearly doubles in size. He goes from waifish surfer bro to boardwalk body builder in three seconds. Worse: He stinks. I kind of want to vomit. But I hold it in. "I'll bite. Why?" I briefly wonder if he intended the bite pun. If so, I want to hit him harder. If not, he totally dropped the villainous banter ball. Shame on him either way.

"First, if this was Buffy, my gay love interest would die a horrible death. That's not gonna happen." He swings a haymaker wide at me. He's strong. He's big. But he's not that skilled. I duck down, and plant three quick rabbit punches to his stomach. They do fuck-all. So I somersault back as he dives to grab me.

"Second?" He stands up again, and stomps toward me. Off in the distance, I see the surfer woman closing in on Natalie.

I dash back toward the fake bay where they hold light shows every night. Where I was supposed to be when Jake decided to fire me. I jump over the "employees only" barrier, I stand on the rocky cliff, and I shrug. "I didn't really have a second. I expected to kill you after the first one, then say that was number two. It was really quite clever, you're just gonna have to take my word for it."

He chuckles once, then growls and lowers into a charge. I take one breath and take a little risk.

As he approaches, I think back to that time I went to cheerleading camp. I was the poorest girl there, but the local fire department gave "scholarships" to send poor girls to camp. The girls all laughed about my ragged, generic sneakers. One of them told me to take them off, and if I beat her in a footrace, she'd give me her Air Jordans. I was an idiot kid who wanted nothing more than to fit in, so I did it. While I was running, the other girls took my shoes. Once I beat her, I looked back, and they threw my shoes into the lake. I cried for hours. One of the camp counselors gave me her old shoes.

The first time they had me top a pyramid, I got to stand on the girl who challenged me to that race. She and her friends said they were going to throw me once I got on top. So when I got up there, I hopped and smashed my heel into her shoulders. I got bruised up pretty bad, but I broke her shoulders. I got sent home, but it was totally worth it.

I jump. I land, planting my feet on his shoulders, then kick my heels down. I use him as a springboard and jump again. He flies into the bay water, and falls on one of the laser light stems, impaling him. I land and roll, then run for Natalie.

The woman's got Natalie on her knees from behind, and is biting down, feeding. Natalie's paralyzed. Maybe it's the feeling. Maybe it's the power. I don't know. The blonde smells, too. It's like rotten meat and honey. I can't tell if it's disgusting or sweet and delicious. Maybe both?

"Yo." I snap. The blonde looks up, but doesn't stop drinking. "You're gonna want to stop drinking from her right fucking now, for your own sake."

"Oh yeah? Why?" She mumbles, pulling away just enough to get the words out. Her fangs are huge, like tusks.

I rush forward and kick her right in the fucking teeth, shattering them. "That's why."

She screams and grabs at her mouth, her eyes going red and her body growing just like the man did a moment ago. I don't give her the time to finish the change. I grab the stake out of the corpse on the ground, ripping it from his chest and charging forward. I feel kind of like a medieval knight with a lance on a horse as I yell and shove it through her sternum. Her skin pulls taut. She gasps her last, dying breath.

Frankly, I'm surprised it works. Usually that takes two or three tries at least. I dust off my hands and bend down to help Natalie up. Her eyes go wide, then my senses go black as something slams into my back.

I don't know how long passes. A couple of seconds? A couple of minutes? Everything's spinning. My arm hurts, burns. It's definitely, definitely broken. As my vision returns, I see that I'm lying on the ground next to an uprooted, upturned park bench. I guess someone must have thrown it at me.

I scan the area.

Surfer bro.

He's marching back for me. Red eyes. Fangs extended. Huge hole in his chest. He's not fucking around.

"Let him pounce you. Just keep his teeth away." I hear Natalie's voice inside my head. I nod to nobody in particular. I don't see her.

I put my non-broken arm up, and lie there crying like a victim. It's not hard. He puts his arms up and dives to grab me. I don't stop him, but I keep my arm ready to block his first bite. He snaps at me, and I smash him in the face with the bottom of my hand. *Shuto-uchi*, my first teacher called it. He growls and tries again. I smash him again. He grabs my arm and yanks it out of the way.

Just then, Natalie bites down on his neck from behind, and pulls him back. I roll to the side while she feeds. He's trying to buck her away like a goddamned mechanical bull. "GRAB HIM." I hear in my mind from Natalie. I don't hesitate. I dive for his legs and toss him to the ground along with her. Then, I roll him to the side and put him in a rear wrist lock. It hurts like a son of a bitch, because of my broken arm. It's not just broken—the bone's splintered, and penetrating my skin. I'm bleeding all over. But I can't let it stop me. This is life-or-death.

She keeps feeding. I've never seen it that fast, that menacing before. I watch as his skin pulls tight from the blood loss, and she goes bright red as she goes beyond her fill.

Then, he decays. His body falls apart into dust.

"If I give you blood, your arm will heal, but..." I hear her voice. *The blood makes you feel for the vampire. It's how they make blood slaves.*

Counterpoint: I'm bleeding to death. No amount of Tylenol or Oxycontin or Zeolite is gonna fix that.

"I know. Do it." I say, and sit up from the pavement.

She bites her wrist and kneels in front of me. I take it with my good hand, and put it to my mouth.

It's not like I've heard. It's not actually that good. It's kind of foamy. Kind of earthy. Like licking the head off a room temperature beer. It's strong. Sweet. But kind of difficult to process.

I feel my arm coming back together. I feel the bones move back into place. I expected it to hurt, but it doesn't. It just sort of... happens.

"Sorry they ruined our night together." Natalie says softly as I drink, as my arm knits itself up.

"Hm?" I say, pulling back and gasping. It wasn't good, but it was overwhelming.

"They ruined our night? Tried to kill us? Remember? I know it was a while ago." She says, doing a shockingly good job of lightening the mood.

"Oh fuck them. We're still going to the ferris wheel."

She looks to me for a moment, staring, considering. "You're not joking, are you?"

24

#VAMPIREMAGIC

"What about security? The cops'll get called, won't they?"
Natalie sort of whines as I take her hand and start toward the
ferris wheel.

"For one, security won't do anything. I've got a contract..." I
stop. "Shit. I've got a contract." I release her hand and grab my
iPhone. I snap pictures of the three bodies.

*$15,000. Maybe vampire gangs should try to randomly murder
me more often!*

I submit them to iHunt, smile wide, and walk toward the ferris
wheel. "And cops, well, you know how to handle cops."

"I..." She takes a deep breath in, pauses, but then follows
along. "I don't like manipulating cops... or people... unless I have
to. But I will."

I stop. "Yeah? Sorry I sorta assumed there."

She shakes it off and keeps walking. "It should be fine. Let's
just move on."

The thing about these really extreme cases is, people just sort
of don't want to believe them. So they sweep them under the
rug. It's not like there are actual remains, anyway. Vampires clean
up after themselves. They leave some dust and clothes, but that's
about it. It can cause you problems every now and again, but
most people just want it to be somebody else's problem.

Especially tourists and the wealthy. That covers all the guests. The employees are taught to avoid any real crisis situation, and just call for security. I always wondered if that was because somebody in the know didn't want stuff like this getting out.

We get in line for the ferris wheel. It's not that long. I wonder if we played any part in that. "So why do you think they attacked us?"

She thinks, and shrugs. "They attacked you. At least, first. Then they went after me. They're new recruits in Elisa's army. They want me because I'm not a loyal soldier. They want you because you're kicking their asses left and right. The one time I went to their compound, they had posters of vampires who they wanted taken out. I bet I'm on that list now."

"Wait. The one time?" I tilt my head. That agent said they were there all the time. I had times and dates.

"Yeah. Right after I was made, they took me there. I knew it was bad news, so I kept away. Why?"

"I dunno. When was that?" We move forward bit by bit, every time the ferris wheel has another load.

She shrugs. "I guess it had to be like August? Maybe late July?"

Is she lying? Is she covering something up?

I shake it off.

It doesn't matter if she's lying. I have to assume she's not. If I don't start trying to proactively trust her, this'll keep being a problem.

"Hm. I don't know what it means, but the company I work for, there are these third party agents that can give you information and things for a fee. They gave me a whole bunch of schedules and photos of you guys. They had all these repeat records of you at the compound."

Her eyes went wide. "Huh? Were there pictures?"

I think for a moment as we get up to the gates. We're on the next load. "No. All the pictures were on the resort district."

"I don't know what they gained from telling you we were there. Hm." She's thinking a mile a minute, looking around contemplatively. Then she takes a few steps over to one of the park employees and whispers something to her. I know her—her name's Angela. She's pure, embodied drama. But she nods to whatever Natalie said to her. She comes back and sighs. "I know this must all be really messed up. It's hard to trust anyone. I'm sorry. I wish I had a better answer. But, that's vampires."

I shrug. "I hunt monsters. I know how that stuff works. And if it's any consolation, I trust you."

She glances over at me, and a smile creeps to her face. "Why? I don't think I've given you any reason to."

"I want to." I shrug. "I kinda think trust comes down to that. I want to trust you. I think you deserve someone who trusts you."

Angela lets everyone off the ride, then opens it up for us. Natalie gets into the caged gondola, then I do. They lock the door behind us. Natalie looks out the side window, away from me. "You know, vampires are afraid of heights."

"I didn't. Wow. I've never heard that before."

"Because it's bullshit." She says, and turns back to look at me with a smile. We share a little laugh. She takes my hand.

One by one, the gondolas fill up. They move us a little bit forward, and we go a little bit up each time. Every time, we see a little more of the park, and of San Jenaro off in the distance.

Natalie squeezes my hand. "I'm ready to talk now. If you don't mind." I nod, and give her a reassuring smile. "My brother left." I tilt my head, but don't say anything yet. "The one you followed to the Tropicana a while ago. He left San Jenaro. Said it's too dangerous. He tried to get me to go with him. I tried to talk him into staying. But he's gone. Back to where his human family lives in Florida."

"Why didn't you go?" I say, turning a little to face her, to make sure she knows I'm listening.

"I don't even know. I thought maybe I should have. It's not like I'm on good terms with my family. I just don't want to leave. And like, he's not my real brother. We weren't even created by the same vampire. But we're all we've had since we got into this whole mess back in July. Now it's just me. And vampire politics. And cults and militias. And vampire hunters. And it's just a lot to take in, you know?"

"I do. But, you don't have to worry about any vampire hunters at least. I've heard they're jerks. If I see one, I'll beat their ass." I smile, wide and full of teeth. She fights a smile for a second, but fails and looks down, shaking her head and blushing.

The ferris wheel goes all the way around, then starts letting people off. When it comes to our gondola, they don't stop—they keep sending us around. I peek around, and notice we're the only ones on the ride. "I thought you didn't like manipulating people?"

She sits back in her seat, looking to the night sky. "I didn't actually do anything vampiric. I just asked her. Sometimes, just saying the right thing's just as good as vampire magic."

"Oh? What'd you say?" I consider it. Of course, you can convince a park employee to do a whole lot with the right keywords. The most important ones are, "I want to propose," and, "my child has cancer and only has three months to live." I doubt she used either of those.

She shrugs. "So anyway, brother left. My first instinct was to run back to my creator. He told me he'd talk to me. That he'd make it all alright. So I went to see him, and it got weird. I don't know if he was mind controlling me or what, but he wanted to fully induct me into their cult, and I started getting into it. 'Drink from the family blood,' he told me. I guess maybe I wanted to belong, I don't know. It's all a little blurry. But it got all hot and heavy. We were feeding from each other and stuff and…" She bites her bottom lip. Tears are welling up in her eyes again.

I wrap my arm around her and adjust so I can watch her eyes. "It's okay." I whisper. Like that actually means anything.

"I had this vision. This idea of what I'd be like as one of them. It felt good for a second. Like I could really belong. Like I could be something. Like I wouldn't have to worry about who I needed to be. But then I thought about all this… About you. I don't really want to be a monster. I'm a vampire. Not a... well, you know...

vampire vampire." The way she accents "vampire," I know exactly what she means. "I knew if I turned him down, he'd kill me. He'd brand me a family traitor. A betrayer. That the only way I was getting out of that situation was if he was dead."

"Ah." I say softly, nodding.

"So, to not be a serial murderer, I had to murder him. And that means execution if they find out."

"You think maybe that's why they sent those three?"

"No. Those three were shits. New recruits. If it's murder, they send the elites. You don't just fight your way out of that." She leans into my shoulder.

I wrap my other arm around her and pull her into a hug.

I want to offer her my blood. Maybe it'll help. They say it's like a drug. If I was feeling the way she's feeling right now, I'd want a drug.

She shakes her head against me. "No. I don't want to have that relationship with you. Can we not?"

"Huh?" I say, holding her, running my hands through her hair.

"You were thinking really loud. Sorry."

"Oh. Yeah. We can do that."

Damn. That feeling's been creeping into my mind every day since that party.

"I'm sorry." She whispers, and pulls in a little closer, burying her forehead in my collar.

"No. I'm sorry. I'll get over myself. You're more than a pair of fangs."

The gondola stops at the very top of the ferris wheel. We're overlooking the city. I can see half of everything, and all the way to the Pacific. That's my city; there's nothing else in the world like it. Natalie nudges her head up. I look down to her face. I see a million of San Jenaro's lights reflect against the green of her eyes. She closes them and kisses me. I feel her jaw quiver against mine, and I kiss back. She puts her hands to the sides of my head, and pulls me down toward her.

I slide out my tongue. She moans and parts her lips for me. I push in and probe, running my tongue along hers. I scratch it against her fang, but withdraw so as to not complicate things. I put my right hand to her breast, and cup it, pressing in gently. She draws sharp, quick breaths, tilts her head, and hungrily kisses me back. I can't tell if it's her blood or whatever, but I don't care. She feels so fucking good right now.

God damn it, I need this.

My phone buzzes. Pulses. Three quick pulses.

That's not just a call. That's my emergency line.

I gave Vanessa and Denny that line. I told them to only call if it's an emergency.

"Answer it." She releases me and put a hand on my thigh, massaging it.

"Sorry." I say, digging out my phone. She shakes her head, and begins kissing my shoulder, looking me in the eyes while I answer. "Yeah?"

It's Vanessa. "Lana. Someone broke into your apartment."

"Huh? How do you know?" I nuzzle into Natalie's hair, and kiss her eyelid.

"I had this weird feeling I should go there. I did. And the place was trashed. Busted open. The cops have it blocked off. I'm here with Denny. We're afraid to go near."

Natalie pulls back and looks to me with a soft frown.

"I'll be there soon as I can. I'm at MovieLand. Thanks."

"Sure thing boss." She hangs up.

"I'm going with you." Natalie nods. The gondola starts its descent.

I consider arguing. But I don't. I nod.

25

#HOMEWRECKER

Natalie and I leave, walking as quickly as we can through the park without seeming too suspicious. You know, too suspicious for two women who just murdered three vampires along the promenade before a romantic ferris wheel ride.

"We didn't even get any churros." I take Natalie's hand as we push through the turnstile and move to the parking lot.

"The park will be there tomorrow. We'll go another time."

"Promise?" I tease.

"Promise."

#

We get out of my car about a block away, just in case. Vanessa wasn't lying. There's eight cop cars surrounding my place, most have driven up onto the curb, onto the lawn. It looks like a drug raid, not an investigation. Regina's standing outside in her night gown, watching them. Vanessa and Denny are across the street, watching from Julio's parking lot.

"Lana!" Vanessa says as we approach. Denny turns to note us as well, and does a double-take. I up-nod and we approach.

"Hey. Natalie, this is Vanessa and Denny. I know it looks weird. And it is, but she's cool."

Denny butts in. "No way. That's the girl from the resort. She tried to kill you!"

"Not right now." I say, and turn to look at the apartment, watching the cops.

"No. It's okay. I did try to kill her. It was a mistake. I was caught up in revenge. We've worked it out. She's forgiven me I think. I hope you can, too. I understand if you can't."

Denny blinks, looking her over, like he was expecting something completely different to happen. "Um, okay."

"Anyway." I sigh, and walk across the street. Natalie stays beside me the entire time. Vanessa and Denny watch.

"LANA!" Regina notes me and starts yelling quickly in Spanish. It's not that I don't understand what she's saying—I just don't understand the velocity with which she's saying it.

"What happened?"

"What happened? Your fucking DEALERS came to collect your money, and you weren't here so they took what you owed them." She's got a finger in my face. I try my best to ignore it.

I look at the apartment. The cops are fingerprinting everything. The door was ripped off the hinge. This wasn't a robbery; this was a raid.

"I don't have any fucking dealers. I don't owe anyone any money."

"I don't care. You're trouble. I want you OUT." She stomps once as she says that.

I am so not here for your shit tonight, Regina.

"Well. California law says you've gotta take me to court. And that if you unlawfully evict, you're liable for $100 every day that passes until it's resolved."

She spits on the ground in front of me.

I... don't think I'm going to stay out my welcome.

"Lana Moreno?" A police detective approaches. I nod. "I understand this must be a difficult time for you, but we're going to need you to answer some questions."

#

The apartment's devastated. There's nothing untouched. Most everything's shredded, maybe with a bowie knife. There are huge holes in the wall, the kind you get from sledgehammers. "STAY AWAY" is sprayed in red paint along the walls inside, with letters as big as people. Detective Washington sits us down and goes through every boring, meaningless question in the book.

"Do you have any enemies?"

"Do you owe anyone any money?"

"Do you know who could have done this?"

"Who would tell you to stay away?"

"Do you know that falsifying a police report is a crime?"

He doesn't seem accusatory, just thorough and completely stumped.

I hear Natalie's voice in my head. "He thinks there's something you're not telling him. He knows this isn't a random robbery. He thinks it's a cartel."

I think back. "Can you steer him away? Make him write it all off?"

She takes my hand. I hear, "No. Not when there's this many of them. He'll act weird. They'll get suspicious. Best let it run its course."

I nod.

"Miss?" He says.

"Nothing. Sorry. Just, this is a lot to take in."

I feel like I should be crying. Panicking. Everything I own's in this apartment, destroyed. But truth be told, it's not too much. My laptop and all my hunting supplies are in my car. It's mostly just clothes and appliances and a fridge full of rotten food. That's the advantage of living the lifestyle of the lone warrior-philosopher.

Detective Washington tells me to call him if I'm leaving town. He gives me a copy of the police report to file with my renters' insurance. Joke's on him—I don't have renters' insurance.

"So." I say, walking back to Vanessa and Denny with Natalie by my side. "Guess I need to find a place to crash tonight..."

Vanessa's eyes light up. Her lips move like she's going to say something, but she stops and just smiles silently.

Natalie crosses her arms and says with a mousy tone, "I'd invite you over, but I imagine they hit my place, too."

"Damn." I snap my fingers. "I had a joke prepared about lesbians moving in together after the first date, and you had to go and ruin it."

Denny looks away, and motions to Julio's shop. "I'm gonna get a Coke."

Natalie shrugs. "I guess we could get a hotel or something."

"Yeah, maybe that's a good idea." Vanessa butts in, seeming a little uncomfortable.

"Oh? Why's that?" I can't help but to pry.

"Well, I mean, it's good. That you guys are safe. Together. You know? In case there's a problem. Or a... thing?" She's practically tripping over her words. This isn't the Vanessa I'm used to.

I'm honestly shocked she didn't offer to let me stay with her. There's got to be something wrong.

"Is everything okay?"

"Yeah. Just... I'd invite you over, but I've got some stuff to work out. If you really, really need it you know you can call me. But it's just weird and hard to explain. Are we still doing the hunt tomorrow?"

The succubus. I almost forgot.

"Yeah. Tomorrow. Meet me at..." I think about it for a moment. "I guess I'll text you tomorrow afternoon, and let you know where to meet me."

"Sure thing boss." She gives me a two-finger salute, then nods to Natalie. Natalie smiles and nods back.

#

A while ago, a few of us tried out an app called SafeHaus. It was basically a network of secure crash places for hunters in need. In our line of work, we sometimes end up hunted in response, and need to go into hiding for a while. It didn't really work, because there just wasn't the saturation necessary to make it reliable. It's cool to be on the ground floor of something big, but when it's life-or-death, you can't really rely on "it's gonna be great eventually."

So, we just use Airbnb. It works. You can find quick places for cheap, and you don't need to show ID. There's pros and cons with everything though. With Airbnb, there are three big issues:

First, it's a private person's property. This means you have to be careful about stuff like bloodstains. It's just common courtesy to not fuck up someone's place, and they don't generally have the same cleaning tools available that hotels do. They'll also charge you an arm and a leg for whatever cleaning they have to do.

Second, you're generally in a residential area, so you've got to be careful about sounds and weird behavior. At a hotel, you're surrounded with people on the move who don't give a shit. The staff's used to strange people. But if you're in a quaint, quiet neighborhood, and rush around with mysterious duffel bags, you tend to get the cops called. Don't even think about getting a MedPDQ doctor to go to an Airbnb stop.

Lastly, a lot of these places are shared rooms, even if they're pretending they're not. The last time I got one, it was a guy who bought a studio loft apartment. He put up some drywall to turn it into four rooms so small that he had to have built the walls around the beds. The drywall didn't even go floor to ceiling—you could reach up and over it into the other "private rooms." In this line of work, you need at least a little secrecy. You can't talk battle plans against the creatures of the night when the only thing separating you from your neighbors is a little gypsum plaster and corrugated paper. To get around this, it's best to rent houses or multi-bedroom apartments just to be sure. It costs a little more, but it's worth it.

Oh yeah. Also, Airbnb contributes to gross gentrification problems and lobbies against the kinds of tenant laws that protect the innocent and the poor. But, in a pinch, monster hunters have to play fast and loose with ethical concerns in the face of existential danger.

I luck out, and we get a tiny house in Ava Blue for about $70. I do the mental math and realize that's not much more than my shitty studio apartment. But it's the off season. I'm sure this place goes for three to five hundred a night during peak tourist season. The listing talks about how it'd be a "great backdrop for filming." That's code for, "You can film porn here."

You know the place. Big picture windows showing off the pretty little pool and some palm trees, but with hedges that block view from any of the nearby properties. A bunch of faux leather furniture that's super easy to clean. As we walk through the little two bedroom, I picture Natalie outside in this adorable orange bathing suit. I imagine myself walking out there. "Excuse me?" I say. She explains that her boyfriend told her this was his apartment, and that they were going to spend a romantic weekend together. I laugh and tell her it's my place, and that I was supposed to be gone for the season, but I got called back in to Palo Verde for an audition. She gets embarrassed. Then her boyfriend texts her and says he's held up in traffic. I, cleverly, take her phone from her and use the Find My Friends app and figure out that he's actually at a strip club. I tell her that he's ridiculous going and paying to look at girls that can't even compare to her. She says, "Oh yeah?," and I tell her I'm the luckiest woman in San Jenaro right now.

She says, "I wouldn't wear an orange bathing suit. Orange looks terrible with my skin and hair. It makes me look like I'm fighting food poisoning."

"Huh?" I snap to attention, then blush. "Hey. No reading my head porn."

"I wasn't reading your mind. It's just that sometimes your thoughts are really, really loud. I can't avoid hearing them." She goes to the picture window and closes the curtains.

I check the fridge. Sometimes with Airbnb, previous tenants have left beer. And in this case, I'm not disappointed. "Why close them? The view's great. Nobody can see in thanks to the hedges." I grab two beers, and walk over to offer one to Natalie.

She shakes her head. "No thanks. And I need to sleep before long. I don't burn in the sunlight. At least, not like some vampires. But I hate the sun. It messes with my skin. I get sunburns when it's overcast."

I go to put the second beer away, and crack mine open. "The real curse of vampirism. You thirst for blood and SPF 45." I take a drink and walk back over to her.

"Not vampirism. It's called being a redhead. It's actually gotten a little better as a vampire, since my body naturally regenerates."

She steps in and rests her head on my shoulder, putting a lazy arm around my back. I hold her there. "Can we go to bed? I'm really exhausted. Thinking too much."

I nod, kiss the side of her head, and put aside the unfinished beer. She gets a handkerchief out of her purse, and bunches her hair back into it. Then, we go to bed.

26
#TELENOVELAS

When I wake up, Natalie's curled up next to me, asleep. She colder—dormant. She looks dead at first glance; she's not breathing, she's paler than normal, and I can't feel her pulse. She has dark blue and red veins peeking through her skin all over, but they're no more obvious than your average body builder's. But she moves at my touch, shifting, groaning, and clutching her pillow. There's something that feels really honest about the way she looks right now. I've only ever seen vampires who can't handle the sunlight sleeping before, since it's the best time to kill them. They're perfectly stationary, indistinguishable from corpses. Natalie's subtly alive, but somehow preserved. Like she was dying, but stopped half-way.

I hear a buzzing, a faint hum. I quickly realize it's coming from her. She's broadcasting her thoughts. I wonder if she's dreaming about bees. I untie the handkerchief around her hair. It whips out of the way and her hair bounces outward, like a caged animal released. I pet her hair and the buzzing changes. It's still buzzing, but it's more soothing, the way it sounds around a hydroelectric dam. I remember going to Hoover Dam with my family as a child. We got there, and my parents realized it costs money to go into all the interesting places, so we just hung around and took pictures outside. My parents fought about it. My mother said my stepfather should have known. My stepfather said it was her fucking idea to go there in the first place, and he wanted to go fishing. The sound of the hydroelectric is my best memory from that trip.

I sit and watch her for a while, relaxing in the sound of her dream. I feel like the creepy protagonist vampire from a shitty young adult vampire story. After a while, I get up and take a shower. Once I finish and step out, Natalie gets in quietly and takes a shower of her own.

"You alright?" I say, towel drying my hair.

"Yeah. Just a lot on my mind." She turns on the shower.

"What were you dreaming about?"

"I dunno. Why?"

"No reason. Just, I thought I heard you dreaming. It was nice."

"Oh yeah? What did you hear?"

"Nothing specific. Just sort of a vibe. It was nice."

She doesn't respond. We get everything together in silence, and leave the keys in their designated spot before leaving. As I'm locking the keys in a little combination lock box, she turns to look at me. I raise an eyebrow. She leans up and pecks the corner of my mouth. "I've got a lot on my mind. I know I probably seem standoffish right now. It's not intentional. I think I'm gonna go look for at least a short-term housing solution. Would you..." She glances away, then looks back to my chin. "Is there anything you might want in a place? If you want to stick together for now?"

I look at her for a long second. "Just you."

She blushes.

"Well, and first floor, in case I have to stumble in late at night with a gunshot wound."

She pushes my chest and represses a laugh. "That's not funny."

I don't have the heart to tell her it wasn't meant to be funny.

#

I meet with Vanessa early, at my gym. Our gym now, I guess. We train a little, and I give her the basics about succubi and thought forms. I brief her on the untrustworthy sorcerer, and his weird plot to get his powers back.

Then, we do spy shit.

#

The Chadwicks live in another nice house, a few blocks from the sorcerer. It's not quite up to the legendary pedigree of his place, but their house is still a small mansion. I do a little Googling. Frederick Chadwick is a renowned architect. Not the kind who makes places you see in magazines. But he still makes ridiculous money doing what he does. My first thought is, there's no real excuse for a guy who makes that kind of money to have such a boring house. It looks no different than any of the other mid-range Ava Blue mansions.

We scope the place out, hiding in the bushes.

"So what are we going to do here? There's someone inside." Vanessa says, motioning to a blue Maserati convertible in the driveway.

There's a TV on inside. I grab my binoculars, and scope it out. It's a telenovela. I think it's Las Muñecas de la Mafia. My aunt tried to get me to watch it a while ago. I tried a few episodes. Which is to say, I binged every one of 58 episodes while on my period, ate about four pounds of Ben and Jerry's, and hated myself for weeks afterward. "It's probably his housekeeper."

"Wife." Vanessa whispers.

"No way a guy in Ava Blue would fuck a brown girl on paper. *Maybe* she's a mistress."

"No. She's his wife." Vanessa says back.

The student is getting a little big for her britches.

"Okay. I'll bite. How do you know?"

She taps my shoulder. I look over to her. She points to the edge of the property. An older woman with a boob job, a nose job, a tummy tuck, and a blue one-piece bathing suit with "CALVIN" printed down the side is holding the leash to a gorgeous white, fluffy Samoyed. It's peeing.

"Look at that rock."

I look. It's big. Comically big. Like, "this is the reason California constitutes the third biggest world economy if you count it as its own nation" big. "Shit."

A big delivery truck pulls up. On the side, it says, "Making Ends Meat Catering."

Ha, ha, ha.

Two men get out and get hand carts, then start loading up big plastic bins. The woman clasps the dog's leash to a fence and walks over to them. "Bring them inside. Leave them by the front door. I'll get them from there." The men oblige.

Vanessa looks to the men and the truck. "Chicken and black bean taquitos in adobo and sour cream." She says quietly. "How many do you think they're serving?"

"Huh? How'd you know that?" I look all over for labels, for hints, for anything.

"Distinct smell. I guess if they're in styrofoam boxes, maybe sixteen per bin? And there's six bins? Are they feeding like a hundred people in there?"

There's no smell. I can smell taquitos from a mile away. I don't even think a vampire could smell something inside one of those plastic bins.

"No way. There's gotta be something more to it."

The men leave. The woman goes inside. A minute or two pass, and she comes back out, arms the alarm system, and gets in the Maserati to drive off.

While we're sneaking around, I get a text message from the sorcerer.

"You have to kill Chadwick. Immediately. If he lives through tonight, it'll all be for naught. Do not talk to him. Kill him."

I'm not an assassin. I hunt monsters. I don't kill humans. I mean, I would if I had to. But for ten grand? No fucking way. I fire back a response.

"Why should I kill the guy?"

He replies.

"I can't explain it right now. You're just going to have to trust me."

"Well, here's our chance." I move out of the bushes, keeping low and creeping toward the house.

"How are we supposed to get past that alarm system?" She follows along, looking all around.

"Intrusion 101. First off, scope your escape routes." I motion around a little bit. "All those ways are dead ends. Bad idea." I slide a ski mask on. "However, over there, you see there's a hole worn in the bushes? That's how a neighborhood dog or other big animal like maybe a raccoon gets in and out. The path is pretty worn, so that tells me they don't know anything about it. Which means it's a pretty safe path."

She nods, raising an eyebrow in disbelief. She then slides on her mask as well.

"Second thing we do is look for cameras. I've already done that. There's one at every corner of the house." I motion to the three that are visible from where we're kneeling. "See how they pan? We use that to our advantage, and go underneath them, close to the wall."

She nods again, and takes the initiative to dodge under one of the cameras. I follow suit.

"Third thing we do is look at the actual security system. See those little silver boxes?" I motion to the windows, and point to small installations on each. They're two silver boxes up against each other, each about the size of deck of cards. "Those are magnetic sensors. You have to use a highly specialized tool to get through those. If they open, the alarm sounds and you have private security here in three minutes, cops within five."

She nods along. "You have that tool, right?"

I fish through my backpack, and pull out a paper thin refrigerator magnet that says, "WELCOME TO THE GOLDEN STATE!", with a picture of a rocky shore and a sunrise. I hold it up. Her eyes go wide.

I sneak over to one of the windows in the livingroom. "She turned the TV off. That means we have a while." I slip the magnet into the crack between the two boxes. Then, I slide the window open.

27

#NEEEFFDAARSOT

The house isn't very lived-in. It's nice. They spent a fortune on interior decorating. But it's all very new. There's no personality here, just money. The first thing I notice is, most of the rooms have their own electronic locking mechanisms. That's weird. But rich people are weird. The livingroom has a ton of sitting space. They definitely have parties or big events in mind.

"Where'd they take the food?" I say, wandering around, checking out the inside, getting an idea of the floor plans.

If she could smell through that plastic from thirty feet away, she can smell where they took that shit.

"Through that door." Vanessa motions to a metal fire door. The kind you might put on a bomb shelter. There's no getting through it. I can pick a lock. But this is a goddamned vault, with a high-tech electronic lock.

"Wonder what they're doing down there."

As I poke around, there's a massive... thing covered in white sheets. Maybe four feet high and twelve feet across. Vanessa notices it as well. "What's that?" She looks it over.

I pull up the sheets. It's a stack of boxes. I pop one open. It's a neon sign with gold inlay. The cursive letter "N." "Check this out." I say, and pull out the huge letter. "These must have cost a fortune."

She digs through them as well. We find three Es, two Fs, a D, two As, an R, an S, an O, and a T. "What's it say?" She says, looking them over.

"I dunno? NEEEFFDAARSOT?" I shrug and cover them back up. It looks like they could be outfitting an upscale Vegas casino with those things.

I drop the sorcerer a message.

"What are the Chadwicks doing? Their house is strange."

I poke around a little more. Not only is the place freshly decorated, there's practically nothing unique in here. No pictures. No degrees. No nothing. The kitchen silverware is all in sealed blister packs. The plates and cups all still have plastic wrapping. All of the cabinets have packaged, unopened linens. Ironically, it seems like they're setting it up as an upscale Airbnb.

He responds.

"I don't know what they're doing. Kill them immediately. You won't get another chance."

He's going to move in on their business. Whatever it is they're doing, he's going to take them out and take over. I fucking knew it.

That doesn't mean I don't still need the money.

"Lana..." Vanessa says. I look over. "There's someone here. Different car."

"Fuck." I listen and look to the windows.

It's going toward the window we came in, so we can't go out that way.

"Let's go upstairs. We can't go out that window. We'll have to find another way out."

She moves toward the kitchen, toward the back of the house. "Let's go out the back. Fuck the cops. We'll be out in three minutes. We'll just run for it."

She's not wrong.

I quietly jog in that direction. "Let's hide. Maybe we can figure out what in the hell they're doing." I motion to a walk-in pantry. "If they come in here, we'll jump them."

I unlock it, and we slide inside. It's all bulk non-perishables. One of my teachers was an apocalypse prepper. From my experience there, I'd say this is enough food and supplies for at least six months for a smart family.

A man is speaking loudly from the other room, sounds like he's talking to his phone. "Are we going to be ready for a Friday night opening?"

It's Wednesday. That's two days from now.

"Sorry Mister Chadwick. Sorry Mister Chadwick. Is that the only thing you know how to say? Sorry Mister Chadwick?"

Guess that's Mister Chadwick.

I briefly wonder if we shouldn't just take the opportunity to jump out and kill the guy. I don't want to. It doesn't feel right. My gut says it's a stupid idea, and I don't trust our kindly ex-sorcerer at all.

"I have people on all sides trying to move in on my business, Dane. I need results. Do you understand me? Friday, we're opening. It's going to be the party of the century. We're all going to make a whole lot of money. I'm busy tonight. But if you need my help tomorrow, I'm free all day. I just need you to do your part today."

He seems nicer than some of my former bosses. I bet he doesn't drug test. I wonder if he's accepting applications.

"Lana. There's something wrong." Vanessa whispers. I look back to her. She's shaking. Sweating. I feel it as well. I feel warm. Ready. I could really use a good fuck right now.

"Succubus is here. She probably follows him most of the time."

She nods. I want to jump out. To do something. But I don't want to give away our position. I need to know more.

The man continues. "Look. I've got a thing I've got to do before my stuff tonight. I'll be around late tonight maybe. If you're still having problems, stop by the house. I have eyes in all the necessary places—you don't have to worry. Later."

At least we know where he'll be later tonight. He leaves, slamming the door behind him. He revs his car and pulls out. I poke out of the pantry and look around just to be sure. He's definitely gone.

"Is the feeling supposed to stop?" Vanessa says, following out behind me.

I shrug. I still have it as well. "Could take a bit to wind down, you know? Just like when you get turned on and it doesn't go anywhere."

She nods, accepting it at face value.

I round the corner into the livingroom, and I feel a hot hand on my wrist. "Please. You have to kill me." It's this fucking luscious sort of Italian accent. Husky. Breathy. Like she just pulled up from eating you out for fifteen minutes straight. I look over. She's this tanned olive woman, in a sea foam green dress with exaggerated curves. Her lips are big, pouty. If I was casting a porn parody of Passion of the Christ, she'd be my Mary Magdalene.

Vanessa turns to face her just as I do.

"Huh?" I look her over. I can't help but to stare a little. That's the problem with succubi—it'a hard to give them whatever attention they're due, because they're exactly what you want right then and there, cranked up to eleven. My mind goes all over the place. I feel like I'd do anything for her right there. But kill her? That's just absurd. How could I kill something like her?

"There's going to be a ritual. It'll shred my soul. It'll turn me into a mortal. A human. But soulless. You can't let that happen. You must kill me. Please. I'm begging you."

"And this ritual... let me guess. It'll turn a mortal into a sorcerer? Give them a... *To ti esti?*" I try my best to emulate the sorcerer's accent.

She nods. "So you know. You're not here to capture me, are you?"

Well shit.

I take a deep breath. "Well. I kind of was? But what if I help you escape?"

She shakes her head furiously. "No, no, no. He'll hunt me to the ends of the Earth, and further. If you don't capture me, somebody else will."

She pauses. "Lana..."

Succubi always know your name. It's sexier that way.

"They'll enslave me. I'll be soulless, and unable to fight. You can't let this happen, Lana."

Motherfuck.

"Alright. So. I'm not going to kill you. Not right now. I will later."

She tilts her head and releases my wrist. It's very, very hard to not grab her and kiss her. I feel like maybe I should take her and run off to Tahiti or something with her.

I want to have her babies.

"Time is of the essence. If you don't capture me, somebody else will. I can't go far for now. I'm tied to this area. Bound to the region."

"I'll be back. I promise." I look to Vanessa. She shrugs. And I go to the window and leave.

28

#WITCHHUNT

We get out of Chadwick's, and we jog toward the sorcerer's.

"The car's that way, Lana." Vanessa says, keeping beside me.

"We're visiting the sorcerer. You heard. He's going to destroy her soul. Turn her human. She wants to be killed."

"Then why not just kill her?"

"Because the sorcerer's been messaging me and telling me I need to murder that Chadwick guy. So, I need to get in his face about it."

"Whatever. You're the boss."

#

"Just a bloody minute." The old man yells through the door as he approaches. "Did you finish it?" He says as he opens the door. He's in his same robe as before.

"No. We need to talk."

"What?" He opens the door and motions us in. "We don't have long. The cards said it'll all be over soon."

"The cards? What cards?" I say, and step into the main hall. We stand there; he doesn't seem interested in inviting us to the library.

"I performed a divination. Since I don't have my sorcery, I have to lean on the old ways for answers. Weaker. Cruder. But, they still work. Now tell me why you haven't acted."

"Because we spoke to the succubus. She told us about your ritual."

"What? The succubus? My ritual? What are you talking about? She wouldn't know about my ritual. I devised the formula in the past few days. I've been researching it for weeks in privacy. There's no way she knows about it."

"Well, she sure as hell thinks so. She seems to think you're going to use a ritual that'll shatter her soul, and leave her a husk, a mortal slave."

"I think she's mistaken. That's one of the old ways. The darkest art. That's not how I'd recover my *to ti esti*. That's how you create a new sorcerer."

I look to Vanessa. She looks at me. "Huh? So what's your ritual?"

"It's an enlivening ritual. A succubus can take the human soul to immense heights. Properly harnessed, the sexual energy intensified by a succubus's power can awaken the dormant seed of sorcery."

"Huh?" I pause. He opens his mouth to explain, but I put a hand up. "So, you're saying your magic power's like asleep or something? And that if she fucks you, it'll wake your powers up?"

He rolls his eyes and nods. "In the crudest possible terms, yes."

"Those aren't the crudest terms."

He sighs. "I can imagine. Anyway, the ritual she's speaking of is dark magic. Far beyond anything I would dare use. I was just reading about it recently."

"Wait. You were? Where did this happen?"

"In the library. Would you prefer I show you?"

"Yeah."

He shows us to the library. As we walk in, Vanessa's attention snaps up. She points to a tiny video camera on the high, vaulted ceiling. "Up there."

"What's that?" The former sorcerer looks up, squints, and pulls glasses from his robe. "I don't understand. What do you see? I see a red dot?"

"It's a security camera." I say.

"That's impossible. I don't have any cameras in this house. It's too dangerous."

"It smells like the Chadwick house." Vanessa says.

"Oh god damn it." I slam a fist down on one of the tables. "We've got to get over there, right now."

#

Sorcerers are a paradox. All of the great things you can use to kill monsters, they work on sorcerers. Silver bullets? They kill sorcerers. Stakes through the heart? They kill sorcerers. Beheading? Definitely kills sorcerers. Sorcerers, for all intents and purposes, are normal humans. But paradoxically, they're gigantic pains in the asses because their magic makes them really fucking hard to get to.

The way my mentor described it, we all sort of wade through reality. We barely send any ripples as we pass through the sea of the universe. Sorcerers, on the other hand, grab reality and rip it apart. This isn't their magic, at least not the part you see. But it's the cause of their magic. If they rip open the part of reality that says "this place isn't on fire," guess what, this place is now on fire. It's really powerful, but also really crude, and really unpredictable. Irresponsible sorcerers blow themselves up all the time. Smart hunters go to great lengths to not get blown up when hunting them.

This is all to say, they're dangerous. They can slaughter you if you're not careful. You can use some minor symbolic talismans to protect yourself, but they're sort of hit or miss. I've had the best luck with one my mentors gave me. It's a small iron hammer on a leather necklace. He said iron symbolizes the way humankind has imposed its collective will on reality. It dampens some of what a sorcerer can do to you—it's a sort of mystical way of being defiant, and saying to the wizard that congratulations motherfucker, *you're not special.*

We run to my car, grab that, and grab a couple of handguns. "You know how to use these, right?"

Vanessa looks at me like I'm stupid. She takes the gun and looks it over.

"Is that a, 'of course I know how these work, Lana' look? Or a, 'of course I have no idea how these work, Lana' look?"

She opens the chamber to verify there's a round in it. She flips off the safety.

"How am I supposed to know? Most people have never used

a gun before."

"My daddy made me very aware of the Second Amendment."

We start back over to the Chadwick house.

"Good to know."

#

The blue Maserati's back. The telenovelas are back on inside. We wait around the corner.

"Do we wait? Or do we try to use her to find out where Chadwick is?"

Vanessa shakes her head. "I don't know. What do you think we should do?"

This boss shit is too much responsibility.

"Let's talk to her. We've got to find him, and quick."

She nods. We approach. I knock.

No answer. No answer. No answer.

I ring the bell.

"No habla ingles." She shouts from inside.

What a fucking liar.

"Un momento por favor?" I shout back.

She grunts audibly, then walks to the door. She opens it and looks us over suspiciously.

"We're supposed to meet with Frederick Chadwick tonight at 6."

She thinks about that for a moment, then shakes her head. "No you're not."

I pull my gun and put it to her chin. I push her inside. The

Samoyed starts yapping. Vanessa pulls her gun and steps in after us, kicking the door shut.

"I don't want to do it like this. But we need to find Mr. Chadwick right fucking now. I don't want to shoot you or your dog, but I will."

Honestly, I kinda want to shoot the dog. It's really annoying.

She puts her hands up and steps backward with me. "I don't know where Mr. Chadwick is. He's supposed to be back this evening. Maybe you should come back then."

I shove the barrel against her cheek. "I don't think you understand how this works. I believe you don't know where he is. But I also believe you can find it out if you really want to."

She huffs and nods. "I can call him and try to find out where he is. I promise you he won't return early though. Not tonight."

I take a few seconds to think it over.

What if she tips him off?

What if she tries to escape?

What if she tries to attack?

What if this is all just a big misunderstanding?

"Fine." I jam the barrel to her chin, forcing her to look up. "But if I think for a second you're trying to give him a hint that there's something wrong, I'm gonna see if I can get your brains on the ceiling. Understood?"

She swallows hard and nods. "I understand. My phone's on the table. Can I get it?"

I nod, and lead her over to the table. She shows the face of her phone to me as she opens it. Her wallpaper's the Hope Diamond. She flips through her recent calls, and taps the one that says, "Frederick." Then, she hits speakerphone.

The phone rings. Once. Twice. Three times. Four times. "What is it, Lorena? Can it wait?"

"It can't wait." He sighs. "The guy who brought you the special rock? He brought over a couple of old papers. He said you're going to need them. That what you're doing won't work without them. Should I bring them to you, or can you swing back by here?"

"Damn it." He snaps. "No. Neither. I can't risk it. Not now. Get my iPad and take photos. Get about three pictures of each page and message me with them. I'll get them printed."

She looks to me and winces.

"Originals?" I mouth.

"He says you need the originals. It's not what they say. It's that they have to be present. He said your... business... he said it won't end well. I can get them to you in no time."

"That doesn't make any sense. Look, I'll call him."

"No!" She snaps. "You don't have long enough to handle it. I've got to go quick. Where should I take them?" Her face is red and white. She's deathly afraid. She looks to me and shakes her head.

"I can spare a minute. I'll conference him in."

"You don't need to. Stop being obstinate and just let me take the damned papers to you, Frederick."

"I'll do what I fucking want. Know your place. Take care of the girls, and leave the business to the men."

God fucking damn it.

A few seconds later, we hear ringing. Ringing. Ringing. It goes to a "this customer doesn't have voicemail set up on this line" message.

She sighs with relief.

"Now can I take the papers to you? We need this to go right."

"You know what? I'm going to take my chances." He hangs up.

She looks to the two of us, pleading. Her hands are shaking. She dials him again, and it goes straight to voicemail.

"Wait. What did he say about the girls?"

She looks to me suspiciously. "I'm confused."

"What do you mean, you're confused. What fucking girls is he talking about?" I hold the gun to her stomach now.

"I thought you knew. I thought that's why you were here. The girls for the club—and the boys. Let me go and I'll take you to them."

Vanessa and I share a glance. Vanessa says, "They're downstairs. You're going to take us to them, then we're going to figure out whether or not you get to go."

I nod to reinforce Vanessa's statement.

"Fine. But if I'm here when Frederick gets back, I'm as good as dead. Either let me go or kill me. But please, I'm begging you, don't let him get to me." She takes a keycard from the table, and leads us to the door.

#

It's a prison. There's at least thirty young men and women down here, most from Southeast Asia. Each has a small cell, maybe six feet by six feet, with wire mesh walls barely thin enough to fit a finger through. They're all in cheap clothes, but well-groomed. They all have professional haircuts and manicures. They all look well-fed, if completely distant and shaken.

The basement has padded, thick concrete walls, and rubber on the ceiling. Completely soundproofed.

I look to their faces. Thirty two people, eleven men, twenty one women—all in various stages of shock. They remind me of my mom. When I was about eight, she had my baby brother. We were living in an apartment in San Maria Cay. When I got home from school, she was just waking up. I had to watch my brother until he was in bed. She worked second and third shift at a truck stop as a waitress. The guy who owned our apartment also owned the truck stop. She didn't have her papers, so he paid her under the table.

Sometimes, she'd come home haggard, with this look in her eyes. She looked distant. Defeated. Not fragile—utterly broken. She didn't look like she might cry; she looked like her tear ducts had completely dried up. When she came home like that, we'd pull the blankets up over our heads and pretend to be asleep. We knew not to talk to her, because she might break into a screaming fit.

When I was about thirteen, mom sat me down in one of her

lectures about how much she had to sacrifice for me, and how I was such a disappointment, and how she regretted ever having me. She told me that on the nights she came home like that, her boss, our landlord, made her fuck the truck drivers. She'd protest, but he'd threaten to call immigration. She told me it was never just sex. They were always violent. Always aggressive.

She told me that's why Dad left. He couldn't imagine her being with another guy. And instead of supporting her in her time of need, he walked out on us. Until I learned that, I thought Dad was great. I saw him every two weeks, and he always bought us a new toy or video game, or took us to MovieLand or Oceanside or something. After that, I never spoke a word to him. I told the judge I didn't want to see him again.

That look? Most of these prisoners have that look.

I almost shoot Lorena in the back, right then and there. But I'm interrupted by a woman's scream from upstairs. "Watch her." I say to Vanessa, and I run back up.

#

The succubus is crumpled on the ground, crying. She looks the same, but... pathetic. Her body's identical, but there's nothing sexy or primally desirable about her. She's just a person.

I move over and kneel next to her, and put a hand on her back.

She looks up to me, her face tear-stained. "He finished the ritual." Even though she's crying, I can absolutely see that she's soulless. She looks like one of those religious cult guys that comes to your door and offers to tell you the good news. There's nothing behind her eyes. No fire. I feel like you could pass a video of her off as evidence of an advanced android intelligence.

"Where was the ritual? Where is he?"

She shakes her head. "I don't know where it happened. I was in the soul stone. He's on his way here now."

"Okay. Fuck. Gotta prepare." I get up and pace, looking over the space, trying to come up with a plan.

I go back to the basement door to get Vanessa. "Hey." As I crack the door, I hear snarling. Growling. Screaming. Crying.

I run and open the door to the downstairs. It's a bloodbath—blood and entrails are strewn all over the floor and walls. The caged people all appear fine. At least, figuratively fine. Some have a bit of the blood spray on them.

I try to focus. Try to figure out what's going on. Then I see it. A werewolf. Black, shiny coat. I can't tell if it's just shiny fur, or because she's covered in blood. Maybe both?

It's definitely Vanessa. I see her clothes, shredded in a pile on the floor. She slaughtered Lorena. She doesn't seem to care about the prisoners. That's good at least.

Shit. I don't have time for this. A werewolf that can pick her targets is not a werewolf I have to worry about right now.

I close the door and head back upstairs, and get ready to kill a wizard.

29
#WIZARDSDUEL

The thing is, monster hunting isn't really about dramatic appropriateness. It's about efficiently murdering monsters. It's about tricking them. It's about doing whatever you can to gain an edge. It's not about fair fights. Most of the time, good traps just work. If it worked the way it did in TV, you might as well not even bother using clever traps, because the monster always figures out a way to ignore them.

I go back to my car and grab a shotgun. I run back to the house. I use a little nylon rope and duct tape, and set up a really crude pulley system. I rig it to the door, tape the shotgun to the wall next to the door, and affix the rope to the shotgun's trigger mechanism. I tape an empty gallon milk jug to the shotgun's barrel to serve as a sound suppressor, just in case. You can't use that kind of silencer at a distance, but it's great for the kind of intimate, point-blank shot I'm going for here.

Chadwick pulls into the driveway. He's got a halo about him. It looks like the hazy air above an oil fire. His eyes are glowing a coal red.

Usually you only get these strong visual cues if sorcerers go above and beyond, and do some seriously terrifying shit with their magic.

He's already high on his power. Great.

"I'm home!" He shouts. He looks around, standing next to his car. "I have visitors. Visitors who would kill me?" He laughs.

Oh fuck you, you insufferable prick.

I hide behind a sofa in the living room, watching him. "Well isn't that just special. Who is my visitor?" He pauses. All of the shelves and cabinets in the kitchen fly open. Dishes and silverware burst out of their packaging. The ceramic all shatters. The silverware and debris fly up and begin spinning.

"Lana? Your name is Lana? Lana Moreno. Fascinating..." Shards of ceramic and some errant silverware starts flying and swarming into the living room like a nest of angry hornets. I jump out of the way of most of them, but a couple nick me.

This isn't going to go well. Gotta act quick.

I lean up over the couch and fire off a few shots. "How about you come over here and show me your superpowers, shit lick?"

One of my shots should have hit him. But as he stared right at me, the bullet flew off to the side.

More silverware and plate pieces start flying into the living room. I roll to the side, taking a few more hits, a few more cuts.

These things are gonna tear me apart if I don't think fast.

I grab the top of the sofa, and pull it back over me like a tent. Like a tiny fortress. The debris rattles it. I hear fabric ripping. That fabric could have been my skin.

"You cowardly piece of shit! You gonna kill me like you killed your first wife?"

Lightning strikes. I hear it. I see the flash of light even through the sofa. "Sore point, huh? Why don't you show me a lesson, you big man, huh? You big wife-killing man, you?" It's not the most eloquent, but it seems to be pissing him off. Hopefully it works before he decides to burn the place down.

Just then, I hear the tell-tale sound of a shotgun blast. Then there's a crash of metal and ceramic shattering. The ripping fabric and flying debris sounds stop. I peek out from the sofa. Frederick Chadwick's dead. Very dead. Head splattered all over the wall. Very modern art.

#

"What do we do?" I look to Vanessa. She's naked. I flip the switches on a box that looks kind of like a circuit breaker. It releases the locks on the cells.

"I don't know. Do you think the cops'll be here?"

I shrug. "Hard to say. I think maybe the shotgun could have been mistaken for another thunderclap. Then again, who knows?"

The doors to the cells start falling open. Some of the captives stand and pensively push the doors the rest of the way. I look to them. I realize I'm crying. Just openly crying. I can't point to any one specific thing. It's a little bit of everything.

"I can't think of anywhere to put them up. And the cops'll just send them back to... fuck knows who. It'll probably be even worse."

Vanessa nods. "There's food upstairs. Maybe they can stay here until we figure things out? If the cops don't show up right away, they probably won't for a while."

"Yeah." I look to them. "Do you speak English? Espanol?" A couple of them nod. Most don't. Some even shake their heads. "You're free. At least, free of these people. I think tonight you're safe to stay here."

One of the women turns back and translates (I think), speaking to the others. Many of the others nod.

Friday. They've got to be out before Friday. That's the "party." I imagine they were the guests of honor.

"You'll have to leave tomorrow. I'm going to try to find you a place to stay."

The woman turns back to explain. Some of them nod again. One of the women shakes her head and begins shouting loudly, pointing at Vanessa. A couple of others join in.

I look between the women and Vanessa. Vanessa puts up a hand and goes upstairs.

I have to speak up. "I'm sorry you had to see that. If we could have done it any other way, we would have."

Some of them are listening. Some aren't. I look to the interpreter. "Can you manage this? We'll do what we can."

She nods. "I can. Maybe some of them will leave. But the rest, I can manage."

I grab Lorena's phone and wipe off the blood, handing it to her. "Here. I'm gonna call you tomorrow."

She takes it and nods. "Thank you."

I force a smile and head upstairs. My eye twitches. I can feel the blood pulsing in my eyelid.

Vanessa says, "Sorry Lana. I didn't want to tell you until I had it all sorted out. I've been working with a guy, and..."

I put up a hand. "Not right now. No offense. I just can't talk about it right now. It's not you. It's me. We'll talk soon. I don't hold it against you."

She nods and swallows. "Can I get a ride home?"

I nod. "Gotta make a stop first if you don't mind. I've got an emergency poncho in the car you can wear."

#

I talk to the sorcerer. He decides to give us the killing fee, even though we didn't kill the succubus. He said we still more or less solved the problem. He then explained that the former succubus would never be a full human, unless she could somehow get a soul. But, of course, that means removing a soul from someone else, which requires magic just as bad as the ritual which made her.

I let the interpreter know to take care of her while we figure something out. She tells us it's not a problem, and that she owes us.

I get a message from iHunt. I missed an appointment with the client for the movie script consultation, so she canceled the gig.

Whatever. It wouldn't have even paid out this year anyway. If at all.

#

Natalie lets me know she found a place for cheap, all cash, no ID. It's a little ranch house in The Flip, San Filipe. It's not the best area. It's not the worst area. But given our specific needs, beggars can't be choosers.

When I get there, it's empty save for an air mattress with a couple of blankets, a beer fridge, some Chinese takeout, and a trash can.

Well, and Natalie.

I break down and explain my day. The sorcerers. The succubus. Vanessa. Everything. She just sits there on the blue air mattress, my head in her lap, ranting and bawling while she pets my hair.

30
#THECLUB

"I have a plan. Tell me if it's stupid?" My eyes flutter awake and Natalie's petting my forehead.

I shut and open my eyes a few times to work out the gunk and get focus. "Have you been there all day?"

"Kinda. But I was asleep for most of it, so I cheated. Anyway. Plan?"

I roll over and sit up to face her. "I'm listening."

#

We go by the Carver's, the 24 hour chain big box store. You can buy anything there. But for the discerning poor person, it's also a makeshift bank. For 3% of a check's value, you can cash a check or receive a money wire.

Why would you pay 3% of your check to cash it?

Well, there's this company called ChexSystems who basically exists to tell banks not to work with you. If you bounce a check or overdraw your account, and the other party reports you, you get flagged. If you're flagged, you can't open accounts pretty much anywhere.

Who bounces checks? People who can't afford to pay them. So, who can't open checking accounts? Poor people.

Thus, if you're poor and have a flag on ChexSystems, you go to Carver's, you pay your 3%, you take your cash, and you grumble. I'm currently sitting on a backlog of $18,000 through iHunt. Unfortunately, Carver's only lets you draw $1,000 from a wire service every day. Except it ends up being $970, because of the 3%. If I go there every day for almost three weeks, I can draw out all my money for the low, low price of $540.

But, I need to get my money quickly. So, we hit a check cashing place. They charge 5%, and have a limit of $3,000 a day. So I withdraw $2,850, and pay $150.

We find another place, and draw another $3,000. They only have a 4% fee. So another $2,880 for $120.

Thanks to the almighty poor tax, I now have $6,700 of my cash, and it only cost $300 and three hours of driving around. I try to not think about how much we've spent in gas.

Ironically, I even have a bank account. ChexSystems doesn't close your current accounts, they just keep you from using new ones. But, the IRS has guaranteed I can't even use that account for... who knows how long.

I hate, hate, hate carrying cash. I can carry about $40 before I start to get nervous. Anything over $200 is completely unacceptable. I always imagine myself losing it, or getting robbed, or it getting accidentally torn, or covered in blood, or whatever. I count it out for Natalie once we're in my car. I keep picturing dropping the bills, and watching them fly out the window and all over San Jenaro. The windows are closed. There's no way in hell it could actually happen. But I can't stop the anxiety from imagining it.

"This should be a good start. I've got about five grand stowed away in my post office box. I think we can make this work with ten grand." I sigh, take her hand, then take her to a branch post office to get her stack of cash.

#

We stop by the licensing bureau. Natalie talks to an officer about getting a liquor license. Apparently, they've gotten more expensive since she took her bartending classes a few years ago. The application's $15,000. Then there's some other thing that's $20,000. Then there's surveying fees. And zoning fees. And it's ridiculous. She tries a few of her mind tricks, but unfortunately he doesn't have any access to the actual process—he just files paperwork.

So, we walk. She fucks around with her phone while we walk.

"Sorry. Maybe it just wasn't in the cards." I try to assuage her defeat.

"Fuck that." She's driven. Googling like her life depends on it. "Here."

She points to her phone. I look it over. There's a bar owner who just evaded a bunch of charges thanks to a suspicious mistrial. Child porn. Domestic violence. Human trafficking. Real winner.

"Oh that's great." I scroll through the story. "We kill him and take his money then use it to buy a liquor license. Two birds with one stone."

She shakes her head. "We're not going to buy a liquor license.

We're gonna use his. And when we're ready, he'll give it to us."

"So we didn't need to take out all this cash?" I say, doing a little research on the area on my phone. It's on the edge of Palo Verde.

It's right on the border of upscale and trashy. I like that.

"It's probably for the best. Even with mind control, it's best if you make it at least a little believable. We're going to come with a... business proposition. And a little seed cash."

#

Natalie's kind of amazing. Academically, it's scary. She talks circles around this guy. I can tell when she uses the mind control, and it's minimal and subtle. She doesn't just tell him what to do. She makes him agree and come up with everything she wants out of him on his own.

Within an hour, we have a deal. Lou will be renovating, changing the name of his establishment, and letting us run it. We offer to cover the renovations. And we'll be splitting proceeds. He'll be getting a modest 20%. And the ability to avoid the controversy of putting his name on the place.

Natalie speaks to my mind while we're in there. She wants him dead. She says he's slime. But, she says, he'll have to sign over everything. And we'll have to be patient, so it doesn't look too suspicious.

#

I borrow a van. The old type, easy to hot wire. Natalie gets an Airbnb house for a month, over near the bar on the south side—

the worse side of the neighborhood. I call the interpreter, and tell her we have a place for them to stay for the time being. Apparently, seven of the captives left. She doesn't know what they're doing. The other 25 will take us up on our offer.

We take every bit of food we can from their storehouse, and take three trips with the van to get all the former captives to the house.

Natalie and I sit down with about half of the prisoners, while the rest—mostly the ones who don't know English—are getting adjusted. Then, we open their eyes. We tell them about vampires. We tell them how they were trapped by a sorcerer. While they initially disbelieve, Natalie speaks to their minds, and they quickly start to understand.

She lays out her plan. I mostly stay quiet, watching, listening, admiring. She tells them she wants to start a bar that's friendly to vampires, where they can safely feed. It'll be a normal bar as well.

She explains that I hunt errant vampires. So I'd be security. If anyone stepped out of line, I'd get rid of them. She tells them that of course there's some risk for those selling blood, but there would be tight security, and there would be plenty of jobs that didn't require blood exchange.

I'm mostly just shocked that none of them seem shocked. They're a little curious, and a little nervous at times. But most of them are relaxed and agreeable. They just want stable jobs, to not be deported, and to not live in cages. I'm just proud we can make that happen.

31

#GIRLTALK

"So when did you find out?" I slide into a booth with two coffees and slide one across the table to Vanessa. It's about a week later. The club is already looking great. Natalie's got an eye for design. I pitched silly shit like black with red silk trim. She went for this really cool 1920s purple and silver wallpaper she found. We didn't know what to do about furniture, but she stumbled on a country club in Ava Blue that was closing down, and she got all their seating and wainscoting for next to nothing. The place looks ridiculously classy for the neighborhood. It looks like the kind of place that would turn me down at the door, or tell me that the service entrance is around back.

"Really early on. A few days after the fight. I started growing hair so fast I had to shave every day. My nails grew so fast I could almost watch them get longer. It wasn't a hard jump to make, you know?" Vanessa smells her coffee, and looks over to me. It doesn't take a mind reader to know she's nervous. She's worried about how I'll respond.

"I just wish you would have told me. I would have liked to know for the hunt, but also as a friend. I want you to trust me enough to come to me. I don't know a ton about werewolves. But I know people who know."

"No offense, boss, but the stuff you know about werewolves

is all about hunting and killing them. I needed first-hand information. That's why I went searching. I found some people in the suburbs. Other werewolves. They know what it's like. How to deal with it. I planned on telling you once I had a handle on it. I didn't want to add to your stress." She sips her coffee.

I feel kind of jealous in a way. Not because I want to be a werewolf. But because she's gorgeous. She's confident. She's strong. Even when she's dealing with one of the most fucked-up things that can happen to a person, she's just sitting here talking to me like it's nothing. She's nervous, but she's keeping her cool in a way I could never. "I appreciate the sentiment, but in the future, I'd appreciate it if you'd let me make that choice. When you're hunting monsters, every variable could kill you. Like, I get it. I do. But in the future…"

"Yeah. In the future." She takes another drink. "Do you want to keep doing this with me? I like it. But I could understand if you didn't want to."

"Why not? We should probably avoid hunts during the full moon for obvious reasons. But any other time, so long as you've got it under wraps, it's an asset more than a liability. I've always wanted a companion that can survive gunshot wounds." I smirk and take a drink of my own. The roast isn't perfect, but it's getting better every day. Natalie said we have to keep at least half of our receipts as food and non-alcoholic drinks. She said Lou was cheating the system, and using a liquor license for a restaurant in the bar because it's way cheaper, but she wanted to keep everything on the up-and-up. We've been looking for a chef, but in the mean time, she's been mastering the art of coffee.

"And what if someone takes out an iHunt contract on me?" She looks at me with curiosity, as if testing the waters.

"Then the contract might as well be on me, too. Because I'll rip a motherfucker a new one if they try to take out one of my friends. Besides, I'll just report the contract for spam and stuff. Usually you need a good foundation for a contract. Nobody puts a bounty on someone that hasn't fucked with them real hard."

She nods. "Denny says he wants out of the game. He says it's not a good fit. That he wants to play it safe. Finish college. All that."

"Good. He's not well-suited for hunting, anyway. His heart's in the right place, but he doesn't have the fire. He's not a bad guy —there's no sense in him getting himself killed. Which is exactly what'd happen."

"But..." She pauses. "He asked if we can let him know if there's a contract in the resort district he can help with. Or if library access might be useful since they've got a big occult section. He said he wants to keep his eyes open and help us out any way he can."

"Fair." I nod. "That's kind of common, actually. Good hunters, we build up networks of people like Denny. People who want to help, but aren't in a good position to get their hands dirty. Denny's got good eyes. He's been able to spot a few things before they happened. He'll be useful."

"So maybe this is a little ahead of myself. But how do I get on iHunt?"

"It takes a little time. You have to have three registered members vouch for you. Of course you've got me. We'll work that all out soon enough. Usually, we do apprenticeship though. I'll get you registered as an apprentice. We'll just ignore the part of the application that asks, 'are you currently a supernatural entity?'"

She laughs. "It doesn't say that, does it?"

I shake my head. "No. There aren't any real questions. You just fill out a W-9 form. They're going to start filing taxes."

"Speaking of that: Did the IRS get back to you?"

I shake my head. "I got a letter from them a few days ago. But they're telling me it'll take an indeterminate amount of time. It could be years. It's all bullshit with the courts and stuff. Messy. They did take the blocks off my bank accounts though. So that's good?" I take another sip.

"That's definitely good. Also, I forgot to say, friends is friends. It's probably stupid, but if you want to use my management discount, you've got it. 30% off everything normally priced. And 75% off clearance. But clearance, I can just write off if there's something you like."

"Marry me." I laugh. She laughs.

#

The demon in Schuster Park feels like a joke. It's a six hour job. It's just a minor imp, going around possessing students at the community college and making them do silly shit, pranks, sex, and minor vandalism. One of the history professors took out the contract, because he was a little in-the-know. One of the first things you learn in this business is that every college or university has at least one professor in the know. They also usually have at least one professor knee-deep in the supernatural.

I spend a little time tracking it down, but it's just too obvious to miss. I don't even bother getting Vanessa for it—she's on a shift at her real job. The imp leaves drops of honey whenever it's committing one of its "jokes," so I follow it out to the parking lot. There's an old Chevy Suburban with a camper bed way in the back. There's fucking going on, the tell-tale rocking says to me.

These kinds of imps, they don't do coercion. They're not rape demons or anything like that. They can really only make people drop some inhibition and do things in inconvenient times and places. These two people would have likely fucked if put in the same room long enough. They might have already. But, I guess the imp thinks the school parking lot is a harmful location for whatever reason.

On a hunch, I look around. I quickly figure out why. There's a security camera on an electric pole. It's got a good view of the truck, despite the Suburban having curtains in all its rear windows. I wrap my denim jacket into a makeshift rope, and use it to scale the pole. Once I'm up to the camera, I grab it and jerk it to the side.

Once I'm back down, I take a can of salt out of my backpack, and draw a rough circle around the underside of the Suburban.

Then I go up to the back and I knock on the rear window. The rocking stops. I hear some movement inside, and some whispering I can't quite make out. I wait a few seconds, and knock again.

A man, maybe 45 or 50, cracks open the window just enough that I can see his eyes. There's a pile of blankets behind him. Curiously, it's about human size. "Can I help you?" He says, putting on a pair of glasses.

"Yeah, I'm gonna need the both of you to get out of the truck."

"Both of you? I'm afraid you must be mistaken. I'm just getting some supplies for class."

I roll my eyes. "Look. This can go two ways. This is public indecency. Either you can both get out of the truck, or I can call the police, professor." I take the gamble.

It works.

"Dana, you heard her. Let's get out." A young brunette, probably not old enough to drink, pops her head out from the blankets. She puts a hand up to hide her face, which is about as red as a person's face can safely be.

The two of them get out. The professor's in khakis, Italian leather loafers, and a soft brown button-down shirt. Kind of cute, if you've got a professor fetish. I did when I was younger. The woman's in jeans and a red t-shirt with a picture of the Little Mermaid in black hipster glasses. Also kind of cute, if you've got a self-aware hipster fetish. I did when I was younger.

"Alright. Now what do you want?" The man says, nervous.

"I swear to God, Eugene. If anyone finds out..." The woman butts in.

"That's it. Nothing. Just go inside. I don't care what you do. Hit the cafeteria maybe. I saw they've got grilled cheese and tomato soup special for $3. That's a great December lunch."

He looks at me, confused. But he throws his hands up and walks in that direction. The woman, embarrassed and volatile, rushes for another car in the lot.

Once they're out of the way, I speak up. "Alright. Show yourself. I haven't got all day."

The imp appears in the back cab. It's small, maybe about the size of a three year-old human. It's slender, naked, with reddish brown skin and no hair at all. It has wings kind of like a bat's, but that aren't big enough to do much of anything, and a long prehensile tail. It hisses at me.

"You understand humans enough to play the games you're playing. That means you can talk."

It hisses again, and little puffs of smoke come from its nose and mouth.

"Fine. Have it your way." I shrug, and pull a perfume bottle of holy water from my pocket. I spray about twelve times, saturating the cab. The little imp howls and hisses and slams its body against the sides of the truck. As its skin dissolves, I pull out my phone and shoot a video of its last twenty seconds of so. Once it's done dying, its last remains are consumed in a quick flash of fire. The smell of sulfur is horrible.

That Suburban will never, ever smell okay again. Suits that professor right.

I check in with iHunt, and leave the client a message.

"Photos attached. You have a professor at the school, first name Eugene. He's sleeping with students. You should do something about this."

He responds with a "Thank you, he'll be dealt with," and full payment within a half an hour. Perfect gig.

32
#FEUDALISM

A few weeks pass. We open the club on New Year's Day. The first day, we have four vampire clients. We average about one a day for the next two weeks. That's not bad, since each one nets $2,500, with half going to the donors. Natalie says she has some ideas to bring in clients, but she's not too concerned. The food's nice—it turns out one of the women was a chef in Cambodia, and her food gives the place a unique air. Sure it's a vampire bar, but it's also a hip but authentic Cambodian restaurant.

With expenses, we're not yet breaking even. Natalie doesn't seem too concerned, so I trust her. She says no bars break even in their first year. Besides, we've got Lou to bleed dry, and he's got quite the credit line. I think the plan is, he'll die once he's fully maxed-out in debt.

It's a Tuesday, an hour before the bar opens formally. There's a loud knock at the door. Before we can get to the door, there's a second knock, even louder.

I'm trying to fix a clog in one of the sinks. Natalie gets the door. "Can I help you?"

I peek over. There's a large Hispanic man in jeans and a cornflower blue work shirt. Behind him are two burly white guys in cheap, nondescript t-shirts.

"Do you know who these men are?" The man says, motioning

back to them. They're dopey. Wavering. Like they're sleepwalking.

I hear Natalie's voice in my head. "He's a vampire."

"You think?" I think back, continuing to mess with the sink, so as to not let him know I'm aware, just in case. Also, just in case, I pull my knife and palm it. He's strong. I don't know this because of any specific thing. There's no vampire radar. There's no power meter that tells you a given monster is off the charts. But he is. I've only once experienced a vampire with this kind of presence, and that was when I fought one of Dracula's five hundred year-old children.

Natalie shakes her head. "No. Care to tell me?"

"United States Immigration and Customs Enforcement. Would you like to know why they were at your bar this afternoon?"

She takes a long breath in. "I think I have a pretty good idea. Who are you? And what do you want?"

"I'd like to be invited in, if you don't mind. I'll send these gentlemen on their merry way."

Natalie thinks back, "Should I invite him in?"

"Yeah. All it's gonna do is piss him off if you don't. I don't know if you can tell, but he's strong. Really strong."

"Come on in." She says, moving aside and motioning him in. "Come have a seat."

He looks back to the men, and just looks them in the eyes for a moment. They walk off. He comes in, and sits at the bar. "My name is Ramirez. Formally Minister Ramirez. But you can call me

Ramirez."

Natalie goes behind the bar. Her jaw is quivering. "I'm... Natalie. Can... I get you something to drink, Ramirez?"

"I've heard you have good margaritas. I'd like to try one." He puts down a $20 bill on the bar.

Natalie goes to get it. I keep fussing.

Natalie thinks to me, "This is the leader of the city. The guy who hired you for the resort gig."

"I know." I think back. "I'm ready in case shit hits the fan. Don't worry Natalie. You've got this. I believe in you."

"Behind the bar. You're...?"

"Lana." I stand. "I believe you hired me."

He smiles softly and nods once. "Yes I did. You've done very well. Tonight's not the night for it, but I think perhaps we should discuss further work away from that infernal telephone app."

Telephone app? Okay. I think I can forgive the ancient vampire lord for not knowing the right lingo. But he'd better know how to pronounce "gif."

"Any time, sir." I say, and clean up the area around the plumbing.

Natalie comes back with a margarita. "So, was this just a social call? Or do you make a habit of protecting other vampires from immigration?"

He sips the margarita, then taps it, nodding. "This? This is good." He takes another sip. "I wanted to speak with you, but my schedule's been horrendous, what with the new year and all. It seems you're doing relatively well so far. That's good to see. The vampire bar model's been lucrative in a number of cities. It never picked up in San Jenaro. But I hope you can prove the exception."

She nods, and begins cleaning glasses. "Me too. So what did you want to speak with me about?"

He takes another sip and pauses for a few seconds. He's very patient. Very slow about his movements. I guess you get that way on a timeline like his. "I want you to do well. But, as you might know, there's a war going on right now. I want to make a deal with you."

"A deal?" She says. I perk up, listening closely.

"Very simply, what you're doing here can be an invaluable resource in an uncomfortable situation like we find ourselves in. Blood supplies are complicated and dangerous. Safe, accessible blood is priceless. However, you're putting a price on it. That's smart. I want to work with you. I often have to deal with new vampires created without permission. As you're well aware."

She nods, and gulps. She's trying very, very hard to be confident. But it's hard. This guy's oozing power.

He continues. "When someone's in need, I want to refer them to you. For the new vampires, I'll be paying their tabs. I'd like a 25% discount for those referrals. Call it... civil service."

Natalie nods, and responds without even thinking about it. "Of course."

"I'll refer others to you. They'll be paying their own bills, and at full price. I wouldn't have it any other way. Also, if you're interested, I think we can hold the occasional meeting here. However, that'll take preparation, as it'll be taxing to the blood supply."

She nods again.

"That said, I need something from you."

This is where the other shoe drops. Oh shit, oh shit, oh shit.

Natalie nods.

"We're entering a new century as vampires of San Jenaro. Everything is changing. Everything is complicated. While we've always been secretive about our ways, we need to be doubly careful. If we're going to do this thing, if you're going to be a part of this new century, Natalie, then you need to be fully on board."

"Of course Mister Ramirez." She blurts out. "What can I do?"

"You need to put this place in a position where scrutiny will not devastate it. I can hold off these immigration officers for a few weeks. But, I need you to get everyone legitimate. Everyone needs papers. Everyone needs verifiable accounts and identification. And I'm sure you're aware the owner is quite the monster. He'll need to be removed from the equation soon."

She nods again. "Of course. Of course. That's all stuff I planned on doing soon enough anyway. What else?"

He shakes his head. "There's nothing else. I want you to be a legitimate businesswoman I can be proud to send people to. I want you to be a flawless cog in the well-oiled machine of San Jenaro's future."

"Wait." I say, like an idiot. "You don't want protection money?

You don't want kickbacks? You don't want us to kiss a ring or anything?"

"Damn it Lana!" Natalie thinks to me, while glaring. Her glare said it without the telepathy.

Ramirez shakes his head. "No. I'm a manager, not a mafia don. I manage my city. If you work well, we'll work well together. When you're successful, I'm successful."

"That's way too reasonable." I tilt my head. Still not convinced.

"I get that sometimes." He says, standing. "I'm sorry I cannot stay and enjoy another drink. I did want to address one final topic. Your criminality." He looks between us.

"Excuse me, sir?"

"I know you murdered your creator."

There's the other shoe. Fuck.

She stammers. "I, I..."

"You were acting in self-defense. You were also created without permission. I'll be forgiving that crime, so long as it remains a one-time affair."

"Umm... Thank you sir?"

He nods, and starts for the door.

Natalie rushes to grab the $20 bill from the bar and make change. "Um, I owe you $12.50."

"Keep the change." He makes his way out.

Once the door closes, Natalie rushes over and kisses me. It goes on for I don't even know how long, and it's perfect.

"Well hello..." I say as the kiss ends. I hold her there and look to her eyes.

"What was that?" She says, smiling, still shaking.

"I dunno? I think we won. I think we're okay. I don't really know what success looks like, but I feel like it's close."

My phone buzzes. It's two alerts from iHunt. Natalie adjusts to look at my phone as I scroll through the notice.

"Quick $2,500 job. New ghoul spotted in Casino Mesa Del Oro."

I swipe right.

"Zombies in the Flip. $500 a head, up to a maximum $10,000."

I swipe left.

"Did you just turn down a job?" Natalie teases.

"Yeah. I think maybe that's the closest thing to success we get in this line of work."

Thank you for reading #iHunt: Killing Monsters in the Gig Economy! As a little added bonus, I've included three chapters of the second full-length #iHunt novel, #iHunt: The Chosen One.

If you like what we do, you can check us out on Facebook at https://www.facebook.com/iHuntSeries or on Twitter at https://twitter.com/machineageinc. You can also sign up for our mailing list at http://eepurl.com/dhfD-f. We only send one or two emails a month, so don't worry about spam.

This edition of the book features a new cover, to coincide with the cover of the upcoming tabletop roleplaying game set in the San Jenaro universe. We think you'll like it. It's slated for release by the end of 2019, or maybe the beginning of 2020 depending on the practical realities of game design.

The San Jenaro book series has actually gotten pretty big, so here's a little outline of the current novels:
° Blood Flow
° #iHunt: Killing Monsters in the Gig Economy
° Reaching Out
° #iHunt: Frankenstein's Monster (Sort Of) (But

Not Really)
  ◦ #iHunt: A Transylvanian Prince in Southern
California
  ◦ #iHunt: Mayhem in Movieland
  ◦ ULTRA
  ◦ #iHunt: The Chosen One

-01-
#MONOLOGUE

Imagine, if you will, a fist fight against a moving car. I said moving, this isn't the bonus round in Street Fighter. When the car's coming at you, you only have one chance to hit it. You punch it, then you die. Win-win, right? Wrong. You hurt your fist, you don't hurt the car, then you're dead.

Worst fight ever.

Fighting vampires can be like fighting a car. They're fast, strong, tough, and if you use your one chance to punch them by, you know, punching them, then you end up dead and it's the worst fight ever.

Instead of fighting a moving car with your fist, you fight a moving car with a wall. It's like bull fighting in Looney Tunes. You get it to chase you. You make it think it's gonna plow into you and kill your ass. Then you dodge out of the way so it smashes into a brick wall.

Do the same with vampires.

Just like Looney Tunes, fighting a vampire has a lot to do with comedic timing.

Except, instead of a brick wall, you've got to be clever. Use, say, a picket fence. Get them to jump on a picket fence, and you've got all their speed and strength going toward jamming a big piece of wood in their chest. It's a win-win. You don't have to hurt your wrist trying to jam a stake through their heart, and you look completely badass if it works. If it doesn't work, they're still impaled on a fence post, which is simultaneously a tactical miracle and hilarious.

Impaled vampires will flail for a good twenty seconds before pulling themselves off the post. I've timed it.

Long story short, Luke's a vampire. Luke is also impaled. He doesn't think it's very funny, because he has zero appreciation for comedy. I'm not killing him because he doesn't appreciate humor —I'm killing him because I've got a contract on his head for $5,000.

Sucks for him, but on the bright side, I'm alive.

Vampires come in three main breeds in San Jenaro. Bats, wolves, and rattlesnakes. Actually, those are proper nouns. Bats, Wolves, and Rattlesnakes. Luke's a Wolf. Wolves are very strong. That means not only did he impale himself on the picket fence, unfortunately not hitting his heart, but he pushed the damned thing all the way out his back by almost a foot. It's gruesome. Vampires don't really bleed, not the way you think of it. Their blood's thick and icky and kind of alive. It pulls back to the body like mercury or the prototype series 1000 Terminator. But when you get them real good, say, by impaling them on a fence post, you've got all this blood from all over the place slithering slowly back to the body. It's really gross. You're just gonna have to take my word for it.

"I'm gonna kill you!" He growls out, grabbing at his chest, clutching at the painted white plank in his tummy.

"Oh my god."

He gnashes his teeth and jerks his head back toward me.

"You guys all say that. Think about that for a second. Is that really the first thing that comes to mind?" I imitate his growly accent. "I'm gonna kill you." I roll my eyes. "You sound like a fucking idiot. Do you think I've never been told that? Do you honestly think you're the strongest or smartest vampire to ever tell me that?"

He looks back at me and blinks. I roll my neck. Proper stretching is important on the hunt. More hunters have died from a lack of stretching and cardio than from hellfire. I don't have the statistics on that. Then, I take my machete out of its sleeve.

"What's your point, bitch? I'm still gonna kill you." He's grabbing at the post, trying to force himself off of it. He's fighting against his own weight and the traction from the old, ratty wood. It's all slippery from his weird mercury Terminator monster blood.

"Um, no you're not. The point is, bitch, that you're not the best vampire to say that to me, and if that's the case, you've got to assume it's not gonna happen, right?"

He stops fighting and raises an eyebrow. "You're gonna kill me anyway. Why does it matter what I say?"

"Fucking shit. You're new at this, aren't you?" I sigh, and hop up to sit on the small of his back. This pushes him further down on the post.

He screams. I can't really blame him for that.

"What? Maybe five years? Tops?"

"Seven!" He snaps and tries to bite me in the thigh, but from where I'm sitting, he can't bend his back far enough. He looks like a dog trying to bite his own tail.

"Seven fucking years, and you don't know the value of a good villain monologue?" I sigh, and shake my head.

His face is red, his eyes are red, and his fangs are fully bared. Vampires usually retract their fangs. When they get pissed, they draw them out like that's gonna change anything. Vampire teeth are not effective weapons. Imagine trying to bite someone in a fist fight. You'd look like a jackass and you'd get your face smashed in. He roars out and starts gnashing the way you might expect an alligator to. It's really kind of pathetic.

"You practice your villain monologue and you make it compelling. You make it new and interesting, that way I'm captivated and impressed and you have a chance to escape. Didn't anybody ever teach you?"

"KILL ME ALREADY!" He shouts and grunts, glaring at me.

"No can do, buddy." I shake my head and look down at him. Thanks to his extra pale face, and exposed blue veins all over, I can tell he's running down his blood supply. Vampires go through blood when they exert themselves. It's like me with enchiladas and cheap cocaine. He's losing self-control. A few more minutes and he'll be a mindless death zombie who will stop at nothing for blood.

"WHY?" He's flailing and trying to reach back with his hands. I bat them away with the flat of my machete.

"I saw what you did to that guy back there. You weren't just feeding. You were torturing him. You take pleasure off that shit. You could have just bitten him and walked away. Fuck, if you had to kill him, you could have just killed him and moved on. But NOOOOO. You had to toy with him. Tease him. Let him know what was coming, then make him feel helpless."

"So fucking what?" He spits a gout of blood on the ground in spite.

Vampires are so wasteful.

"So fucking what? Um, I'm doing that to you, that's what. This is poetic justice, and I really don't think you're appreciating the hard work I'm putting in here. I'm giving you a narrative arc that justifies your inclusion in the story. You did a thing. You get punished for the thing. Instead of some jack off nameless vampire, you get to be Luke, the Greek motherfucking tragedy. You should be thanking me."

He jerks to the side hard enough that I almost fall off. I hear the wood of the fence cracking.

I hop off and the fence shatters. He stands tall and howls out. Then he laughs and turns to face me. He's got this huge grin, teeth and fangs all covered in blood, with blood dripping down his chin. Very black metal album cover. "Oh I'll thank you. For the meal!"

I sigh and throw my head back. "For the meal? Jesus Christ. At least say, 'for the holy communion you're about to give me' or some shit. Fucking vampires today. No sense of drama. Besides, you've already lost."

"Me? Lost? I'm free. I'm not gonna fall for your shit again."

I laugh. "Remember how you killed him? You let him escape for a second? But then he tripped because you broke his toe? That way you could give him the illusion of safety?"

He raises an eyebrow and nods.

Then the cherry bomb I planted in his back pocket goes off with a little gunshot pop.

He jumps, turns, and grabs his ass. I rush forward and jam my shoulder into his side, knocking him to his stomach. I jump and thrust the heel of my shoe into his spine, pinning him to the dirt.

"You empowered him then took it all away. All to suit your perverted little power fantasy."

He snarls back at me.

"So now I'm gonna cut off your fucking head just after you thought you could turn the tables. How does that feel?"

He stares at me in disbelief. "You're just like me. You're enjoying this."

"Wrong."

"No. I can see it in your eyes. You like it. You're having fun. This isn't about justice. This is about amusing yourself. You're just as much a monster as we are."

I shake my head. "I'm worse." I shove the shoe deeper into his back. "You're doing it for a meal. I'm doing it for money. I'm doing it because it's important to evaluate your work-life balance, and understand that when you're overworking yourself, it's important to eke out a little fun wherever you can find it."

His eyes go wide. "Work? This... you're not the chosen one?"

I laugh. "Sorry bro. No chosen ones here. Just a broke-ass woman you keep calling a bitch, and the $5,000 bounty she's standing on."

He tries to say something. But in the end, my millennial internet attention span wins out and I swing my machete down at his neck like a golf club. The head doesn't come off in a single swipe, but it's enough to sever the spine.

Sometimes the drama doesn't work out, so you've got to settle for functional.

I pose him like a scarecrow on the remains of the fence, with his head dangling down by what little bit's left of his throat. His body's decaying quickly, so I snap a couple of pictures. Then I realize my flash is off and I take a couple more.

I post the pictures to the #iHunt app. Then I post them to my private Discord server.

"Got to him first. Sorry everyone. Y'all get the next one."

I like having a chat server full of hunters. It's like a water cooler for people who murder murderers for a living. You get to brag a little, you get to pick up jobs when others can't finish them, and you get human interaction with people you don't have to lie to when they ask what you do for a living.

The #iHunt client's already responded. Five stars. They left a comment.

"I think perhaps the dramatics were unnecessary, and unnecessarily violent, but I can't complain about her results."

That's really me to a T, isn't it?

I'm Lana. I hunt monsters.

-02-
#EXPOSITION

I feel like maybe I should do a little self-introduction. This isn't my first rodeo, but it might be your first experience with me.

Understand that I'm trying very, very hard to resist "I'm Lana, and I'm an addict" jokes. I'm not an addict—I'm really a very high functioning drug user, and frankly, addiction isn't funny. Impaling monsters and posting selfies with their decaying bodies? Hilarious. But making fun of very real health struggles? That's just too far.

Imagine, if you will, a Venn Diagram of urban fantasy novel protagonists. I hunt monsters for a living. That's its own big circle. Pretty common in the genre, right? I'm not super powered. That's another circle. I am super sarcastic. That's another circle. These three circles actually don't overlap very much. You might get two of them, but the three aren't too common.

Next, I'm pointedly self-aware. I get things like narrative beats and dramatic irony. Sometimes I knowingly make choices based on how good they'd be for the story, instead of just making the best choice within my universe. I like to think that combined with the other aspects of my identity, I'm fairly unique.

So now, let me tell you about my super cute vampire girlfriend, Natalie. Usually a woman protagonist that hooks up with a vampire finds a man. Dark, brooding, haunted, you know, the kind of guy you have to save. While I have fucked a few men who were vampires, they were insufferable and definitely not long-term dating material. She does own a bar, though. If we were just looking at Natalie without any other details, she's kinda cliche. Unfortunately, while she's super cute, we actually don't have a particularly functional sex life. Blood makes things complicated. In fact, my whole sex life is complicated and dysfunctional. I think that makes me unique within the genre by itself. Protagonists like me, we're supposed to have heaving bosoms and fawn over turgid members or some shit.

Also I do a lot of coke. But it's not a character flaw as much as a statement about societal bullshit I have to deal with and the things I have to do to get ahead. Performance-enhancing cocaine, if you will. Some people don't wake up without coffee. I don't kill monsters without coke.

All those circles overlap in exactly one tiny point, and that point is me, Lana Moreno, professional murderer murderer. I don't murder professional murderers. I professionally murder non-professional murderers. Well I guess maybe some of the monsters I kill are professional killers, but that's the exception, not the rule.

So we've got the action scene to start everything up. We call that "in media res." It's a good way to dump characters and themes in an engaging fashion. Then, straight up exposition. Except, I did it with a motherfucking diagram. Consider that when leaving your Amazon review. Remember, anything less than five stars gets stuck in algorithm hell.

I feel like maybe I overshared a little about my situation with Natalie. That's probably the kind of thing you should see, not hear, right? Well, I can't just take that back. So pretend I didn't say it.

After my fight with Luke, I head to Natalie's bar. It's a vampire bar. She pays her workers very well to consensually give up bits of blood to clients. This means the clients aren't murdering as many people as they might otherwise. I like to think of it as a public service for profit. Kind of like what I do when I kill vampires for cash. Natalie doesn't have to murder anyone to do what she does, but when I do my job, I don't have to worry about my targets killing anyone ever again. It's give and take, you know? That's what we like to call "moral gray areas." They're pretty common in the genre.

Her bar's called Eden. We argued for weeks about the name. She ended up using it because we had some neon lettering left over from a sorcerer I killed and it saved her some money. The place is cute. Not exactly my thing, but classy and dark. She's got this whole velvet and fake leather thing going on. Everyone seems to like it, and not everything has to be for me. It's maybe the calmest bar I've ever been to. The whole atmosphere has to be pretty chill. If a vampire loses control, she has to know immediately so they can be stopped before they seriously hurt someone. For a while, she had me doing security work there. But it was boring, and the patrons didn't like that I was also killing vampires. They considered it a conflict of interest. Like these motherfuckers have any room to judge.

"Hey Nat." I plop down at the bar.

"Hey…" She says with a smile. She's all red and black tonight. Black jeans and a tank top with a dark red fake leather jacket. I don't really like that jacket on her since it clashes with the much brighter red of her hair, but whatever. It's not for me. Everything's gotta be blood blood blood blood blood. "How'd the hunt go? Can I get you a drink?"

"Hunt went well. He was a sadist. But not anymore. So I can't complain." I think for a moment and look around. I feel like somebody's watching me but I can't pinpoint it. That's sort of the problem with vampire bars. All the damn vampires. If someone's invisible and watching you, there's no good way to tell. Out on the streets, that's different. But you've got to expect at least a couple of invisible vampires in a place like this. I don't know why this would affect my drink choice. "I'll take that thing you gave me last time with the maple and whiskey and apple."

She smiles. "Got it." She darts off to get a few more orders.

I like Natalie. I like her a lot. A lot a lot. Otherwise, you wouldn't catch me dead in a bar full of vampires. Particularly since most of them know exactly what I do. This means I get a bunch of dirty looks and nobody will sit next to me.

Okay, it's not all bad.

Pro tip for ladies looking to have a drink without a bunch of motherfuckers getting in your personal space, demanding your attention: Murder some of them. They'll quickly stop getting in your shit. Well, the ones you murder will stop immediately. But I mean the others.

Because I hang out with Natalie here sometimes, everyone knows who I am and what I do, and sometimes I'll catch someone crossing a street to stay away from me. I guess they're assuming that if they see me in public, that means I'm probably hunting them down. They don't get that if I was hunting them, they wouldn't see me until it's too late.

These vampires must really think I'm a shitty vampire hunter if they think they can just cross the street to avoid me.

"Here you go hon." Natalie puts down a glass. "I'm a little busy, so maybe give me a few? I'm out at 1."

I look at the clock above her head. It's still only 11:25.

"I might drink this and meet you back at your place?" I say, sipping the sweet maple whiskey apple thing I can't remember the name of.

"Yeah." She sighs. "I'm sorry. Just, duty calls."

"It's cool. It's good to see you either way."

She smiles and wanders off to handle the other murderers at the bar.

#

Natalie's place is nicer than mine. Of course, she makes more money than I do. Part of it's about location though. Her bar's along the edge of Palo Verde, which is full of movie studios and animation offices and ad firms, so all the apartments nearby have been gentrified into very hip, very spacious things compared to the rest of San Jenaro. On the outside, they look like they came straight out of a Raymond Chandler novel. On the inside, they're all white and hip and bleached and boring but expensive-looking. She's gotta live close to her bar, because day and night get really complicated and she's got to be at work damned near the moment the sun falls.

To be honest, it really doesn't have much to do with money. Natalie uses her vampire powers to get free rent. I can't blame her. Landlords are assholes that don't create anything, and I'd sure as fuck do it if I could. It's not like a Palo Verde landlord really needs every last cent, anyway. These are multi-million dollar apartments and every building has a ton of them. Hell, some of the landlords are keeping places empty just to drive up the rent costs from demand. That's iconic California. You buy twenty apartments on a block, that way you can leave five empty and charge more for fifteen of them.

It's bigger than my place, too. Every time I'm here, I spend a lot of effort to stretch out and take as much space as possible. Otherwise it feels empty, like it's a waste. I'm kicking a leg up on the white leather sofa and reaching an arm back behind my head when she comes in.

"You stretch like a cat."

"Sorry Nat." I say. Heat rushes to my face and I scramble to sit like a normal human being, knitting my fingers together on my lap.

"No, it's cute." She says and tosses a black leather messenger bag onto the coat rack. "By all means, don't let me stop you."

"So... how was work?" I say, crossing a leg over the other. It feels very sophisticated, until I bump my ankle on the coffee table and yelp. That doesn't help with the blushing.

"Work..." She looks to me and shakes her head. "Work was okay. How was it for you?"

"You know. Normal night. Normal things."

"Kill anyone?" She says and hangs her long wool coat up. I keep telling her that thing doesn't look appropriate in California. She never listens.

"Yeah. Like I'm wont to do. Real skeezy motherfucker. Kept calling me a bitch. So I strung him up like a scarecrow. It was really badass."

Her eyes go wide and she just stares at me.

"I guess you had to be there."

"I guess." She sighs and walks over, falling onto the other end of the sofa.

Natalie's weird about my work. She's supportive. At least insomuch as she knows that I kill vampires for money, and doesn't try to stop me. It also disgusts her. Which I guess I understand, because she's a vampire, and I'm fairly open about, well, being very good at killing vampires. I don't blame her. But sometimes it hampers my style. I'm very proud of myself. I take pride in what I do, because it's the only thing I'm really good at. Every time I talk about a good night's work, she looks like she's gonna vomit.

"Sorry." I say, slumping my shoulders.

"It's okay. It's just... His name was Luke." She bites her lower lip. A little of her lipstick comes off on her teeth. She looks like it hurt to say that.

"You knew him?"

She shrugs. "Yeah. He'd come by the bar sometimes. It's just weird, knowing I'm never going to see him again."

The blushing turns to a hint of anger as my mind flashes with memories of Luke. Of how in the moment, it was me or him and he wouldn't have hesitated to kill me if the tables were turned. "He called me a bitch, Natalie."

"If he was human and he called you a bitch, would you have killed him?"

I grit my teeth. I want to argue. I want to tell her I would. But we both know I wouldn't. It didn't even have anything to do with calling me a bitch. It had everything to do with the cash. He could have been a perfect gentleman and I'd still have done the deed.

"Nevermind, Lana. I'm sorry. I understand. He's a murderer. If you didn't kill him, who knows how many others he'd have taken down over the years."

"Yeah. Murderer." I sigh.

"Um!" She says, snapping to attention, and turning to face me fully, legs crossed on the sofa in front of her. "Anything else going on? Non-vampire things?"

I also perk up at the chance to change the topic. As much as we'll never see eye to eye on the "I professionally murder people like her" thing, she knows when stuff's getting too tense and can diffuse an argument before it gets there. I appreciate that.

"I start classes tomorrow!"

"Huh? Classes? Hunter classes?" She tilts her head. I realize I never told her I enrolled in part-time classes.

"No. College. I'm taking three classes this semester. I'm really excited."

"College?"

"Community college."

"Oh."

I sigh. "I think the response was supposed to be, 'Oh Lana that's wonderful! I'm so proud of you!'"

"I'm proud of you?"

She's not proud of me.

"You don't sound that convincing."

"I don't know what to say, Lana. I feel like that's the kind of thing you'd have talked to me about. You're just really good at making big decisions without even asking me, and it... it kinda hurts, y'know?"

"Oh. I'm sorry. It didn't even occur to me."

"Yeah." She sighs.

"I..."

Five seconds or so pass. It feels like an hour. Then she reaches forward and takes my hands.

"What classes are you taking?"

I force a smile. "Oh. A basic math class. Theater. And gothic lit. I figure I'm kind of an expert there, so it's an easy grade."

"You're an expert at gothic lit? What else don't I know about you?"

"Gothic lit is full of vampires and Frankenstein monsters and stuff, right? I'm an expert on that shit."

She drops her face into her palm and shakes her head. "You're not an expert on Frankenstein's monster."

I nod a few times quickly. "I killed one."

"No you didn't."

"We're just gonna have to agree to disagree on this, Natalie."

-03-
#GOTHICLIT

"Lana Moreno?" I raise my hand. The professor scribbles some shit on her paper. That's not literal—she's just writing things. I just say shit a lot.

"Veronica Vanderbilt?" I look over to the blonde next to me, raising her hand. She's tall, strong, cute, but really, really not my type. She's got a sweater from Tommy Hilfiger, red, white, and blue, and blue eyes that sparkle like a bad parody of a Japanese cartoon.

Why in the fuck is someone like this in community college? Did her daddy's business go under because Trump passed a tariff daddy thought would Make America Great Again, so now she's gotta go to the dirt people school?

The professor scribbles on her paper, then calls for someone else and someone else like she called for ten someone elses before me.

"Welcome to Gothic Literature 101. I'm Carrie Shockley. I hope you're all prepared to do a lot of reading this semester." She says, and pats a stack of novels on her desk.

Professor Shockley is such a stereotype. Nothing wrong with that. But she's got this really very brown hair that doesn't have much luster, a white peasant shirt, with a gray jacket that doesn't really match the gray of her tweed skirt. She doesn't look bad, but if you gave me a police lineup and told me that one of them was a librarian who killed her rapist ex-boyfriend, I'd pick her without hesitation. You know, except I wouldn't give her up to the cops for that, so nevermind.

Anyway, point is, she seems cool.

Not the kind of professor you expect to get high with, but cool.

"Has anyone here read Dracula?" She says, holding up an old, beaten up copy of the Stoker novel. It was on the syllabus, but they were asking $40 for a fucking paperback and I fought Dracula a while back so I figured I could save myself the $40 and just use personal anecdotes.

"I saw the movie." Veronica says with a smirk.

Professor Shockley sits on her desk. "Which one? Lugosi? Christopher Lee? Frank Langella? Leslie Nielsen? Duncan Regehr? Gary Oldman? Gerard Butler?"

"Um, that was a joke." Veronica says, rolling her eyes. Like eight people laugh, which makes about zero sense to me but whatever. Everyone's a critic.

"You look like you've read Dracula." Shockley says. Everything goes quiet for a second, until I realize she's talking to me.

"Me?" I raise an eyebrow.

"Yeah. You seem the Dracula type."

I laugh. I can't help but to laugh. Maybe it's a little disrespectful, but, I laugh. "Why's that?"

She shrugs and smiles. "Call it a hunch?"

I briefly wonder if she knows something about me. If she's actually a vampire's servant here to spy on me. But if so, why would she give herself away like that?

Then I look down and realize I'm wearing an old, beaten up Night of the Living Dead t-shirt. I tap my shirt and look up to her. She nods with a smirk.

"I've read it before. That was a long time ago. To be honest, I don't read as much for fun as I used to. That's one of the reasons I took this class, I wanted an excuse to read more. Seems like these days, I only get to read for work."

"I know the feeling." She pats her stack again. "So, does anyone know what defines the gothic novel?"

#

In the hallway right after class, I feel a tap on my shoulder. I clench a fist and turn, ready for the kill. After all, I still can't assume Professor Shockley isn't a vampire slave assigned to kill me.

It's Veronica Vanderbilt.

"What's up?" I say. I'm really not looking forward to whatever comes out of her mouth next.

"I just wanted to say hi and see if you wanted to go to the cafeteria and grab some lunch?"

I tilt my head and look her over again. She's about my age. Which is to say, she's about Professor Shockley's age. She's tied with the two of us for the oldest in that room. The community college is like that. Most everyone's coming straight out of high school, but every room has someone in their thirties trying to make up for lost time with a shitty budget. Well, two if you count the adjunct professors.

"I, um..." I feel like I should say something clever here.

"Come on. You need to eat." She laughs to herself. "I don't even know what that means. I don't know if you need to eat. Is it the cafeteria food? We could go out and grab something if you wanted."

"It's not the cafeteria. Cafeteria's fine. I like the $3 grilled cheese meal. Just... not used to people coming on so strong. Do you invite everyone who sits next to you in class to lunch? Or do you have some elaborate plan to pour pig blood on my head? Because I promise you that will not go well."

"I like you." She laughs. It's somewhere between high school cheerleader giggle and girl who thinks she has to laugh at your bad jokes and get wasted on tequila with you to get in your pants, but then the next day she acts like it was all your fault and she tells all her friends you gave her herpes.

Hypothetically.

"You know what? Sure." I say. "I'm Lana."

"I know. I'm good with names. I'm Veronica. But you can call me V."

"I feel honored." I say and turn toward the direction of the cafeteria. "You never answered me about the pig blood. I'm gonna need you to address that before we go any further."

"No pig blood. It's just, I'm new in town and I work really

hard. I've got to make the most out of what little study time I can get. So I thought I'd connect with someone who seems to know her stuff. Study buddies?"

"Why do you think I know my stuff?" I say and grab a tray and get in line. I order a burger and some fries.

She grabs a tray and gets a tiny, prepackaged salad and some mineral water. It's like looking into a dark mirror, except instead of a mirror it's more like a person who does all the bullshit people have expected of me since childhood. She's like healthy, white, perky, overachiever Lana. She's like if Lana were cast in an #iHunt TV show.

"You obviously know your stuff. You should have seen your face every time Professor Shockley said something about vampires. You clenched up like you wanted to correct her. Like you knew more about the subject."

I look over to her and hold back laughter. "But she was right. She knows Dracula better than I know how to do my eyebrows."

"But you know more. Like, the deep stuff. I just... feel like you're a subject matter expert. So I want to hang around and see if some of that might rub off on me."

"You know this stuff is really easy though, right? I'm not gonna tell you anything revelatory about Dracula that'll get you a better grade than just reading the book. These kinds of classes are easy A grades. Most everyone in that class is in there because they know it'll help their GPA."

She shrugs. "Or they like to have sex in graveyards."

I fight back a laugh. I feel like that might have been accidentally funny, and I don't want to reward her unless I know it'll be a pattern. "Don't knock it until you try it." I get a can of Monster and lead her over to a table.

"Ew. For one, sliding around in moss. For another, tombstones are like sandpaper on your back."

I do laugh that time. "I never would have pegged you for the type."

"To have sex in graveyards? Not really. I've dated some really weird guys. But never like that."

"So why gothic lit?" I say and take a bite of my burger.

She looks at my burger and winces a little, like she might throw up. She opens the clear plastic cup her salad's in. "It's important for work. You know, research. I figured I'd kill two birds with one stone and get some college credit out of it."

"What kind of job does Gothic Lit help?"

You know, except my job.

"Oh, it's hard to explain. I'm in..." She sips her mineral water. "Um. Pest control."

"Pest... control?" I say and take another bite of my burger.

"Yeah. Pest control. Gotta kill those pests!"

Pests? Really?

"You keep on surprising me, V."

"Why? Don't think I can kill, um, rats, and bugs, and things? Pests?"

"I just think that if you think studying Gothic Lit is gonna help you kill vampires, you've got another thing coming. It causes more problems than it solves. You know most of this shit was written as propaganda, right?"

"What do you mean, vampire hunters?" Her face goes red. Like, "I'm at a party with people smoking pot and daddy just walked in with a baseball bat" red. Like, "I'm a really fucking bad liar and someone just called me on it and I'm not used to being called on my bullshit because I'm pretty and white."

I have to try to get through to her. "You heard me. You know Anne Rice was working for them, don't you? She's gotten more vampire hunters killed than you can count."

I'm not assuming she can count very high, to be honest.

She sighs and leans forward, whispering. "How did you know?"

"Pest control? No offense Veronica, but if I had to guess, I'd say you're qualified for five, maybe six jobs. And none of them involve poisoning animals. Girl like you, I'd say you wanted to be a marine biologist growing up."

Her eyes grow wide. "Can you read minds?"

I can when they're Little Golden Book level.

"I..." I sigh and shake my head at the Poky Little Puppy before me. "Have you ever actually killed a vampire before? It's not what it's cracked up to be."

"I've killed a lot of vampires. In my old city, I killed off the entire vampire population. Now I've been tasked with saving San Jenaro."

"Saving… Tasked?"

"There's like a million vampires here. You have no idea."

I picture myself being thrown out a spaceship's airlock. It has to be better than this.

Made in the USA
Coppell, TX
25 January 2021